GO THE DISTANCE

A TWISTED TALE

For more Twisted adventures, check out:

A Whole New World by Liz Braswell
Once Upon a Dream by Liz Braswell
As Old as Time by Liz Braswell
Reflection by Elizabeth Lim
Part of Your World by Liz Braswell
Mirror, Mirror by Jen Calonita
Conceal, Don't Feel by Jen Calonita
Straight On Till Morning by Liz Braswell
So This Is Love by Elizabeth Lim
Unbirthday by Liz Braswell
What Once Was Mine by Liz Braswell
Almost There by Farrah Rochon
When You Wish Upon a Star by Elizabeth Lim
Fate Be Changed by Farrah Rochon
Sally's Lament by Mari Mancusi
How Far I'll Go by Keala Kendall
Adventure Is Out There! by Liz Braswell

GO THE DISTANCE

A TWISTED TALE

JEN CALONITA

Random House New York

Random House Books for Young Readers
An imprint of Random House Children's Books
A division of Penguin Random House LLC
1745 Broadway, New York, NY 10019
penguinrandomhouse.com
rhcbooks.com/disney

Cover art by Jim Tierney
Cover design by Scott Piehl, Gegham Vardanyan, and Tanya Mauler

Library of Congress Cataloging-in-Publication Data is available upon request.
ISBN 978-1-368-06380-7 (trade) — ISBN 978-1-368-06584-9 (ebook) —
ISBN 978-0-7364-4740-9 (paperback)

Originally published in hardcover by Disney • Hyperion, an imprint of Buena Vista Books, Inc., New York, in 2021. Previously published in paperback by Disney • Hyperion, an imprint of Buena Vista Books, Inc., New York, in 2024.

Manufactured in the United States of America
1st Printing

For Tyler and Dylan—
Always go the distance.

—J.C.

PROLOGUE

Some time ago . . .

"Excuses! Excuses! You give the same ones every week!"

"They're not excuses, Thea! It's the truth!"

"Truth? You expect me to believe you leave this house every day and go to *work*?"

Their voices echoed through the small home, inevitably reaching five-year-old Megara as she sat in the adjacent room at the window. She didn't flinch as their argument grew louder and more heated. As cutting as their words might be, Megara didn't understand them. Her parents' arguments had become as common as the sun rising in the morning and the moon shining at night. Even her mother seemed to anticipate them coming now, like she could feel an impending storm. As the sun began to fade each day, she'd move

Megara to the home's only other room minutes before her father would walk in the door.

"You wait here and play, Megara," her mother would say, sounding tired before the yelling even began. "Be a good girl now and keep quiet."

Her mother usually placed the *stromvos* in front of Megara to keep her busy. The top her father had once whittled her was the quietest of all of Megara's toys, though it had never been her favorite. That would be the *platagi*, but the rattle was deemed "too loud" by her father, and the *spheria* rolled all over the floor. One time her father had tripped over the marbles when he walked through the room and yelled so loud, Megara swore the walls rumbled. What she really wanted to play with was a doll with moving arms and legs like the ones she saw the girls at the market carrying, but somehow she knew not to ask for such an expensive gift. Most days her mother struggled to make enough from her mending to buy Megara milk.

"Where did you spend the money you made, Leonnatos? We need it for the rent! Maya will be here any minute to collect."

Megara rocked the stromvos back and forth between her thumb and index finger.

"I don't expect you to understand what it is like for me while you do nothing all day but sit here with her."

"*Her?* You mean your daughter? The child who is your spitting image? The one you all but ignore while I mend and clean for others to feed her, since you can't?"

Megara gave her fingers a small twist and watched the top take off, spinning wildly across the windowsill, the colors in the wood melting into one.

"It is hard enough to feed one mouth! You expect me to provide for three when there is no work in all of Athens?"

"You mean none that *you're* willing to do, Leonnatos. I see you when I bring Megara into the market. You stand around with those other louts all day laughing and doing nothing! While I fight to buy her milk!"

"Enough!"

Her father's roar reminded her of that day with the spheria, when he'd landed on his back after catching his foot on a marble. She momentarily looked at the door and held her breath, wondering if he would burst into the room and start yelling at her for doing absolutely nothing wrong, as he sometimes did.

"I can't do this anymore, Thea. I never wanted this life."

"Yet this is the life you have," her mother said sadly. "Rent is due today, the food is all gone, and there is a child in that other room who needs us."

"I have nothing to give her." His deep voice broke. "This is on you now. Goodbye, Thea."

Megara watched the top wobble as it neared the edge of the windowsill. If Megara didn't put her hand out to catch it, the stromvos would fall off.

"Don't you walk out that door!" Megara's mother shouted. "Leonnatos?"

The door in the other room opened and slammed shut.

Her mother gave a strangled sob, then was quiet.

The stromvos wobbled for a moment more before it fell onto the floor and skidded across the room, landing in front of the door. Megara turned to retrieve it, but the door opened first, sending the top back across the room and under a chair.

"Megara, get your things." Her mother swept into the room, gathering blankets and clothes and shoving them into a giant sack. Her pale face was tired and her brown hair was pulled high above her head in a messy bun held up by one of her sewing needles. "We're leaving, so move quickly."

"Are we going to the market?" Megara asked hopefully. Her stomach growled as if to remind her how hungry she was. They'd had nothing but a roll to split the day before. The money her mother made mending clothes never made it to the end of the week. By the last day, Megara would be lucky if she had one meal to sustain her. Megara recalled the jug with coins being empty that morning when her mother had peeked inside to see what was left. "Maybe today your father will bring home some pay," she'd said hopefully, but Megara had said nothing. Father never came home with money.

"We're moving," her mother said, not looking at her. "We need to get out of here before Maya comes to collect the rent. Rent we don't have because . . ." She exhaled hard. "Your father causes nothing but pain."

Pain. "Is he sick?" Megara asked, not understanding.

"Yes. Sick of us," Thea mumbled under her breath and then looked at her daughter. Her face softened, and she dropped the bag and knelt at Megara's side. "Look at me, child." She held the bottom of Megara's chin with a single finger. "Your father left us."

Meg blinked, unsure what to make of this statement. "Father went to work?"

This made her mother laugh, but the sound was bitter, like the taste of Kalamata olives. "No." She looked her straight in the eye. While Megara's deep red hair and pale skin resembled her father's, she shared her mother's unusual violet eyes. Their eyes were so magnetic a day didn't go by when someone in the street or at the market didn't comment on them. Today, her mother's eyes looked as if they were on fire. "No. Your father is gone and isn't coming back. It's just you and me now. I need you to be strong."

Gone. Megara blinked rapidly. He wasn't coming back. The way her mother was staring at her, Megara sensed this meant something that would change all she ever knew. Her eyes filled with tears.

"We will not cry, Megara." Her mother pushed a strand of Megara's hair behind her right ear. "We are better off without him. You'll see." She held her chin high. "Let this be a lesson, child. Don't ever let a man dim your light. In this world, you can't count on anyone but yourself."

Megara sniffled, but said nothing.

There was banging at their door. "Thea? Leonnatos? It's Maya. Are you in there?"

Megara and her mother looked at one another. Her mother put her hand to her lips. "Grab what you can and go to the window. We're going."

"Window?" Megara whispered. Their home was only one floor, so there was no need to worry about falling, but she'd never come and gone by window before. "No door?"

"No door." Her mother pushed her toward the window and opened it. "There's no pleading with that woman," she said as she dropped their sack outside. "You think she'll feel bad for us that Leonnatos left? That we can't pay to stay here and she's placing a child on the street? No. All she'll see is lost rent money."

"Thea? I know you're in there!"

"We will find somewhere else to stay," her mother told her as the banging grew louder. "I promise."

Megara looked around at the small home they had rented. The sparse furnishings, the tattered blanket on the bed they all shared, the small table where her mother sat to do her mending, the fresh orchids in the vase (the one luxury Thea allowed herself). None of the possessions being left behind were their own, but there was something about the space she'd lived in for five years that Megara somehow sensed she'd have a hard time finding again: a true home. Their world wasn't much, but her father had robbed her of it. Her eyes caught sight of the forgotten stromvos under a chair. That top was the one and only thing she recalled her father ever giving her. Instinctively, she went running back for it. Her hands closed around the top just as she felt her mother's hands on her back.

"Megara! What are you doing?" Thea hissed, pulling the child into her arms and lifting her up and out the window.

The stromvos slipped from her fingers as her mother dropped her over the side of the window. Megara could hear it hit the floor as she landed on the other side, but she knew not to ask her mother to retrieve it. Her father and the top were gone, and there was no use crying over them. Megara looked up to see her mother climbing out of the window behind her.

Maya appeared in the window looking angry. "You owe me your rent!"

Thea ignored Maya and reached for her daughter's hand. The two started to run.

"Thea!"

Megara could still hear Maya yelling from the window as they disappeared into the crowd at the end of the street.

If there was one thing Megara had learned in her short life already, it was this: love wasn't worth the trouble.

ONE: In Thin Air

Present day . . .

The view was spectacular.

That was Meg's first thought as Wonder Boy lifted her into his arms and a cloud carried the two of them into the air, high above the city of Thebes.

The second? Don't look down.

She wouldn't let her fear of heights ruin the moment. Hercules was beside her, his body awash in a golden glow that burned like the sun. Meg knew just from looking at him that he had finished his quest. Wonder Boy was now a god, and she was . . .

What was she, exactly?

Was she even alive?

In the last few years, Meg had been to hell and back—literally. She'd sold her soul to the god of the Underworld and spent her days and nights fulfilling Hades's every demand. While she still walked in the land of the living, her life was no longer her own.

Meeting Hercules had awoken something in her. Honestly, she wasn't sure what that something was, but she knew it felt *important*. Why else would she have leaped in front of a falling pillar to save him, causing her own demise in the process? That moment, and Wonder Boy's rescue of her afterward, was a blur now, like so many nightmares she tried hard to forget. The next thing she remembered was air filling her lungs as if she'd held her breath underwater for too long. Then there had been a crack of lightning, a flurry of clouds, and she and Wonder Boy were being whisked into the heavens toward Mount Olympus.

The city sat on a bed of clouds that shone like the sun burning brightly behind it. The majestic home of the gods rose high in the sky with peaks of clouds holding various buildings and waterfalls. As their cloud came to a stop in front of a massive staircase that led to Mount Olympus's pearly gates, Meg could hear cheering. Lined up on either side of the staircase, every god of Olympus was on hand to congratulate Wonder Boy.

"Three cheers for the mighty Hercules!" they shouted

as they threw flowers and blew kisses of gratitude into the air.

At that moment, Pegasus landed on a nearby cloud with Phil. The satyr caught a yellow flower in midair and began to chew happily as he surveyed the celebration.

"You did it, kid!" Phil shouted.

"Can you believe this, Meg?" Hercules said in wonder. "They're cheering for . . . me."

"You deserve it," she said warmly, because he did . . . but something was suddenly gnawing at her.

The fact that Phil was there made sense—he'd trained Wonder Boy on Earth, helping him achieve true hero status. But how had she gotten a front row seat to this party? Her association with Hades, and doing his bidding, had almost cost Hercules this moment. Did these gods realize the woman standing beside their newly anointed god had almost derailed his dream?

"Meg?"

She looked up. Hercules was offering her his hand. At some point, she must have stopped walking, because she was standing still as the cloud swayed slightly.

"Are you coming?"

Meg hesitated, looking from him to the crowd of admirers and those huge steps to the Mount Olympus gates. Her thoughts were coming fast, and not all of them were pretty.

Wonder Boy might have wanted her there, but it was clear a mortal didn't belong among the deities of Mount Olympus. Hercules was a god now. Where did that leave the two of them?

Mortals weren't allowed to date gods, were they?

Was this the last time she'd ever see him? If it was, she was just standing there, totally blowing it. She wasn't saying any of the things she wanted to say . . . which were what, exactly?

Well, there was the way he made her appreciate things in life she had never seen before—fragrant lilies in bloom, the way a kid in the market smiled. He had a contagious optimism that filled with her newfound energy. There were also those stolen moments between Hercules's hero training and triumphs, and Meg's awful meetings with Hades. The two of them would stroll through the garden, talking for as long as they could. They could not get enough of one another, drinking in each other's thoughts and observations like parched farmers reaching for brimming wells; Hercules brushing hair out of her eyes, Meg teasing him, making his ears redden so adorably. They had each challenged one another to see such vastly different points of view, to expand their worlds far beyond the reach of Mount Olympus and the Underworld. Those moments had been just for them . . .

or were they? Did the gods know about all the time they'd spent together? Did they care?

Okay, so it was clear there was a lot to unpack there, and Meg had no clue what the newly minted god in front of her was thinking. *That's* what she really wanted to know. But how did she ask Wonder Boy what he wanted when this was the moment he had worked so hard for . . . and when every god of Olympus was watching?

There was a sudden hush over the crowd and Meg followed the stares of the others to two figures who had appeared at the top of the stairs. Zeus and his wife Hera were a commanding sight: Zeus, a ball of blinding light with a long white beard and flowing hair, with muscles so large they looked as if they belonged to several men; Hera, a vison in pink, her curly hair and gown sparkling like gems.

Meg felt Hercules's sharp intake of breath at the sight of his parents. This was what he'd wanted, what he had been working toward his entire life. He glanced at Meg for a split second before rushing up the stairs to see them. She said nothing as she watched him go, staring instead at his bulging calves as he raced up the steps. Only one thought came to mind: *I should have taken the man's hand.*

Way to go, Meg! Hercules asks if you're coming and you

just stand there like a Greek statue. Why didn't you talk to him? Why didn't you say, "Wonder Boy, I want you to stay. Don't become a god"? Because that sounds selfish, doesn't it? And what right do I have to ask him that after I almost cost him everything? She could tell him the truth. *And what's that, Meg?* she countered herself. *How do you really feel about the boy?*

Meg looked at him as he reached the gates and her heart felt a sudden pull. There was only one thing she knew to say for certain.

"Don't go," she whispered.

He was too far away to hear her.

"Hercules," Meg heard Hera say as Hercules sank into his mother's open arms. "We're so proud of you."

"Fine work, boy!" Zeus punched him in the arm affectionately. His blue eyes that mirrored Hercules's own shone with pride. "You've done it! You're a true hero."

Meg suddenly felt Hera's eyes on her. Every other god in the joint turned to look at the single mortal among the clouds too. Meg shifted uneasily at the sudden attention of the immortals.

"You were willing to give your life to rescue this young woman." Awe coated Hera's voice.

Even Meg couldn't believe that Wonder Boy had almost

sacrificed himself to save her, of all people. And yet here they both were. *Don't go. Don't go.*

"For a true hero isn't measured by the size of his strength, but by the strength of his heart," Zeus told his son as he clasped a large arm around him. "Now at last, my son, you can come home!"

The gates of Mount Olympus opened, revealing a world beyond that Meg couldn't put into words. It was heaven, pure and simple. Paradise. It was a world not meant for a mortal like her.

She felt the shift as her heart—the one she'd only just gotten used to hearing beat again—stopped suddenly at the sight of it all. Any second now Wonder Boy would walk through those gates and never look back. She couldn't blame him. Zeus was offering him his dream come true—immortality, family, and home.

Home. That was everyone's dream, wasn't it? She'd never had a home of her own—not really. For years, she'd bounced from place to place, never staying long enough to even hang something on the walls. She'd never lived somewhere she longed to return to, where she felt loved, where she felt safe; a place she didn't want to leave.

Well, of course, she had felt that way once for a short while . . . and look how *that* had turned out.

The other gods crowded around Hercules, cheering

once more for the boy who was lost and found again. When Meg heard a cry, she couldn't help turning around. The god of love, Aphrodite, a vison in purple, was being consoled by a green god wearing a hat of leaves whom Meg didn't recognize.

"I can't believe we finally have our Hercules back." Aphrodite wiped away tears. "I'm just so happy for this family! Hera has waited so long to see her son again."

"Yes, well, she could have seen him sooner, but you know Zeus. He's so big picture," said the green god, and Aphrodite looked at her strangely. "Oh, don't mind me being dour on such a happy occasion. Just a bit of gossip I heard."

Aphrodite moved in closer. "Gossip away, Demeter."

Demeter was the god of harvest—someone Meg's first love had always prayed to when planting crops for the coming year. She strained to hear the zaftig god with the pink lips.

"Well, I heard that Hera was so inconsolable about Hercules being stolen that Zeus set out to find the boy, and he did. But once he found out the kid was mortal, he left him there. The Fates predicted Zeus's son was the only one who could stop the Titans eighteen years after his birth, so Zeus just waited the time out. Now he has the boy trained up, and strong enough to fight future battles."

Meg inhaled sharply as Aphrodite gasped. "No! He just *left* the child on Earth? Hera would be heartbroken to know that."

Holy Zeus. Was it true? Meg wondered.

Demeter shrugged and half-heartedly waved a palm leaf in the air in celebration. "Well, it's just a rumor, but I'll tell you something: if it were my daughter, I would never have left her sleeping in a cradle to be stolen in the first place. And I'd certainly never let her roam the Earth alone. If I knew where she was, I'd stop at nothing to get her back. Nothing."

Aphrodite patted her back. "We'll find Persephone. Don't you worry. I'm sure the girl is just off wandering meadows and farmland again as she likes to do."

"Maybe. But she has her harvest duties on Earth soon," Demeter said, her eyes on Zeus accepting praise for his son. "Anyway, all I know is I won't rest until I find her."

Phil rushed past the gods, separating Meg from them, with not even a greeting. He ran up the steps as fast as his small hooves would take him. Meg watched him, distracted. She couldn't get what Demeter said out of her head. Did Hercules know his father had located him, had known exactly where he was his entire life and never come for him?

Meg felt cold at the thought. She tried to shake the rumor aside, not let it get to her. She had enough to worry about—including saying goodbye to Wonder Boy in this,

his big moment. He'd opened up a whole new way of life to her—one where sacrifice was rewarded, and people could be good, and heroes could save the world. And now she was going back to Earth alone. There was nothing waiting for her in Thebes. Not anymore.

She had no one else to blame for her misfortune. What did her mother always say—never rely on anyone but yourself? It was true. After her father had abandoned them, she had lost her mother, and finally, her first flame. When would she learn that love was a dangerous game that she never won? Was it any surprise she was about to lose Wonder Boy, too?

Meg felt tears begging to come to the surface, but she refused to give in. She had no clue what she'd do next, but for now, she could stand on this cloud and watch Hercules till he disappeared beyond Olympus's gates. Hercules was home and she was happy for him—truly—even if she felt an urge to scream *don't go* once more.

"Congratulations, Wonder Boy," Meg said softly, giving him one last look. "You'll make one heck of a god."

She'd only made it a few steps before she felt someone grab her hand.

She turned around in surprise. Hercules was somehow standing beside her.

"Father, this is the moment I've always dreamed of," she

heard Hercules say, "but a life without Meg, even an immortal life, would be empty." He pulled her closer and stared into her eyes, making her heart quicken once more. "I . . . I wish to stay on Earth with her."

Her grip on his arm tightened. Had she just heard him correctly?

"What? How? Are you sure?" she whispered, still not believing her ears.

"I finally know where I belong . . ." he whispered back. "And it's with you."

Then suddenly he was kissing her and she was throwing her arms around him as he lifted her high into the air. She could hear the gods cheering, and this time it wasn't just for Hercules. It was for the two of them and their love that somehow defied logic.

Meg started to laugh and then thought she might cry. She stared into his blue eyes and didn't know what to say. But that was okay. She didn't have to rush her thoughts. Now they had time. Lots of time! Wonder Boy was coming back to Earth with her and they had a whole life ahead of them. Had something in her life finally gone right? It didn't seem possible, and yet Wonder Boy's lips on hers were proof. The gods approved. They were happy for them! They were—

"No."

No? At first, Meg thought she'd imagined someone

uttering the word and disagreeing with Hercules's wishes. But one look at Zeus's stern face and Meg knew—the gods' All-father was putting an end to their relationship before it could ever really get started.

TWO: A Change of Heart

The air was completely still. No one spoke a word. Their eyes were either on Zeus or his newly god-anointed son. And he just looked downright confused.

"Father?" Hercules questioned, still holding tight to Meg.

"I said no to your request, my boy," Zeus repeated.

Meg noticed some of the other gods sense the friction in the air and start to move away. It was clear no one wanted to be in Zeus's crosshairs. Only Hera remained by his side, listening patiently to Zeus's reasoning. Phil quietly motioned to Pegasus and climbed aboard the horse's back, flying off without even a goodbye. There went her ride.

"We waited a lifetime to get you back and have you sit beside your mother and me," Zeus explained. "And now that you're here, you want to give that up and remain human?"

"No . . . but I . . . I want to be with Meg," Hercules said, running a hand through his wavy locks, as he did whenever he got nervous. "If I can't go back, can she remain here?"

"No," Zeus said again, laughter escaping his lips. "Mount Olympus is no place for *mortals*."

He said the word "mortals" as if they were the scum of the Earth. *We're the ones who praise the gods, make sacrifices and do their bidding, and we're not worthy of their company?* Meg thought, feeling suddenly defensive even though she had had a similar thought just moments earlier.

"Zeus," Hera started, but he blazed forward.

"Son, when you visited my temple, I was so thankful to know you were alive and well." He grabbed Hera's hand and smiled. "Your mother and I had always hoped and prayed you were out there somewhere and we'd find you someday. Instead, you found us."

Meg's eyes flickered to Demeter's. Her face was blank, but Meg felt her skin prickle. *He's lying,* she thought.

"That is why I sent you on a quest to become a hero," Zeus continued. "We wanted you to become a god again, and you did all we asked and more to make that happen. You fought every beast sent your way and won! You have proven yourself to be selfless and a fighter. You deserve to be a god again, child, and gods, as you know, belong here. You spent your time on Earth with the mortals, and I'm glad you enjoyed spending time with this one." Zeus's eyes flickered to Meg before he looked away dismissively. "But now your place is here with us."

Hercules let go of Meg. "But Father . . ."

Her body went cold. *I'm glad you enjoyed spending time with this one?* Was Zeus serious? Who was he to judge their relationship when he barely knew her? He didn't even know his son! If what Demeter said was true, Hercules had not needed to wait so long to prove his worth as a hero; Zeus had left him on Earth till he needed his help. He had abandoned Hercules, just like she'd been abandoned countless times over. And now he was dismissing Hercules's love for her as if it were nothing? Then again, why was she surprised? When her first love had lain dying, it wasn't Zeus who saved him. It was Hades.

Meg felt a flash of anger. If Hercules was going to stay on Mount Olympus, he deserved to know what his father had done, just as she had learned the painful truth about her own—they'd both been left to fend for themselves.

"Wait! Hercules, you deserve to know the truth!" Meg's voice was breathless. She felt a little dizzy now, the altitude finally catching up to her. "Zeus knew you were alive! Even before you reached the temple. He left you on Earth till you grew up and he needed you to fight the Titans!"

Meg heard gasps and saw Zeus look at her with disdain. She looked for Demeter, but she had suddenly disappeared from the crowd, as had Aphrodite. Smart move. Maybe she should have thought about revealing this news in front of an audience.

"What?" Hercules whispered, his pained expression making Meg's stomach twist.

"Zeus, is this true?" Hera asked, the anguish on her face mirroring her son's. Zeus looked away, his face turning redder.

"How do you know this?" Hercules asked.

"I overheard someone telling the story," Meg admitted, choosing not to reveal Demeter's name. Why have multiple gods mad at you? "You were mortal, so he left you on Earth, waiting till Hades resurrected the Titans so *you* could fight them for him," she continued, feeling the heat rise in her face as she thought of Hercules being a pawn in the god's game. "He only wants to keep you here now so that you can fight his battles." Hercules's broad shoulders sank. "I'm sorry. I just felt you should know what you're signing up for."

"Father?" Hercules looked up at Zeus, whose expression had grown even stonier.

Zeus glared at Meg. "Who are you going to believe, son? Me or this mortal?"

Meg's eyes flashed. "I'm not the one who let his own child be stolen while he slept."

The minute the comment left her lips, she knew she'd gone too far.

The other gods quickly began to dissipate. Hera stayed put, but Meg wondered if she was in shock.

Zeus's face turned almost purple as he seemingly grew three times his size. Behind him, the sky darkened like an approaching thunderstorm and lightning bolts crisscrossed the sky. Hercules instinctively stepped in front of Meg, putting one hand on her arm, but she nudged it away. She'd lived with Hades. She wasn't afraid to stand up to Zeus.

"You dare question my judgment, Megara?" Zeus thundered as the storm clouds rolled in around him. Lightning crashed dangerously close to where she and Hercules were standing. "You, the woman who worked to keep my son from completing his quest?"

On second thought, maybe she *should* be a little afraid of Zeus. Especially now that she realized he was well aware of what she had done.

"Oh yes, I know all about your life, too, Megara," Zeus said. "I suspect much more than my son knows."

Meg felt her cheeks flame. It was true she hadn't told Wonder Boy *everything.*

"You did my brother's bidding for him, trying to cheat Hercules from his rightful place at my side, and you think I should let him return to Earth with you?" As Zeus continued, Hera looked at her.

"I . . ." Meg wanted to explain herself, but Zeus was on a roll.

"You think turning my son against me will allow you to keep him?" Zeus bellowed. "You are not worthy of a god's love!"

"Father, she saved my life!" Hercules shouted. Zeus flinched and the lightning stopped.

"That may be true," he said, his size shrinking back down to normal again. "And it is also true that I could have come to you before, son." Regret laced his voice as he glanced briefly at his wife. "But I saw no point in disrupting your childhood when good people like Amphitryon and Alcmene could protect you and keep your identity hidden until you were old enough to learn how to fight for your right to be a god again. As that is indeed what needed to be done. Only a god can call Mount Olympus home, and you needed time to grow into that role. It would have been foolish and selfish to have rushed you." He narrowed his eyes at Meg. "*That* is why I sacrificed our time together—not because I didn't want you. *Never* because I didn't want you."

Meg felt her cheeks burn and she looked away. *Okay, that kind of makes sense. Nice one, Meg.*

"I was trying to protect you," Zeus added. "Can you, Megara, say the same for Hercules during his time on Earth?"

Meg looked at the ground. They both knew the answer to that question.

"I am sorry, son, but this mortal is not worthy of your love," Zeus added. "My decision is final. You will remain here and she will leave at once."

"No!" Hercules cried. Hera narrowed her eyes.

"Hermes!" Zeus thundered, and his faithful messenger flew to his side in seconds.

"You called, my lord?" Hermes hovered in front of him thanks to the wings on his hat. He rubbed at his fogged-up glasses to see them all better.

"Yes," Zeus said. "Take Megara back to Earth." He looked at his son and his expression relaxed slightly. "You may have a moment to say your goodbyes," he added hastily before gliding up the steps to the gates. The storm clouds slowly began to dissipate.

Hercules looked from Zeus to Meg. "I . . . you . . . Don't go anywhere. I'll talk to him." He ran after Zeus. "Father!"

Hermes flew to Meg's side. "Wow, you really know how to wind up the big guy! Ready to go?"

"Will you give us a moment, Hermes?" Hera appeared in front of her.

Hermes flew off and the two women stared at one another. Close up, Hera was almost blindingly stunning, the epitome of regal with her sparkling gown and rose-colored hair piled on top of the crown on her head. Small gold rings held up the draped sleeves of her dress, which ruffled in the light wind. Unlike Zeus, she bore an open, almost curious expression as she peered at the mortal before her. She held out an arm.

"I think we should talk," the god said simply.

Meg took a deep breath. "Look, about what I said before . . ."

"I will deal with Zeus later; that's not what I want to talk to you about. I want to know why you felt the need to tell my son about his father. Were you hoping to gain favor with him?"

"No, I just thought he deserved to know."

"Because?" Hera prodded.

"Because no one should live with a lie," Meg said.

"And?"

Hera was clearly fishing for something. Meg thought for a moment. "And . . . I owe him. He changed my life."

Hera drew closer. Now that she was getting used to the light emanating from the god, she realized Hercules had her wide eyes. Yes, Zeus also had the same magnetic blue shade, but there was a kindness in Hera's and Hercules's that instantly put her at ease. "And how did he do that?"

Meg closed her eyes and thought about Wonder Boy again. She pictured their rendezvous in a secluded meadow, a surprise picnic at the water's edge—these moments were some of the happiest she'd had in a long time. He had literally saved her body from the river Styx, her soul from Hades, but it was more than that. When they were together, she felt as weightless as the clouds beneath her. What she knew for sure was that she was content when she was by his side, like a piece of a puzzle had slid into place.

But could she say all this to his newly found mother? No way. Best to keep it simple. "He gave me my life back. A girl doesn't forget that."

Hera tapped her chin and looked thoughtful. "I see. Is that the *only* reason you wish for my son to return to Earth with you?" Meg opened her mouth and closed it again. "I assume you do want him to return to Earth, don't you? You didn't protest when he suggested it." A small smile played on her pink lips.

"I . . ." Meg looked back at Hercules, who appeared to be talking with his hands, winding them up as if he were about to throw a discus. "Of course, I'd like to spend more time with him, but if he's happy here . . ." She felt the lump form in her throat and couldn't believe this was happening. She would *not* cry while talking to Hera. "I want him to be happy. He deserves that."

Hera nodded. "And do *you* deserve to be happy, Megara? I suspect *you* make him happy. And if he stays here and you go back there, I don't think either of you will be." She looked up at her son and husband still arguing. "No, this arrangement of my husband's clearly won't work. We need to come up with a different plan."

Was the god of marriage and birth offering her an olive branch? Meg took a deep breath and tried to keep her words in check for a change while she deferred to Hera. "What do you suggest?"

Hera continued to look at her. "That depends. Are you in love with my son?"

"Love?" Meg took a step back. She immediately thought back to something she'd said to Hercules as she lay dying back in Thebes. *People do crazy things when they're in love.*

Was that what this was? Love?

Was she in love with a god?

No.

Yes.

Possibly.

How did one know for sure? Her track record when it came to love was tarnished at best, and she and Wonder Boy hadn't known each other very long. Of course, they had grown close, but in the moment she had uttered those words she thought it was the end of the road. Her experience with love up until then had been messy and painful; she had sensed things could have been different with Hercules if given the chance. But *if* was the key word. She had no clue what she would do next when she stepped off this cloud, and even less of a clue if her world didn't include Wonder Boy. Was Hera giving her a chance to change her fate yet again? Meg looked at the god. If saying she was in love would give her and Hercules time to figure their story out, what was the harm in saying it?

"Of course," Meg said firmly.

Hera clasped her hands together and smiled. "Wonderful! Then there is only one choice: you, Megara, need to become a god."

Meg wasn't sure she had heard Hera correctly. "I'm sorry. What?"

"You need to become a god," Hera repeated, as if it were as simple as buying figs at the local market. "It's the only logical answer to this predicament."

Meg's eyes narrowed. Gods didn't just offer the gift of immortality without reason. People prayed for such an honor all the time, but other than Hercules—who was born a god and lost his status when he was kidnapped—she could count on her fingers the number of gods she knew of who had started out as mortals: Psyche, Thyone, Ariadne . . . Dionysus counted since he supposedly had a mortal mother, but Zeus was his father. She had done nothing to help the gods like they had. All she'd done was anger Zeus. She looked up again at Wonder Boy still pleading with his father, who seemed as angry as ever. "And Zeus would be okay with this?"

Hera waved her hand dismissively. "Let me worry about my husband. Are you interested in what I have to say or not? We don't have much time."

Meg still couldn't believe what she was hearing. "What do I have to do? Let me guess. Save a pair of kids trapped in a chasm? Oh, wait. Hercules already did that when Hades set him up to fail."

Hera's smile faded. "Do you think I am trying to deceive you?"

Okay, maybe she'd overstepped. Again. A rumble of thunder in the distance made Meg choose her next words carefully. "Where I come from, offers like this aren't thrown around so easily. You'll have to excuse me for wondering what the catch is."

Hera's smile returned. "I like your spirit. And you

clearly care about one another. My son wouldn't ask to give all this up if that were not true." She stared at Meg. "I have a feeling you two would make a strong match, and that power is rare indeed—something that, in turn, could help the world. What good is one miserable god when there could be two extraordinary ones? That is why I want to help you. I assure you, this offer is no trickery. If you can prove yourself worthy, I can see to it that you are given the gift of immortality. There are special circumstances where mortals can become gods, and if that were to happen, then the two of you could be together." Her eyes flashed mischievously. "Whether Zeus likes it or not."

Meg was speechless. Hera wasn't joking. The god was offering her something that she'd never even dreamed of becoming. It took her a moment to catch her breath. "A god?" Meg repeated.

"A god," Hera said again. "*If* you can prove your worth."

Meg placed a hand on her hip and cocked her head to one side, her ponytail swishing. "And how do I go about doing that? Start helping kids cross the road and assist old men with their trips to the market?"

Hera actually laughed. "No. If you want to be with my son and become a god worthy of Mount Olympus, I need to see you understand love is a strength, not a weakness. That putting your trust in someone you love doesn't mean you can't stand on your own two feet. It means you know how to share responsibility and accept help when it is needed." She placed her hands on Meg's shoulders. "I want to see you know how to be vulnerable, Megara. And understand that love means opening your heart even if the story doesn't always end the way you want it to."

Meg crossed her arms. "I know all these things already."

Hera put her arms down and smiled at her kindly. "Do you?"

"Yes," Meg insisted, somewhat defiantly.

Hera continued to study her. "Then you've told Hercules about the loves you have lost, I assume. You told him about Aegeus?"

Just hearing Aegeus's name made Meg's lungs burn. The memory of crying and the screams that she associated with the name of her first flame came flooding back. As always, she attempted to block the noise out. "Of course," Meg said, which wasn't exactly a lie. Wonder Boy knew she'd been scorned before. How she'd been scorned, not exactly . . .

Hera's eyes glittered. "And what about your mother?"

THREE: Life and Loss

Before . . .

Thirteen can be a hard age for a girl.

Especially when that girl has to act like the parent.

Megara might not have realized how much her life would change that day her father walked out on her and her mother, but she learned quickly.

Forced to provide for her daughter in a society that viewed women as unequal, Thea couldn't own land or vote. Her place was meant to be keeping house, but since she had no house to keep and a daughter to feed, she had to figure out a way around the laws. Thea took mending work where she could get it, and when she couldn't find that, she'd clean the homes of men whose wives were too busy raising countless children to scrub a floor. (Megara would watch in wonder as her mother convinced men their wives needed an extra set of hands around the house. As harsh as Thea had always been with Megara's father, she was sweeter than nectar to these skeptical men, who almost always caved and gave her work.)

While her mother worked, Megara took care of their own life—cleaning their rented spaces, cooking so her mother wouldn't have to after a backbreaking day, and minding the money her mother brought home. If young Megara had learned anything from her time with her father, it was to hold on to her drachmas. She counted and recounted what her mother earned and learned to keep a budget for food so that they wouldn't go hungry if they could help it. And though girls weren't afforded school, Meg taught herself to read using the stone signs in the square, stealing Homer's works out of the school-aged boys' bags when she could. She watched the merchants in the market accept payment from shoppers, learning how to count coins and what each one meant. So when precious coins she kept in a jar went missing, she went straight to her mother to inquire where they went.

"Oh, Megara, it's just a few drachmas!" her mother would say as she lay on the bed they shared and tried to rest her eyes.

"Those 'few drachmas' were meant to buy eggs

for breakfast this week," Meg scolded. "Now what will we eat?"

Her mother sat up with a start, her eyes bright. "Who needs food when we have this?" Her mother opened up the sack by the bed and held out a tarnished flute. "This is for you!"

Meg stared at it unhappily. "I don't know how to play."

"You'll learn! Music feeds the soul. I always wanted to learn, but never had the opportunity. You, my darling Megara, do! Here. Try it."

Meg bit her tongue. Her mother was excited, but Meg still hated how impulsive she was. How could she think a rusty wind instrument was better than eggs that could feed them for a week? This was just like that time her mother had bought a vase said to belong to the gods, thinking they could sell it for a good price. (They never did.) Another time, her mother bought old copper wares hoping she could trade them for better goods. That didn't work out, either. Not to mention the fresh flowers she still bought every time she could. Meg was tired of it.

"Just think—the more you practice, the more beautiful the notes will sound," her mother said, trying again. She laid a finger upon a divot on its side. "It doesn't matter what the flute looks like. It's the melody you create, child, that can take you away from all this." She motioned to their small rental. "If you learn to play, people will want to hear you. I know it." She put down the flute, grabbed Meg's hands, and held them in her callused hands. "When I saw this instrument, it was as if the gods spoke out and said, 'Megara could be a great musician if you help her!' How could I say no?"

Meg shook her head. "But, Mother, the eggs . . ."

"Child, what do I always say?"

"Trust yourself," Meg repeated alongside her mother.

"That's right!" Her mother looked pleased. "When I saw this flute, my instincts told me that our money would be better spent on this flute for you than anything we could put in our bodies. Learning to play could change both of our lives." She picked up the instrument again and held it out to Meg. "I'm asking you to try."

Meg's stomach growled. How could she play when she could think of nothing but food? And how would she even begin to learn when her mother had never played, either? Why was her mother so infuriating? What if her instincts were wrong? Meg thought about speaking up and then saw her mother's face, so open and hopeful. She relented, taking the flute from her outstretched hands. She put her lips to the reed and blew.

The sound that came out was so dreadful, dogs howled in the distance.

Her mother smiled hopefully. "All you need is practice!"

Practice Meg did. Every time she saw that flute and thought of the lost money, she felt spurred on to make something good come out of her mother's impulsive purchase. While her mother did odd jobs, Meg taught herself notes, then eventually learned melodies. For inspiration, she would sit in the square and listen to musicians play. She tried to mimic them. After some time, Meg got better, which only made her want to practice more. Night after night, she tried new notes, new tunes strung together, experimenting with the placement of her mouth and fingers, with the strength of her breath. The first full song she learned was one about the plight of a white lily. She became swept up in its beauty, and in her ability to pour every bit of herself into it—her frustration at how difficult life had been for her mother and her, her ache for a permanent place in the world, her pride at how far they had come. Before long, her mother encouraged her to play for others.

"They will want to hear you!" her mother said, leading her along through the village square. Megara would never forget her words. "You are a survivor, like me. Remember that. No matter what happens, you can handle it. *Trust yourself.*"

Megara remembered being skeptical, but it turned out her mother had been right again. When she got lost in the music, people stopped what they were doing and listened.

A few even dropped coins at her feet and asked when she'd be playing again.

"Tomorrow?" Megara had said, looking to her beaming mother for guidance.

"Of course!" Thea said, picking up the coins and pocketing them. She put her arm around Megara as they left the square and looked at her daughter. "I told you, Megara, you are meant to shine, and look! You are shining, and you're being rewarded for it." Her mother looked around the village again happily. "I like it in this town. I think we should stay, and you can play here forever."

Megara tried not to get excited at the idea of putting down roots. No matter how smitten her mother was with a new village, the sheen wore off after a few days like on an old vase, just like it probably would here. Megara didn't blame her. Thea had been burned before. Sometimes it would be by a family that refused to pay after a backbreaking week of work or promises of long-term employment that went dry after a few days. Couple that with her mother's razor-sharp tongue and rash behavior, and Megara knew Thea's view of a situation changed like the wind. Thea trusted no one and always feared the little good that came their way was a ruse.

But Megara expressed none of this. Instead she just smiled and said, "I'd love to stay."

Her mother squeezed her hand. "Good."

One week later, her mother came through the door like a sudden gust of wind.

"Get your things, we're leaving!" Thea spun around the room looking for their well-worn travel sacks. She noticed them packed by the door and looked at her daughter suspiciously.

"Did something happen with Argos?" Megara asked innocently.

"Yes, Argos!" Her mother threw her hands up, forgetting all about the packed bags. "I don't trust that man!"

"That man" was the widower brother of Thea's current employer. The two had met the week before when Thea was mending shirts for the family, and Argos had inquired about giving her additional work. Megara had met him and his young son when they had run into them in the market. Megara had recalled Argos being soft-spoken and having long lashes covering his brown eyes. He had asked Megara thoughtful questions about her age and her birthday. Adults rarely talked to children about such things, in her experience. When he had noticed Megara eyeing the dried fruits that were far too expensive for them to even consider getting, he had bought her some. They had tasted sweet, like heaven. Thea had disapproved. "He's probably trying to get me to do his mending for free." Instead, as Megara learned through gossip at the market—which was always the best place to find gossip—Argos was looking for a new wife. Megara hoped against hope that her mother could be that person. And she prayed her mother wouldn't mess things up.

"Argos seems nice," Megara tried. "And his son is sweet."

"Yes, yes, but so young and needy as children are," her mother said dismissively. Megara tried hard not to take offense. Thea looked down, registering the expression on her daughter's face. "Oh, not *you*, Megara. But I have no time to play with the boy when I'm working, and yet, Argos keeps bringing him by! And then today he says . . . he says . . . he's looking for . . ." Megara noticed the fear in her mother's eyes. "It doesn't matter. He was just spinning lies. You can't trust a man. Never rely on anyone but yourself."

"I know," Megara said, knowing her mother's mantra well, "but Argos . . ."

Her mother shot her a look. "We don't need a man complicating things for us. Now we must go. Before he comes by. He said he'd be here in an hour."

"You're not telling him we're leaving?" Megara said, aghast. "Mother, that's . . ."

"Enough, child!" Her mother hoisted the sack over her shoulder and looked around the sparse room. "Let's go."

"Yes, Mother," Megara said and lifted the sack with

the coins in it. Thea hadn't even thought to ask if they had money for travel. Perhaps she already knew that if they had any, Megara would think to grab it. The vase her mother had briefly prized was left behind and all but forgotten. The only memento of their time in that town was the tarnished flute.

Megara kept her head down as they rushed out of the village and tried hard not to think about what her life would have become if her mother had accepted Argos's proposal. But dreaming of a life she'd never have was pointless. They didn't need a man when they had each other.

Until one day that changed, too.

The next town they landed in was no different than the half a dozen they had been to before. Thea still found work mending and cleaning while Megara counted their money and took care of the home and the cooking, practicing her flute in the evenings.

"Thanks for the bargain, Theos," Megara said to the young man in the marketplace who had given her a good price on day-old bread. "It's been a real slice." Then she turned with an expertly timed flip of her lengthening red hair—it was almost to her waist now—and swung her hips as she sashayed away. As Megara grew, she was learning that her charm was a tool she could rely on.

She was almost giddy as she thought about the things

she could make with two loaves of bread. Her mother would be thrilled when she returned from work that evening. But as she approached the home where they were staying, she saw the crowd gathered on the street. There was a lot of yelling, and some tears, but Megara couldn't see what was happening till she got closer. There was Thea, pinned beneath a horse and a cart.

"Mother!" Megara cried, dropping the bread and rushing to her side.

"I didn't even see her! She came out of nowhere!" the guy driving the carriage told anyone who would listen. "She wasn't watching where she was going!"

Men were trying to lift the carriage off Thea, but Megara knew it was already too late. Her mother was fading fast. "Hold on," Megara cried, starting to hiccup as she grabbed her mother's hand. "Don't leave me, Mother!" Her mother's face was white and her eyes were already closing. "Stay with me!" Megara begged. She was crying so hard she couldn't see.

"Megara, listen to me. You'll be all right," her mother whispered as she started to drift away. "Trust yourself. Remember, whatever happens, you can handle it."

Megara froze. It was as if she knew what her mother was going to say next. It was the same thing she always said to Megara when times were tough and it looked like the situation was impossible. Megara would always be the one in their relationship to worry, and her mother would be the one to crack the jokes. This time it wasn't funny.

"You're a big, tough girl," her mother said, her voice fading.

"No," Megara cried. "Please!"

Her mother's eyes closed. "You tie your own sandals and every . . . thing." Her mother's hand went limp. Megara threw herself over her mother's body. Thea was gone.

FOUR: An Offer Meg Can't Refuse

On Mount Olympus . . .

"You've made your point—I need to deal with the loss of my mother. What's that got to do with this quest?" Meg knew she sounded more aggravated than she should considering she was speaking to the mother of the guy she really cared about, who just so happened to be a god married to the All-father of gods.

Thankfully, Hera didn't appear ruffled. She quickly glanced at her husband and Hercules again. "You'll understand with time. For now, all you need to worry about is finding the lost aulos of Athena."

Meg wasn't sure she understood. "So to become a god, all I have to do is track down Athena's double flute?"

Hera smiled. "That's the *first* step."

Ah, there it was. The catch. Finding Athena's flute, which she had to assume wasn't just lost in a clearing or hiding under a rock, wouldn't be as simple as Hera made it sound. The last time she'd made a deal with a god, it had ended with her losing her soul. What would happen if she risked her life for this quest and failed?

Well, one thing was certain: Hades would never let her leave the Underworld again.

Meg shuddered at the thought. She did not want to return there anytime soon. Although, if she became a god, she wouldn't have to return at all.

She'd be a god. An actual god! And when she really thought about it, she'd make a heck of a great one. She wouldn't be all judgy and hurl angry lightning bolts like Zeus. No, she'd forgive people for their mistakes, like Hercules had forgiven her for the countless wrong decisions she'd made before he walked into her life. And as former mortals, she and Hercules would have insight on the world in a way these ethereal gods wouldn't. Together, the two of them could do a lot of good up on Mount Olympus. As she knew from her own experience, the gods didn't always get things right. Meg looked up at the gates to Mount Olympus again and wondered *what if*.

"You should know, I don't make offers lightly," Hera added, starting to sound impatient. "If you find what is lost and complete the tasks that follow, you will rise to Mount Olympus as a god and spend an eternity with my son."

Eternity? The word felt like a water nymph's punch to the stomach, instantly taking the wind out of her sails. Eternity as in forever? Her longest relationship had lasted a year, and look how that had ended. How did she know she and Hercules would even make it that long? Sure, she wanted them to have a chance to figure out their relationship without Zeus interfering, but if she did as Hera asked, could she spend an *eternity* with Wonder Boy? The gods were forever deceiving one another, fighting, and taking lovers. Is that what she and Hercules were signing up for if she did this? But then, what was the alternative?

Hera interrupted her thoughts. "I believe you're familiar with flutes, are you not?"

So Hera *did* know all about her past. Meg hadn't picked up a flute since Aegeus, but just the word evoked memories and music in her mind that she hadn't dared to think about in a long time. "Yes. I know how to play," Meg admitted hoarsely.

Hera nodded. "Good. Music will come in handy on your journey."

"And that's final!"

Meg and Hera looked up. Zeus was storming through Mount Olympus's gates, which closed firmly behind him.

Hercules's whole frame seemed to shrink in defeat, and Meg felt a pull at her heart. It wasn't just the way he always looked at her—with a mix of genuine joy and longing rolled into one—or his appearance, although he wasn't hard on the eyes with those rippling pectorals. She found herself drawn to those kind blue eyes and the hard line of his jaw, which moved when he was thinking. It was the dimples in his cheeks when he flashed her that magnetic smile, and the way his reddish blond hair had a single curl that was always falling in front of his eyes. But mostly it was that earnest nature of his, and his need to find the good in every situation, which was so different from how she viewed life, and gave her hope that the world could be more than she imagined it to be. All she knew was she wasn't ready to say goodbye to him.

Meg looked at Hera. "Thank you for the generous offer. I accept."

Immediately she felt something in her hand. It was an hourglass. Inside it, pink sand, the color of Hera, was piled high on one end. The other side was empty. Slowly, pink grains began to flow to the empty side of the glass.

"You have ten days to complete your quest," Hera said. "I wish you well, Megara." Then the god disappeared.

"Ten days?" Meg froze. Hera hadn't said anything about a deadline. What happened when the sand ran out? "Wait!

I have questions! Come back!" Meg cried just as Hercules reached her at the bottom of the steps.

"I'm so glad you're still here." He placed his arms around her. "Are you all right? What were you and my mother talking about?"

Meg buried her face in his chest and breathed in his scent. She had a sudden desire to stay right there in his arms and forget all about the hourglass. "Oh, you know. Nothing much. Your mother just gave me a quest."

"A quest?" Hercules repeated. "Why?"

So much for forgetting. Meg lifted her head and looked up at him, curious and worried, his brow wrinkling slightly. He really was something. "If I prove myself worthy and complete her tasks, she'll make me a god so that we can be together."

Hercules's eyes widened as he processed her words. Then his face broke into a wide smile. "That's amazing!" He lifted her into the air and spun her around. She laughed despite herself. He gently placed her back down on the cloud, keeping his arms around her.

"Yeah, wonderful for you. You don't have to go on the quest." Meg's fingers traced his ample shoulder blade. "I have ten days and counting." She showed him the hourglass.

"Ten days is a lot of time! You can do it, Meg," he said in

earnest. "You can do anything you put your mind to! I know it." He lifted her again and spun her faster this time.

She pounded her fists on his back, laughing. "Put me down. Didn't I just say I have a deadline?"

"Sorry." Hercules gently lowered her. "I'm just so excited! If you become a god, we can be together forever."

There was that idea again. Meg took a deep breath. "Quests aren't easy."

He looked at her. "Anything is easier than talking to my father." Herc sighed. "I tried to convince him how much good I could do on Earth, but he feels I belong here." He smiled wide again. "But now you can be, too. If my mother believes in us, we can't fail. Hera loves love and she loves me. She wants us to be happy." Hercules cocked his head, taking Meg's hand in his. "What does she want you to do?"

"She only told me my first step—I have to find Athena's double flute," Meg explained as a cloud drifted past them, shrouding them both in mist. "Any clue where it might be?"

Hercules's face darkened. "I heard it was stolen by a river guardian somewhere."

Meg relaxed. "A river guardian? They're not so bad!"

Herc shook his head. "Meg, they're huge and mean! Don't you remember Nessus?" She gave him a look. "Sorry. I know you can take care of yourself. I just don't see how Mother would give you a quest and not offer some sort of clue as to where to find the flute. It's a big world out there."

"That's true." *Come on, Hera, what am I missing?* Meg thought, looking at the hourglass again for clues. That's when she noticed something small etched into the top of the vial she hadn't seen before. It was a single word: KOUFONISIA. "Does this word mean anything to you?" Meg held the hourglass out to Hercules again.

"I think that's an island! It must be one of the Lesser Cyclades. That's right about here." He turned Meg toward the edge of the cloud and pointed to a large swath of blue below with a series of tiny islands peppered around it.

"Whoa! Not so close to the edge." She took several steps back before she got vertigo. If she did become a god, it would take some time to get used to this height.

"Sorry," Hercules said. "Hey! Koufonisia is kind of near Phil's island! You should take him with you."

"Oh, no." Meg backed away even more. "That red-faced mini menace hates me!"

"Phil doesn't hate you. He just thought you were a distraction." Hercules paused. "And he wasn't happy when he found out you were working with Hades, but that's all in the past! Phil likes you now, and he'd be a great guide."

Hercules might not have picked up on it, but she knew

there was no love lost between her and that satyr. "I like your enthusiasm, but I don't need help. I can do this on my own."

"I know." He nuzzled her face. "I just—I still wish I could go with you."

"We both know that's not going to happen," Meg said softly.

Hercules pulled away. "Maybe there is a way I *can* be there—at least for a little bit. I have an idea! Hold on!" He dashed to the other side of the cloud and returned at an impossibly quick speed. Meg couldn't believe he had been a mortal only a few hours ago. To watch him now, one would have thought he had been a god his entire life.

He came closer, gripping two small saddlebags in one hand, and holding out a bright fuchsia orchid in the other. "This is for you."

"It's beautiful," Meg said, taking the flower from him. She'd never seen an orchid like it. The color glowed like the gods.

"This orchid is powerful. Phil told me all about it once. It's as rare as ambrosia, and only grows on Mount Olympus. Think of it like having your own messenger to the gods. If you want to reach me, rip off one of the petals, say my name, and I'll be there."

"Well, I'll be." She gently pinned the stem to the clasp

on her gown. "There's only three petals on here. What happens if I run out?"

There was that crinkle in his brow again. "I won't be able to get another one. This was the only flower fully matured I could find." He touched her face. "But you won't need another. I know you can do this. Then we can be together."

"Yes." Meg tried to push her doubts aside. She'd died, been saved from the river Styx, and been offered the chance to become a god all in one day. It was a lot to swallow for any girl.

"You're my world, Meg." Hercules cupped her face in his large hands. "I can't imagine living an eternity without you. Be careful out there."

For some reason, his warning made her think of her mother. "I'm a big, tough girl. I'll be all right. I tie my own sandals and everything."

Wonder Boy smiled and leaned in for a kiss. His lips had barely grazed hers before they both heard a rumble of thunder.

There was a popping sound and Hermes appeared, the wings on his hat flapping wildly. "Greetings, lovebirds! Zeus sent me here to move the goodbyes along."

Meg could see the storm clouds rolling in again behind them. The last thing she wanted was another appearance by Zeus. She tightened her fingers around the hourglass. There was a trace amount of pink sand on the bottom of it already. "I should go."

Hercules held her tight. "Let me send Pegasus with you." She opened her mouth, ready to protest. "You'll be able to travel way faster with him than you can by foot." The horse trotted over and Hercules hung the two saddlebags on his back. Meg looked at them curiously.

"Supplies," he explained.

She inhaled, taking in Hercules's sweet scent one more time. "Okay." She smiled softly, placing the hourglass in one of the bags as he leaned in again to kiss her. At that moment, Pegasus bumped her from behind, swooping her up onto his back. He started galloping toward the edge of the cloud before Meg could even say goodbye. "WAIT!" she cried, closing her eyes and hanging on to Pegasus for dear life.

"Keep your hands on Pegasus's back at all times," said Hermes as Meg and Pegasus went galloping past him. "Enjoy your ride to Koufonisia!"

Pegasus plunged off the side of the cloud, and Meg's scream could be heard throughout Mount Olympus.

FIVE: The Backside of Water

They were falling. At least that's what it felt like as Pegasus dove straight down and Meg clung desperately to his neck. She could feel the wind rushing past her, whipping her ponytail into her face as they continued to plummet.

Don't look. Don't look. Don't look, she told herself. *You went up. You have to come down. Everything is fine.*

The ride up to Mount Olympus had been almost peaceful. She was alive, she was in Hercules's arms, and he was suddenly a god. Just one of those things was enough to put her in a blissful state of wonder. But traveling with this flying beast was different. And why did she sense Pegasus was enjoying her panic?

Pegasus dipped again and Meg let out another terrified

scream. She squeezed his neck even tighter and opened her eyes against her better judgment. The horse was bobbing and weaving through clouds so fast Meg was sure she was going to be sick. She wanted off this ride.

"Hey! You!" Meg tugged on his blue mane. "If you don't want me to drag you down to Poseidon and make you a sea-horse, then slow down already!"

She heard Pegasus neigh unpleasantly, but he slowed to an acceptable glide.

"Thank you," Meg said, and Pegasus snorted softer that time. Meg loosened her grip on his mane and looked around. Koufonisia was growing closer. They were near enough that she could make out a few mountains and bodies of water on the island.

"Look, Peg—can I call you Peg?" Pegasus gave a half-hearted neigh. "I don't like this any more than you do. Hercules wanted me to take you on this quest." Pegasus quietly continued to flap his majestic wings. "The quicker we find what we're looking for, the quicker we can both go home. Wherever that is," she muttered to herself. "So let's find this flute and get out of here. Deal?"

Pegasus neighed louder, seeming almost happy. As he dipped again, the clouds cleared, giving way to bright sunshine and turquoise blue waters below. They glided so close to the water Peg's wings actually skimmed the waves. Finally they made it to the island's sandy beach. She climbed off Pegasus and patted his side.

"Nice landing there, Peg." She unhooked the saddlebag where she had tucked the hourglass and placed it on the sand. "Why don't you get yourself a drink and take a fly around this island before we explore?"

Pegasus neighed and took flight again, giving Meg a moment to look around. Koufonisia was pretty impressive at first glance. The sandy white beach surrounded a forest full of lush greenery, pink flowered bushes, and orange trees. In the distance, she could see a waterfall atop a green mountain. The sound of birds was the only noise she heard. There was no sign of boats or footprints or smoke. The island appeared to be uninhabited. Meg raised her eyes to the sun and felt the warmth on her face. Maybe Koufonisia was Elysium on Earth. Maybe she could hide out here and no one would even notice. There was no Hades around to torture her, no gods to remind her of her mother's loss or Aegeus's betrayal. Here, she could just *be*. Was it so wrong to want to skip the quest and spend her days lying on the warm sand, eating fruit, watching the waves?

But then there was Hercules to think about. *Do you love my son?* she heard Hera ask again in her mind. Meg looked at the saddlebag a few feet away. He had been so thoughtful, to pack her a few things even in the last few precious moments they'd shared together. She wanted more time with him, of that she was certain. And that meant she had a job to do.

Striding across the sand, Meg pulled the small hourglass out of the saddlebag. There was only a dusting of pink on the bottom of the glass, but grains were falling at a steady rate, almost as if they were taunting her. *You're already running out of time,* they seemed to say.

Turning her attention to the rest of the bag, Meg found fruit and water along with a smaller pouch perfect for holding the orchid and the hourglass. Slipping her hand in, she found something else tucked inside: a slingshot. The Y-shaped handle looked hand carved, while the tubing and the pouch were made from worn leather. Carved into the handle was a small fist, which she took to mean strength. Meg looked up at the heavens.

"Wonder Boy," she said softly, "you're full of surprises. Thank you."

Placing the hourglass and flower carefully in the pouch with the slingshot, she used the cord from the saddlebag to fasten it to her waist; she wanted to carry her most important items with her. Of course, she was kind of destroying the saddlebag in the process, but she could always put the food in Pegasus's other pouch when he returned.

Where was Pegasus, anyway? It didn't look like that big of an island. He could have taken a lap around and been back in a minute, and yet there was still no sign of him.

The hairs on the back of her neck stood up. Why did she suddenly feel like she was being watched? Meg stared at the water, which had gone quite still, then looked up toward the mountains now covered in the clouds' shadows. That's when she saw a speck in the sky. Peg was flying toward her. He swooped down over the beach and landed right in front of her.

"Am I glad to see you. For a second, I thought you abandoned me." Peg snorted in annoyance. "Yeah, I know, loyalty and all that, but you were gone awhile. Find anything good?" Peg reared up on his hind legs and neighed louder. Then he motioned with his head to follow him.

"You did find something, huh?" Meg trailed behind him across the beach, rubbing her arms, which were now cold. "Any chance it's the flute?"

Pegasus galloped ahead, stopping at the edge of a rocky part of the shoreline. Beyond it was a row of palm trees nestled among thick brush. Beyond that, she could hear a familiar sound coming softly from the woods. It definitely sounded like a wind instrument.

She hadn't even been on the island a half hour and

already she'd sort of located Athena's flute! Maybe this quest was going to be easier than she'd thought.

"Nice job, Peg." She patted the horse's side. "I think I'll keep you around." He snorted. "When you flew over the island, did you see the aulos or just hear it?"

Peg snorted and pawed at the sand with his front hoof. She watched as the horse shuddered. Something had unnerved him. She wished she spoke flying horse.

"Why don't you give me a lift so I can give the island an aerial view?"

Peg knelt down on his front legs, bending so that Meg could easily climb atop him. Once she was settled, he took off into the air. This time, she noticed Peg didn't jostle her or dive between clouds at a breakneck speed. Progress.

The flute was nowhere to be seen although she could still hear it, and it definitely sounded closer now than it had on the beach. She had to be getting warmer. Maybe it was on a mountaintop. She wouldn't put it past a god to accidentally drop a beloved instrument midflight.

"Peg, take a right," Meg said, hearing the sound of rushing water.

Pegasus flew lower and the waterfall she'd spotted from the beach came directly into view. The flute's melody grew louder.

Meg directed the horse to a patch of grass next to the waterfall. "Let's head over there. We've got to be close." As she dismounted, the sound of the water overpowered the flute, but Meg could still hear its music calling to her. Where was the wind instrument? Meg took a step closer to the mountain. "It sounds like it's coming directly from the water, as if that's possible. Unless . . ." Meg stared at the swift water collecting in the pool in front of her and wondered. "Maybe the flute is stuck on a rock or something." Meg moved toward the stones and spotted an opening. The waterfall concealed an entrance to a cave. She could just make out a small path. Meg lifted a vine covering the way and the flute hit a sudden high note, causing three birds in nearby trees to take flight. "Peg, the music is coming from inside a cave. The question is, where and *why*?" She paused. "I guess there's only one way to find out." Meg took a step forward and Peg rushed in front of her. "I know it's a bit scary, but I have no choice. I've got to go in there." Peg rose up on his hind legs.

Meg couldn't help thinking of Phil. The satyr would never let Hercules blindly go into a cave emanating mysterious music without a plan. "What if I take a weapon with me?" she suggested. "Hercules gave me a slingshot. I just need a few rocks." She grabbed a few and placed them in the bosom of her dress, afraid that if she added them to the pouch they would squash the orchid. "See? I'm completely prepared for anything now," Meg said, turning toward him. The rocks tumbled out. "Okay, maybe I need a Plan B . . ." She pinned the orchid to the inside flap of the satchel and placed the rocks in the pouch instead. "That will do the trick." Pegasus still looked uneasy, but he didn't protest as she headed toward the entrance again.

Suddenly the flutist started playing louder, the notes coming faster, like a wave, settling into a melodic frenzy. Meg froze. The tune was very familiar. A few more twisted notes sprang out from the water, and then it clicked into place: It was the first song she'd ever taught herself to play—"The Plight of the Lily." She clutched the slingshot firmly in her right hand and felt her pouch for the hourglass to make sure it was still there.

"Guess I'd better get this over with," Meg said to Peg, who started to follow. "No, you stay here." Peg neighed. "I appreciate the sudden loyalty, Peg, but I've got this. Besides, if we need a quick getaway plan, you're it." She held up the slingshot. "I'll be fine."

Peg pawed at the ground, but Meg gave him an encouraging smile. Still clutching her slingshot, she headed under the waterfall, pushing aside thick, intertwined vines. The back side of the waterfall was deafening, making it difficult for Meg to still hear the flute, but she kept shuffling along till the cave finally opened up in front of her—a chasm of rock and dripping water. From here, the flute's melody could be heard loud and clear again.

"Well, well, someone does live here," Meg said to herself as she stared at a series of lit torches lining the stone walls.

At the sound of her voice, the flute suddenly stopped and the torches dimmed, shrouding the cave in shadows.

"Games, huh?" Meg's voice echoed in the darkness. "That's fine. I know how to play games."

Having lived in the Underworld for a spell, she was not scared of darkened caves. Nor of the monsters that lived inside. What did worry her, however, was not knowing the type of monster she was about to face. She grabbed a dimmed torch from the wall and walked slowly, her eyes scanning the dark path in front of her. She didn't see any other tunnels. There was only one way into this cave, it seemed, and one way out. She started walking. When Meg finally looked back, the waterfall was just a speck in the distance. She could hardly hear it anymore. The only sound was the water trickling from the mossy condensation on the stone surrounding her.

In the distance, she heard the flute. It sounded far away again. *How big is this cave?* she wondered, quickening her step. The torches ahead of her roared back to life. The path was widening, too. She was finally getting someplace. The music was calling to her, beckoning her to come closer. And though every bone in her body told her she could be walking into a trap, she had to keep going. *The only one who can save you now is you. Trust yourself.* She was the master of her own destiny. Taking a deep breath, she held the torch in front of her and kept going.

She was not leaving without Athena's flute.

The music grew louder as the path curved downward and brightened. *Are my eyes adjusting to the dark, or is there really a light up ahead?* she wondered. As she turned the corner, she saw a path leading to a waterfall. Was it another waterfall or the same one she'd come from? Had she gone in a complete circle? She wasn't sure. She heard the flute again and turned around. This time the sound had come from the other direction. To her right was a second path. She made the turn and headed down it. At the end, she found herself in a large cavern where a beautiful woman sat atop a throne carved out of rock and played Athena's double flute.

Meg was mesmerized.

The woman was lost in the music, her eyes closed as she played the double reed pipe. Her head bobbed and swayed, her long jet-black hair sweeping around her bare shoulders. She wore a flowing peach gown with a train that swept across the length of the room, wrapping the space in fabric. Meg looked at the flute in wonder.

Legend had it Athena had thrown the flute away in disgust because playing it distorted her face and ruined her beauty. This woman, however, practically glowed as the notes escaped her flute. Meg listened with rapt attention, finding herself overcome with emotion. She played far better than anyone Meg had ever heard before. She felt a sudden pang. Whoever this woman was, she was meant to keep Athena's flute.

It took Meg a moment before she realized she had drifted closer to the throne to listen. Still, the woman didn't look up. Meg closed her eyes and let the tune take her to a different time and place—to that little village and the sound of her mother sleeping soundly in their bed as Meg practiced by the window. Meg was suddenly sleepy, too. Would it be so wrong to lie on the ground and rest for a spell? Meg started to drop to her knees.

Megara!

Megara!

Be alert! she heard a voice in her head command. Meg snapped out of her trance, opened her eyes, and gasped.

The woman was now standing inches from her face, the double flute of Athena held tightly in her hands. Her blue eyes were the exact color of the sea surrounding the island and her skin was a luminescent, milky white. She stared at Meg a moment before circling her slowly. Meg tried to remain calm. She felt so tired, like she could sleep for a thousand years.

"I . . . You play beautifully," Meg said, trying to focus. "I know that tune well."

"Yes?" the woman replied, and Meg noticed the word sounded almost like a hiss. Meg felt her heart beat faster.

"I used to play it all the time." Meg clutched the slingshot tighter in her right hand and prayed the woman didn't see it. The woman looked harmless enough, but every fiber of Meg's being told her not to believe appearances. She stood rigid as the woman's eyes swooped over her face.

"Have you come to play for me?" the woman whispered.

Play? Meg tensed. Hera had said nothing about her having to play the flute . . . had she? She had asked if Meg *could* play. But could and would were two different things. The last time she'd played—*no.* She didn't want to think about that moment. Here and now, she had a chance to get the very thing that would change her fate. She needed to focus. "Some say I play well enough to put Cerberus to sleep." The woman's blue eyes widened. "If you like, I will show you." Meg held out her hands.

The woman surveyed Meg curiously, clearly considering the offer. Finally, she held the flute out to her.

Meg felt her breath quicken. The double reed was beautifully made compared to the tarnished mess she had once owned. She pushed her doubts aside and locked eyes with the woman as she slowly moved her hand forward. Her fingers grazed the reed pipe.

And everything in front of her burst into flames.

SIX: Escape

Meg felt the fire singe her forearms and she cried out in surprise.

This was no woman. Its gown had fallen away to reveal one bronze leg and one hoofed donkey's leg. Its black hair was engulfed in flames, burning bright red and orange as it moved toward Meg, mouth dripping with blood. It had scaly bat-like wings so large they couldn't even fully open in the cave. It was an Empusa. The vampiric beast was known to seduce men and feast on their flesh and blood, but when men were lacking, an Empusa was not going to let any other potential prey go unscathed. And Meg had walked right into its lair.

Meg stumbled, trying to get out of its path, but her arms were burning. She tried to move faster and heard a crunch beneath her feet. She inhaled sharply. What covered the cavern floor was not the train of a beautiful gown. It was a mountain of bones!

The Empusa sniffed the air. "Young blood. Blood so pure." It moved toward Meg, its arm outstretched. Meg watched as it tucked the double flute into a leather strap slung over its shoulder. "I haven't had young blood in a long time. What I wouldn't give for just a taste."

"Sorry," Meg said, climbing over the bones to escape. "I'm pretty fond of keeping my blood in my body." Meg picked up a rather large rock and threw it at the monster.

The Empusa kept coming. "Few come to this island," it said, gliding toward her. "Most realize what's here and leave before they even get near me. But you, child, came willingly, sent here to take something that is not yours."

"It's not yours, either." She pulled a rock from her saddlebag, placed it in the slingshot, and threw it in the Empusa's path. "That flute is Athena's, and she wants it back."

The Empusa's eyes flashed. "If she wants it, she will have to pry it from my dead hands, mortal." The Empusa lunged forward, its long clawlike nails catching on Meg's gown.

Meg felt the nails sink into her thigh and she cried out,

falling onto her knees. The slingshot went flying, skidding out of reach. She lunged for it, trying in vain to find it again, but stopped when she saw the Empusa about to hook a claw into her shoulder. Meg tried to crawl backward on her burned hands and feet as she frantically searched the floor for a weapon. Her nails dug into the dirt as she tried to grab hold of anything that would aid her. Finally, her fingers closed around something large—a human skull—and she lobbed it at the creature's head.

The Empusa screamed and fell backward, one of its wings wrapping around to cover it. Meg grabbed two more large bones and threw them as well, hoping to keep the creature down.

Get up! she heard a voice in her head command, and Meg winced as she stood up and hurried out of the cavern. She tried to get her bearings. Where was she? Was this the main cave? Another path? Where was the waterfall? *What about the flute?* she thought. *It's the flute or your life! Go!* She staggered into the darkness, dragging her badly wounded leg behind her. Her only hope was to reach that waterfall and feel her way out before the Empusa caught up to her. She could hear it hissing. Meg whirled around and saw it rounding the corner, the flames of its hair whipping at the walls and setting the moss that grew in the cave ablaze. The cave quickly filled with smoke.

"I smell you!" the Empusa called. "You can't hide from me, mortal!"

Meg started to cough, her eyes welling from the smoke. She leaned on the rock wall to keep herself upright. Her leg was dripping blood, sending her scent and exact location to the Empusa, no doubt, and the skin on her arms was so badly singed it felt like it was still on fire. The cave was filling with so much smoke, she could no longer see.

I failed, she thought. *No flute. No way out. I'm going to die in this cave.* Meg's eyes started to flutter closed.

Be alert, Megara! Meg heard a voice say, and she opened her eyes and looked around. Still, all she saw was smoke. *Keep going! Hurry! You're almost there!* Meg took a step forward, covering her mouth with her arm and coughing wildly. She squinted through the darkness and saw a new shape in the distance moving toward her. It stopped right in front of her.

"Peg!" Meg cried as she clambered onto his back, fighting through the pain. "Am I glad you don't listen! We've got to get out of here."

Pegasus started galloping back the way he came.

Then she heard the scream. The Empusa was gaining on them, attempting to fly through the cave with its folded wings. It emerged out of the hazy darkness, its fangs dripping with blood.

Pegasus rounded a corner, and Meg saw light up ahead and heard the waterfall. "Move, Peg! We're almost there!" she cried. Then she felt the horse's whole body lurch backward.

The Empusa had grasped Pegasus's tail.

Meg fumbled for her satchel, reaching inside to grab another rock, which she lobbed at the creature's face. The Empusa cried out and let go.

"Faster!" Meg screamed. The horse flapped his wings harder, jerking from left to right to get away, but the Empusa came roaring back, catching the bottom of Meg's gown. Meg shook it off, wincing with pain at the sudden movement. "Peg!" she cried as the Empusa came back yet again.

With a final burst, Pegasus raced toward the waterfall, jumping straight through it and emerging on the other side.

The stream washing over her was just what Meg needed for a momentary revival, the water hitting her wounds and giving her a second's relief. She felt the clean air fill her lungs and blinked hard, trying to get the sensation of smoke out of her eyes. Then she heard the Empusa shriek.

It burst out of the waterfall seconds after them, taking flight on its massive wings and keeping pace with Pegasus. The horse neighed.

"I know! Get us out of here!" Meg cried, wishing more than anything Peg could whisk her away from this island

and take her . . . where? If she left Koufonisia without that flute, her quest was over. She glanced back at the Empusa and saw the double flute still hanging from the strap on the creature's chest. Was there any chance she could still grab it? *Think, Meg!* She looked around wildly for inspiration and spotted another cave on the edge of one of the mountain's cliffs. Above it were several boulders. That gave her an idea.

"Wait! Peg, new plan! Make a hard left to that cave!" Meg cried, and Pegasus started to snort and neigh angrily. "Yeah, I know we almost died, but I need that flute. I have to try!"

Peg continued heading toward the horizon, and for a moment, Meg thought he was going to ignore her. Then the horse dove straight down, Meg clinging to him before he veered left. The Empusa screamed and followed.

"Yes, it's following us! Keep that creature on its hooves!" Meg shouted.

Peg darted up and down, through clouds and around them. The cave was fast approaching. Meg held tight to Peg's neck as he flew toward the cave. She was just formulating her next move when she felt the jolt. Peg was bumped so hard he went sideways and almost pitched Meg off. She heard the horse scream and saw a gash in his side.

"Peg!" Meg cried as Pegasus started to spiral, falling fast.

Meg was sure they would hit the rock wall straight on, but the horse managed to pull up at the last second and glided unsteadily into the cave. Meg looked around. The cave had a wide enough opening. If the Empusa flew in, they could hopefully fly out at the exact same moment and—*BOOM!*

The Empusa barreled into Pegasus, knocking Meg clear off him and sending itself flying. Meg hit the ground hard and heard screams and Peg's nervous neighs. There was a ringing in her ears. The cave came in and out of focus. The Empusa, it appeared, had hit the cave wall and was knocked out cold. She forced herself to get up and was thankful to see Pegasus stumbling toward her. Meg knew what his neighs meant. *Let's get out of here. We won't survive a second attack.* He was right, but she couldn't leave without that flute. She lunged for the instrument still hanging from the creature's waist and her fingers closed around the reeds. Then she gave the strap a hard yank, and the flute came free. The Empusa immediately stirred, and the two locked eyes—violet meeting blazing red. Meg jumped up and started running.

"Peg! Go!" Meg screamed, running after the horse, who clearly wasn't sure if he should grab her or take off first.

Meg reached desperately for the horse's mane and felt the Empusa grab her gown. Meg screamed and Peg started to run with Meg clinging to his tail. Finally, Pegasus leaped out of the cave and took flight. He was slower with his injuries, but he still managed to pull Meg up out of the cave and then above it. But they weren't in the clear. Meg knew if she didn't get rid of that Empusa once and for all, it would keep coming back till it killed them both. She looked down and saw boulders. Meg didn't think. She just let go, knowing Peg would follow. The horse did, neighing frantically as he came down for a landing, but Meg was already dropping the flute into her satchel and pushing a large rock toward the edge.

"Quick! Help me!"

Peg used his snout, pushing on the boulder until it started to roll. Meg heard the Empusa's scream and knew it was coming.

"Keep going!" Meg shouted.

Her arms were burning, her leg was still bleeding, and Peg was losing blood, but together they rolled the largest of the boulders to the cliff. Then Meg stood at the edge, making herself a target. *Come and get me,* she thought.

Peering over, she saw the Empusa flying upward, its claws outstretched to grab her. The boulder had to roll off the ledge at just the right moment or it would miss. *Wait,*

Meg thought as it drew closer. *Wait,* she continued to tell herself as Peg looked to her for guidance. The Empusa was just a few feet away now and reaching out to grab her. "Now!" Meg screamed as she and Pegasus pushed the boulder off the cliff together.

The Empusa only realized what was happening when it was too late. Its red eyes widened as the rock hit the target, slamming the creature to the ground below.

Meg fell to her knees as she watched the Empusa's flaming hair burn out. Then she looked over at Peg in surprise and relief, her eyes welling with tears. With trembling hands, she pulled the double flute of Athena out of her satchel and held it up to the heavens, half expecting Hera to appear and commend her work.

Nothing happened.

Peg slowly walked over, looking the worse for wear. Meg slumped onto his back, her chest rising and falling fast. She was in so much pain, she could barely breathe. *Now what?* she thought. *The hourglass!* she suddenly remembered and pulled it out of her satchel. There was a layer of pink sand along the bottom that couldn't be ignored.

As much as it killed her to admit it, Hercules was right—she needed some guidance. She'd never survive another attack like this one on her own. Meg looked up at the clear blue sky and sighed loudly.

Peg looked at her.

She knew what she had to do, but she didn't like it. Not one bit.

"Pegasus? Take me to that cranky satyr before I change my mind."

SEVEN: The Great Philoctetes

Aaah . . . this is the life! Phil thought as he lay in a hammock, putting his hands behind his head and letting his gut hang out for the rest of the island to see.

Truthfully, there was no one on this chunk of paradise but him, some goats, and a group of nymphs, but that would change soon enough. As soon as word got out that he'd helped Hercules go from a wet noodle to a superhuman to a god, everyone would revere the great Philoctetes!

Not to brag, but he was kind of a living legend, which is what he told those nymphs he'd been unsuccessfully chasing around the island for years. Forget Odysseus, Perseus, and what had become of Theseus. His work with Hercules would be what the world would remember. When the

Underworld finally got his goat, he'd wind up in Elysium for sure. And boy, would he have stories. How many satyrs actually got to visit Mount Olympus? He'd witnessed Hercules's glory and seen the mighty Zeus and Hera in the flesh. Sure, he felt a little bad about leaving before saying goodbye to the kid, but that business with Meg was not one he wanted to get roped into. Geez, Zeus looked hopping mad when the kid had asked to stay a mortal. And who could blame him? After all Phil and Zeus had done for the boy? The nerve! He was just going to try to forget the kid had ever made such a bad call of judgment. Zeus had said no, and his word was final.

Phil closed his eyes and was just drifting off when he heard the birds start to chirp madly. He opened his eyes with a start and looked around. A familiar white figure was flying over the Aegean Sea.

"Pegasus?" Phil scratched one of his ears. "What are you doing back—"

He spotted something slumped over the horse's back and froze. What was that? And why was Pegasus coming in at such a sharp angle and landing way too fast? Phil bleated, jumping out of the hammock seconds before Pegasus crashed into it and collapsed on the ground. The horse had a gash on his left side and was breathing heavily, which was alarming, but even more so was the woman he had been carrying with him. As soon as Phil saw the red hair, he knew who it was. That dame.

"Oh, no," Phil said, backing up. "No, no, no! What are you doing here? What do you want?" His face grew deep red to match his auburn bottom half.

That woman was trouble, and he'd had enough trouble to last three lifetimes.

Red lifted her head to look at him, and Phil noticed how pale her face was. She had bruises on her legs and burn marks on her arms. What trouble had she gotten herself and Pegasus into? Hadn't Hercules just saved her from Hades himself?

"Phil," Red said, her voice hoarse as she tried to dismount Pegasus. "I—"

"I don't want to hear it!" Phil cut her off. "I don't care what happened. This shop is closed, sweetheart." He looked at Pegasus. "I'll patch my friend up here, and then you two are on your way back to Thebes or wherever it is you were headed before you clearly got into some sort of scrape." Red didn't argue, and curiosity got the best of him. "What happened to you two, anyway?"

Red's eyes fluttered open, then closed. "Hercules told me to come find you first, but I didn't listen." She tried again to dismount and winced in pain.

Phil's eyes widened. "Hercules put you up to this? Wait

till I get ahold of that kid! Telling you where I live! Sending you with his horse!"

"He was right," Red tried again, pulling herself slowly off Pegasus's back. "I need . . . help." She stumbled toward him.

"Too bad!" Phil said. "Find someone else to do your dirty work, whatever it is. You caused me enough trouble. Why, I . . ."

Red reached for something in a satchel around her waist and pulled out a double flute. Phil's eyes widened with recognition.

"Wait a minute," Phil said. "Is that . . . Athena's?"

Before Red could answer, she collapsed at his feet.

What choice did he have after that? He couldn't let her just die again.

Okay, so maybe he considered it for a split second, but no one could fault him for that.

The two of them were in bad shape. He brought them home to patch them up, but his door was the size of a tack compared to the rest of the joint. Living inside the hollow head and shoulders of a statue had its challenges. He found Pegasus shelter under a cluster of trees nearby, and thanks to some TLC, Pegasus was recovering nicely. But the redhead was taking longer to come around. Red was out for a full day before she even started to stir, but at least by that point, his burn remedies were starting to work their magic. He'd had to deal with a lot of training mishaps over the years, so thankfully he'd gotten really good at emergency care. She'd be up and running soon. In the meantime, he could do some housekeeping and stick close by. The place certainly needed a good dusting.

He was just about to polish one of Jason's old swords when he heard Red gasp sharply, then start to cough. He made his way over to the bed with a glass of water.

"Drink this. You'll feel better."

Red took a long gulp, then looked up at Phil, confused. "Thanks. Where am I?"

"My place," he said, motioning around the oddly shaped room with artifacts piled almost to the ceiling. He was a bit of a hoarder, but how could he part with things like the mast to the *Argo*? It was proudly displayed, of course, hung on a rope from the ceiling.

Red's signature smirk made a quick appearance. "You felt guilty, huh?"

"What choice did you leave me?" Phil asked, his face growing hot. "When you barged in like that, bleeding all over the place, I couldn't just leave you there."

Her violet eyes widened. "Where is Pegasus?"

"He's fine. Patched him right up. He's already sailing around the island, taking some test flights. Good as new."

"Oh no." Red started frantically removing blankets and pillows. "Where is the flute?"

"Hanging right behind you, along with your satchel," he said, pointing to the wall. "Got to say—I've been really keen to get an explanation about how you got it."

Red opened the satchel and removed an orchid and then a small hourglass with pink sand. The bottom was a quarter full, and the sand on top was falling at a steady pace. "Oh no. No. No. No. No. *No!*" She looked at Phil in alarm. "How long have I been here?"

"A day, why?" He pointed to the hourglass. "What is that thing timing?"

Red slowly swung her legs over the side, noticing the bandages on her legs. "I've got limited time," she said, sounding frustrated. "And I've now lost a whole day lying around here!"

"Hey. It's not like you had an invitation! *You* showed up. You want to go? Go! I've got stuff to do." He took the water glass away from her bedside and shuffled across the room.

"No, Phil, wait." Red sighed and slowly tried to stand up. "I'm sorry, okay? If you hadn't been here when Peg and I landed . . ."

Phil folded his arms across his chest. "You'd probably be on your way back to Hades!"

Red closed her eyes as if to block the thought. "You're right. I owe you one for saving us. And if I had just listened to Hercules and come to you first, I probably wouldn't have nearly died at the hands of an Empusa."

Phil fell to all fours. "You two faced an Empusa and survived? How?"

Red raised her chin defiantly. "Hercules gave me a slingshot and I improvised the rest."

Phil started to laugh hard. "A slingshot and wit? Against an Empusa? You needed fire-resistant armor! And at least three swords, and a bow and arrow to pierce its wings. And a killer escape plan." He waved a hand knowingly. "Those things lure innocents into caves and trap them there."

"Yeah, learned that the hard way." She paused. "Look, I'm not the best at asking for things." She flipped her hair back, and Phil immediately knew she was starting to feel like herself again. "But that's why I'm here. So I don't screw up again." She looked down at the floor, then back up at him. "Would you consider helping me?"

"Me? Help you? With what?" He shook his head. What was he thinking, even indulging her? "I can't. I am retired."

"Congratulations. Look, this wouldn't be a long-term

gig. We're talking eight days tops. The abridged version of whatever you did with Hercules."

Phil snorted. "Help you be a *hero*? In *eight days*? Not possible. No way. Sorry, lady."

Red threw her head back in disgust. "What was I thinking bargaining with a satyr? I'm out of here." She grabbed her satchel and flute and headed to the door.

"Good!" Phil snapped. Some thanks she gave him. Let her leave. Eight days . . . couldn't be done. Phil scratched his right horn. "Hey. Why do you only have eight days, anyway?"

Red stopped at the door, not looking at him. "I'm on a quest for Hera."

"You're on a quest for Hera?" Phil laughed hard. "You wish!" He turned around, grabbed a rag, and polished a gold shield. The aegis displayed Medusa's head, another one of his most prized possessions.

Red turned around, her eyes flashing. "It's true!" Phil continued laughing as she opened the door. "Just forget it. Pegasus and I are out of here." She made her way outside. Phil followed, watching Pegasus trot toward her. Red touched his mane, and he snorted softly. She attempted to pull herself onto his back, wincing in pain.

"Hey, kid, if you want to stay and recover longer . . ." Phil started to say, but Red shook her head.

"It's fine. Don't want to overstay our welcome. Thanks, Phil," she said as she tucked the flute into her satchel. She patted Pegasus's mane and braced herself to make another try at climbing onto his back. "It's time to go."

Phil suddenly realized that if she left now he'd never know what this all had been about. "Hey, this quest you're supposedly on. What is it, anyway?" Red didn't say anything. "Come on, I did patch you up. Least you can do is tell me what Hera asked you to do."

"Hera asked me to find her the double flute of Athena. Once I did that, she said the rest of my quest would be revealed, but I haven't heard a single thing." Red looked up at the sky for answers. "I guess I thought you were the guy to have by my side no matter what was next, so I came here. It was a stupid idea."

Phil almost fell over. Red had just paid him a compliment. "But what's the quest *for*?" he pressed. "Gods don't just go around asking for favors without giving you something in return."

Red pushed her bangs out of her eyes. "Hera said if I proved my worth, she'd make me a god so Hercules and I could be together."

Phil nearly fell over again. "Holy Hera."

Red nodded. "My thoughts exactly."

Phil slumped onto a crumbling piece of the statue he

lived in. "That means you and the kid could be together. Like forever." He thought he noticed her fidget. "No wonder you came to me for help. You can't do a job like this on your own."

Red gave him a look. "Hey, I did survive the Underworld without you, if you'll recall."

Whether she was up for the task or not, no one turned down a god, especially not one offering that kind of payoff. If Hera had given her a quest, maybe she saw something in Red that he hadn't. "Have you looked the flute over for any hidden messages or a note written on the strap?"

"No." Red retrieved the double flute from her satchel and turned it over in her wounded hands. "I don't see anything."

Phil thought again. "Have you tried playing it?"

A strange look came over her face. "I doubt that would help."

"How do you know? Can you play?"

Red hesitated. "Yes, but . . ."

"Blow a few notes through the thing," he said impatiently. "Maybe Hera has to hear it."

She sighed and looked uncomfortable as she stared at the instrument. "Fine. But don't expect much."

The first note came out rather loud and pitchy, but then she seemed to find her footing, quickly playing a few notes that were kind of nice. She didn't play long enough for him to get a sense of her skill. When she was done, she held up the flute and made a face. "Happy?"

"No."

Red, Phil, and Pegasus turned around.

Athena, god of war and wisdom, stood before them in the flesh.

EIGHT: War

Meg knew it was Athena the moment she saw her. Like most Greeks, she'd seen many statues depicting the god, who appeared with an owl perched on her toned shoulders and a shield at the ready in one hand. She used her other to point directly at Meg.

"Where did you get that flute, mortal?"

Athena stood before them on the edge of the cliff, her back to the sun. Her lavender body seemed to glow, the silver on her headdress and gauntlets practically fluorescent. She wore an armored breastplate over her dress and a navy blue helmet that offset her sky blue hair. Her dark eyes looked anything but pleased.

Pegasus shuffled side to side restlessly and Phil was as still as a statue as Athena approached.

"I asked you a question: Where did you get my flute?"

Meg quickly came to her senses and spoke up. "I retrieved it from the Empusa who hid it from you on the island of Koufonisia."

Athena took a step back and it felt as though she were sizing Meg up. "You? A mortal stole my flute from an Empusa?"

Phil bleated involuntarily. "Hard to believe, Athena, I know, considering she had no training from me, the Great Philoctetes, but that is the story she gave me, too."

"Thanks, Phil," Meg said dryly. "It's true. Though as you can see, I could have used some help." She gestured with her bandaged arms. "Are you here to offer some guidance?"

"That depends," Athena said. "What is it you want, Megara?"

She knows who I am. "What do I want?" Meg repeated, unsure.

"Yes." Athena moved closer and looked her in the eye. "What is it that you want?" The god enunciated every word.

Meg thought carefully before answering. "What I want is to know the next part of my quest. Are you here to tell me?"

Athena sighed impatiently. "And *why* do you want to know?"

The god wasn't making sense. *So I can finish my quest,* Meg thought, but somehow she knew that was not what Athena wanted to hear.

"So she can be with Hercules!" Phil finally blurted out. He shot Meg a look. "How can you not understand the question?"

"Is that what you want, Megara? To be with Hercules and be a god as he is?" Athena asked, her voice tight.

Say yes, Meg thought. *But if she catches you sounding unsure, she'll know. She's a god. She knows everything.* "I think so." Phil slapped a hand over his eyes, but Athena looked surprisingly delighted.

"Finally! A real answer!" Athena's owl began to hoot. "I appreciate your honesty, Megara, but the truth will only take you so far." She pointed a finger at Meg's chest. "You are a mortal who does not know what she wants, and because of that you lack purpose. Where is your drive? How do you expect to complete a quest such as this one if you have nothing to fight for?"

"I have purpose and drive," Meg said grudgingly, folding her arms across her chest.

"Do you?" Athena asked almost mockingly. "Is that why

you played my flute so *beautifully* when given the chance? We both know you know how to play."

"You do?" Phil questioned. "It kind of sounded like you didn't. No offense."

Meg's cheeks colored slightly. "I don't play anymore."

"Not because you can't, but because you have lost your will," Athena pointed out. "Therein lies the problem."

"Why don't you play anymore?" Phil asked.

Meg brushed him off. "That's not important."

Athena's eyes flashed. "On the contrary, it's *very* important. You are going to war, Megara. And in war, one must have the will to fight for what they want or they will fall in battle as swiftly as a sword cuts through the air."

Meg stifled a sigh, careful not to offend the god in front of her. *What do I want?* she asked herself. *I care for Hercules, but we've just started to get to know each other. How do I know I want to be with him forever? And how do I actually know I'd even make a decent god? That's a pretty big commitment, too. When have those ever worked out for me?*

"Good!" Athena nodded appraisingly. "Finally, we are getting somewhere. Without questioning where you've been, you'll never understand where you must go."

Meg tried not to look too shocked. So Athena could

hear her thoughts. She supposed it made sense. She had prayed to the gods for answers before. One just happened to be standing in front of her now.

"Wait, did I miss something?" Phil asked.

Both women ignored him.

"But how do I know what I want without having the time to figure it out?" Meg questioned.

"War waits for no one," Athena said. "You have a deadline. To find answers, you must look to both the past *and* future for guidance."

Meg still wasn't sure she understood. How was someone supposed to understand something like love? How would she know what she wanted out of Hercules, out of *herself*? How could she be a god like Athena when she did not know the answer to those questions?

"Yes, like that!" Athena said, again seeming to hear her thoughts. "The more questions the better! I want to see fire in your belly, Megara. I know you have it, or you would not have been able to beat that Empusa." The god studied Meg. "Perhaps Hera was right to put her faith in you. If you do as I say, you'll do well on the journey ahead."

Meg inhaled sharply. The next part of her quest! "What do I have to do?"

Phil, Pegasus, and Meg looked at Athena. Her dress blew softly in the light breeze and she seemed to consider the question. Finally, she spoke. "You must go to the Underworld to retrieve a lost soul."

Meg felt as if the earth beneath her feet had dropped out from under her. Her mouth went dry. "The Underworld?" This had to be a cruel joke. Hera couldn't expect her to travel to the land of death and be able to return a third time.

"But we just got her back from there!" Phil sputtered.

Exactly! Meg wanted to cry, but she was too afraid to speak.

"Quests are not for the faint of heart," Athena said simply.

Hades did not just let souls come or go. Charon, the ferryman, only shuttled the dead, and even if one could get past him, there was Hades's three-headed dog, Cerberus, at the entrance to the Underworld to keep mortals out. This was an impossible task. Meg rubbed the bandages on her arm and tried not to let her fear show. "Do you know whose soul I'm looking for? The Underworld, unfortunately, is a rather large place."

Athena staked the tip of her sword in the dirt and squared her shoulders. "Her name is Katerina. I believe she captured the heart of someone you once loved."

Meg felt the world start to spin. "Katerina?" She reached out for Peg. Her knees felt like they might buckle.

"Katerina?" Phil repeated. "Who is Katerina?"

Meg wasn't sure she could answer that question without opening up an entire new can of worms. "He left me for Katerina."

Phil scratched his right horn. "Hercules?"

"No!" Meg felt herself grow impatient. Her chest felt like it was constricting, and it was suddenly hard to breathe. "Aegeus."

"Who is Aegeus?" Phil asked, but Meg couldn't speak.

Athena had to do it for her. "He's the one Megara gave up her soul for."

NINE: Do or Die

Years earlier . . .

Adrift. That's how Meg would later describe the years after her mother died. She was a ship lost at sea with nowhere to anchor, drifting from town to town, never staying in one place for too long. Her reasons for being nomadic weren't the same as her mother's had been. No, Meg found herself moving on anytime she noticed something that reminded her of her old life with Thea. It could be a song being hummed by women doing the wash, or the way a small girl with red hair called for her parents, or even the sight of fresh flowers in the market, but when Meg felt that pull, she couldn't stay a minute longer. She ran from her mother's ghost until she could run no farther, taking only one thing from her old life on her travels—the rusty flute Thea had given her.

She played that flute till her fingers callused and bled. She poured her pain and her grief into song, creating melodies that she played at dawn, midday, and in the middle of the night. The skill she had once turned her nose up at because it had cost her a week's worth of eggs suddenly became her most cherished possession. And it turned out her mother was right about one thing—music saved her. Meg was not one to take handouts or rely on the kindness of strangers. No. Her mother had warned her about living life that way. Instead, she used music to afford rent and food. With age and talent, Meg found herself getting more and more invitations to play her flute at performances with other musicians.

It was at one of those concerts she met Aegeus.

"You have a gift," she recalled him saying to her one evening as she walked off the amphitheater stage. "And a gift like that shouldn't be wasted playing alone. Play with me instead."

Meg remembered being ruffled by his words. She'd seen him earlier that evening. He played the lute like no other musician she'd ever seen, and she couldn't help being taken by his thick black hair and green eyes that shone against his tan skin. "Kind of forward, don't you think, Curly?"

He half smiled. "I had to say something to keep you from getting away." He held out a hand. "My name is Aegeus."

She hesitated for a moment before shaking it. "Megara."

The minute her fingers connected with his, she was adrift no more.

For the first time since Thea had passed, Meg found herself opening up to another. It had been so long since she'd shared someone else's company for any length of time that she'd almost forgotten what it was like to connect with another human. It wasn't long before they were playing music together on stage, and she found herself falling in love despite her better judgment. Her mother had said to never put her faith or trust in another, and here she was making future plans with a man she barely knew. But Aegeus wasn't like the father from her faint memories. He never raised his voice, and she'd only seen him cross once—when a merchant refused to pay them for a performance he had requested. Life with Aegeus was easy, and it didn't hurt that she now had someone to create music with.

"Your skills make me feel like an imposter," Meg lamented one night. Aegeus had played her under the table with a fast-paced arrangement on his lute, and she wasn't happy.

"You sell yourself short," Aegeus told her. "You're good!"

"I'm decent."

"You're masterful!"

"I'm your apprentice," she argued, as she nuzzled into his chest in front of the fire he had made for them.

"Don't say that." Aegeus ran a hand through her hair. "You don't become a master by acting like an—"

"Apprentice," Meg finished. It was one of his favorite sayings. "I know."

Aegeus picked up the lute again and his fingers plucked the strings so quickly, it seemed as if the instrument played itself. "You're self-made, Megara. You've never had a single lesson! Talent like that is a gift from the Muses. Who knows? Someday your skill may help you put Cerberus to sleep."

"And why would I ever need to learn how to put Cerberus to sleep?" she'd said with a laugh.

"Orpheus did," Aegeus reminded her. "When his beloved Eurydice died, he played so beautifully he tricked Cerberus into letting a mortal enter the Underworld to retrieve her soul." He reached out a hand and caressed her cheek. "If there ever comes a time when I have to do the same, my love, I, for one, will play like a master and sail by Cerberus as he sleeps to come find you."

She cupped his face in her hands. "And I would do the same for you."

Aegeus had mended her broken heart. What more could she ask for in life? She knew that soon he would ask for her hand in marriage—he hinted at it daily—and without question, she would say yes. Would her mother approve of the marriage, of her putting her trust in another? Probably not, but her mother wasn't always right. Was she? Aegeus would never betray her.

Though, of course, the rest of the world might.

One day, Aegeus fell gravely ill. Meg tried to get help, but she didn't have the funds for pricy herbs. She went to their fellow musicians, but they turned her away. "If he's sick, that's punishment from the gods," several said with a jealous tinge to their voices. They had never liked that Aegeus had outshone them on stage.

"And if he gets well, is that a gift from the gods?" she argued angrily. But she didn't wait around for their answer. Why would the gods punish Aegeus? He had done nothing but bring her joy and offer beautiful, moving music to the world. Despite her argument, she began to pray to every god she could think of to heal him. And yet, Aegeus grew sicker.

As he lay in bed, struggling for every breath, Meg found herself thinking of her mother. *I told you,* she'd say. *No one will help you. People are no good. You can't trust others.*

But Aegeus is good, she'd tell the voice in her head. *He deserves to live. I need him! Please, gods, save him!* But Aegeus's condition only worsened.

Perhaps I am praying to the wrong gods, Meg feared one night when she thought Aegeus was about to take his last breath. Their friends had abandoned him. Money for treatments had eluded them, and no aid came. But maybe there was another way. *Cerberus,* she mused, thinking of the Underworld. Her thoughts had turned dark and the path of darkness led to none other than the god of the Underworld. She placed her lips to her flute and played her most cherished tune—"The Plight of the Lily"—in his honor.

Hades, Meg silently prayed as she played, *if you save my love's life, I will give you anything you ask for. Just don't take Aegeus too soon as you did my mother. I'll give anything.*

Anything? a voice inside her head asked.

Meg looked up and stopped playing. *Was* this a voice in her head, or had a god finally answered her prayers?

"Anything!" Meg repeated, this time aloud. She held tight to Aegeus's hands to stop hers from shaking.

Including your soul? the voice said.

Meg looked down at Aegeus, so weak and pale she knew he wouldn't last the night. She loved him like she'd loved no other. He'd given her so much these last few months—a companion, inspiration . . . a home—she couldn't imagine walking the Earth without him.

"Yes," Meg said firmly.

It was the last word she spoke before she suddenly felt

her body begin to fade from Aegeus's bedside. She reached out to grab Aegeus's hand, but felt it slip through her fingers. Her flute clattered to the floor.

"Wait! Wait!" she begged when she realized what was happening. "I'm not ready to go!"

She didn't even have time to see Aegeus open his eyes.

She was falling, fast, into a never-ending darkness that made her scream die out before she hit the bottom. Her body went from cold to brutally hot. Her lungs felt like they were on fire and she was sure her skin would begin to melt, but instead she kept falling until she finally hit solid ground and felt dirt beneath her fingers.

The breath knocked from her stomach, Meg inhaled sharply, gasping for air. She sat up fast and looked around. "Aegeus! Aegeus, where are you?" she cried, her voice echoing in the darkness, but there was no answer. She blinked rapidly as her eyes adjusted. She was in a cave that glowed by torchlight. The air was thick and unbearably warm, and she could hear screaming in the distance. Suddenly, three hooded figures appeared out of the darkness and Meg screamed once more, trying to retreat farther into the shadows.

"Are you sure this is her?" croaked a tall, grayish being with empty eye sockets. She had a pointed chin and nose and long, spindly fingers. She held a pair of scissors poised against a string two others were holding taut.

"Because if it's not—*snip, snip*," said her short, squat companion. This one bore a pinkish skin tone and had a single eyeball in the center of her head.

"Every soul must be accounted for," said the third, who had empty eye sockets and a nose twice the length of her face.

"Who are you?" Meg cried. "Where is Aegeus?"

But there was no answer.

"You can back off, ladies," said a deep voice in the shadows. "This one is mine."

A god with a flaming blue head and hollow, deep-set eyes stepped forward. He smiled, revealing his razor-sharp teeth. "Hello, my little Meg-let. Glad you could make it."

"Hades," Meg whispered.

"In the flesh!" Hades bowed. "And hey, so are you. For the time being."

This shouldn't have been possible. She'd made a deal with the devil and he'd come to collect. Meg worried she was going to pass out. She was in the Underworld, and Aegeus was back on Earth dying. "Aegeus! Aegeus!" Meg shouted, feeling her way around the rock, looking for an opening so she could run straight for Cerberus and play her way out of there, except . . . she felt around, panicked.

The flute was not with her. She had left it behind with . . . "Aegeus!"

"He can't hear you down here. No one can." Hades folded his gray hands. "Well, except me, so can you cut it out? I'm not used to souls being all alive and stuff when they get here."

"That was your choice," croaked the one with the pointy nose.

"Who are you?" Meg cried.

"Meg, meet the Fates. Fates, meet Meg," Hades said. "She's going to be working for me for a while, as long as she behaves. Otherwise it's as they said." He made a cutting motion. "Snip, snip."

The Fates. Meg backed away again, her backside hitting cold rock. The Fates not only knew all, they *decided* all, and they were currently holding her life—literally—in their clawlike hands.

"But if you do as you promised, all will be fine, great, superb!" Hades said as he took Meg's string from them and pocketed it. The Fates shuffled out of the room. "Don't worry, Aegeus's thread stays intact." He clapped. "Yay! You got what you wanted. Your guy lives!"

Meg's heart was beating so fast she thought it would stop. "Aegeus is okay? He's going to live?"

"Yes, and so will you, technically and all that. It's kind

of a sticky situation." Hades waved his hand around and she noticed it turned into a stream of smoke. "Mortals aren't supposed to be in the Underworld. Against the rules and all that, which is why the Fates are all up in arms and eye and whatnot. But I can't do what I have to do on my own from down here." His eyes yellowed as he approached her. "I need someone up on Earth to do a bit of housekeeping, as it were. Big things are happening! Huge! It's exciting times down here in the Underworld!" He paused, staring at her expectantly. "Don't you want to know why?"

Meg met his gaze but said nothing. Her thoughts flew about wildly as she tried to comprehend what was happening. She was in the Underworld. She was in the Underworld. She was in the Underworld.

"Okay, okay, stop needling me for the dirt, you're embarrassing yourself. If you must know, I've got some business coming up with the Titans. They're making a comeback. *Hopefully*. And if all goes right, I'll be getting a promotion; we can save the details for later. The point is, I'm giving you a job!"

Earth? Job? "So I'm alive?" Meg repeated, unsure. *Aegeus. I have to get back to Aegeus.*

"Alive, yes. Can you see your guy at the moment? No." Hades's face darkened. "Your soul belongs to me, remember?"

Meg wiped the sweat from her brow. She was so hot she couldn't stand it. "But I'm alive, which means I can't *stay* here, right?"

Hades powered over to her in seconds in a haze and whispered in her ear. "Technically, if someone found out a mortal was here, things could get a bit dicey for me. But we're not going to tell anyone, are we?" His smile faded. "Wouldn't want anything to happen to Aegeus before you can repay your debt. That would be a real shame, especially after I just saved his life. So we're all copacetic. Anyway, I'm sending you topside to work, which means you will indeed get outta here."

Topside? Earth? The land of the living? Aegeus? Her next words tumbled out of her. "I'll do whatever you need to pay off my debt. Anything! I'll start right now. Please. I just want to go home." Meg hated how pathetic she sounded.

Hades looked at her. "Not that I don't admire the work ethic, but are you sure you even want to get back to this guy?" He whirled his hands around and shot smoke toward a fireplace she hadn't noticed in the corner. An image appeared in the sudden fire. "Looks like he's back on the market already."

"Aegeus!" Meg rushed toward the blue flames, then quickly took a few steps back as the heat sent a shock through her system. She stood, holding her arms, and found that through the flames she could see an image as clear as day. There was her love, rushing through the marketplace in their village. He looked well! A sob escaped her lips. Aegeus was all right. Hades had saved him! "Wait," Meg realized. "How can he be in the market? It's the middle of the night." She peered closer. "Is it daytime already?"

Hades shot smoke at the flames and the image disappeared. "Yep! Time travels fast down here. You want that boy to remember you, you better get a move on."

And so, Meg went to work for the god of the Underworld. The days marched on as she met with the nastiest of creatures all over Greece, creatures that usually never showed their faces in the light. She negotiated with river gods and harpies, a Nemean lion and a Minotaur, convincing them to join Hades in his quest to topple ol' Zeus, and she didn't feel bad about what she was doing. It wasn't Zeus who had come to her aid to save Aegeus; it was Hades. And besides, one more deed for the god down meant she was one step closer to returning to her old life, and to her love.

When she'd counted seven days in his service, Hades congratulated her.

"A week together, my little Nut-Meg," he'd said, throwing an arm around her. "And what a week it's been. You're good at your job, Meggie. You managed to get five new allies on our team this week."

"Yeah," Meg grumbled, turning away from him. "And I almost gotten eaten by one."

"The Minotaur? Nah. He's harmless. Just wanted to scare you. But, uh, you've performed far better than I thought you would, so I got you something." He reached behind his back, and through the smoke she saw something familiar floating toward her.

"My flute," Meg said in surprise, reaching out to grab the precious instrument. She clutched it to her chest and forced herself not to tear up. She wouldn't give Hades the satisfaction of knowing how much this meant to her. It would be just another thing for him to lord over her. "But how?"

Hades shrugged. "God of the Underworld, remember? I have my ways. I have to say, it's not much to look at, though. Rusty old thing."

Meg stared at it. "It holds a lot of memories."

"Of dear old Mommy, huh?" Hades asked.

Meg froze. She looked up at him, a wild idea popping into her mind, one she couldn't believe she hadn't thought of before. "Please . . ."

"Nope! Can't see her. Sorry. No good for her, and no good for you! I placed a veil as soon as you arrived so she wouldn't hear about your comings and goings." Meg started to protest, and Hades held up a long hand. "You have to concentrate, and Thea will just distract you. Besides, the residents would get twitchy if they knew there was a mortal staying among them. Unless . . ." He sidled up next to her. "If you wanted to stay for good. Then maybe I could arrange a reunion."

"No! You said once I paid my debt, I could blow this joint!" Meg's scowl returned, as it seemed to do more often than not in the Underworld. "Unless you want a certain someone to know I'm here," she threatened. "I haven't prayed to any gods as of late. . . ." That was about the only thing she could use against the guy.

"No, I know. I know. You want to get back to your love," he said, talking fast as he did. "You miss him. He misses you! Or at least he did . . . till he met *her*."

Meg whirled around fast, her heart almost leaping into her throat. "What her?"

"Oh, it's no big deal." Hades shrugged. "I shouldn't have even mentioned it. Hey, should we go over your schedule for tomorrow? I need you to go see a griffin."

"What. Her?" Meg repeated slowly and the god looked sheepish. "Hades!"

"Okay, okay. I wasn't going to say anything because I know you've been through hell and back—literally. Ha! But, uh, there's been a development with your boy." Hades motioned to the fire and a new image appeared. Meg walked over, flute in her hand.

Aegeus was standing near the ocean, his arms wrapped around a woman with long blond hair. She couldn't hear what he was saying, but they were talking closely as he nuzzled his cheek close to hers. The the woman planted a kiss on his lips.

Meg felt bile rise in her throat. "No. This is your trickery! Aegeus loves me! He was going to ask me to marry him before he became sick! You're just trying to make me crazy."

Hades looked forlorn. "Meg, I may be a lot of things—a bad guy, a cheat, a scoundrel, the leader of the Underworld—but what I'm not is a magician. This is real." He pointed to the blue flames again and Meg watched with despair as Aegeus lifted the woman in his arms and spun her around. The two of them were laughing. "I hate to tell you this, but the world is a cruel place. Didn't your mother ever tell you that?"

Yes, Meg thought miserably.

"You can't trust people, because they will always let you down. Aegeus has moved on, my little Nut-Meg. He's a guy. They can't stand being alone. It's in their nature."

In that moment, Meg knew Hades was right. This was no witchcraft. Aegeus didn't love her. If he had, he wouldn't have moved on to another woman a week after she'd sacrificed everything to save him. One *week*!

"Look, I know this hurts—you gave up your soul for the

guy, and this is how he repays you? Ouch! But this guy isn't worth it. You know it. I know it. Channel that anger into something we can work with and complete your sentence so you can get topside again. Isn't that what you want?"

You gave up your soul for the guy. Whatever hope she had left seemed to fade away like Hades's infamous smoke. "Who is she?" Meg whispered.

"Come on." Hades looked sad. "Does it matter?"

"Tell me her name!"

Hades sighed. "Katerina. Her name is Katerina."

Katerina. Meg looked down at the flute in her hands and squeezed it till her fingers almost bled. Her mother had been right. The only person she could rely on was herself. Love was for fools, and she had been played for one.

Meg felt a guttural sound emerge from her throat. She raised her hand and pitched the flute into the flames as Hades looked on in horror. Aegeus was dead to her.

It was time to get back to work.

Meg looked at Hades. "So tell me about that griffin."

TEN: A Fateful Choice

Back on Phil's island . . .

Meg knew one thing for certain: this quest was beyond cruel. It was vindictive.

Hera, it seemed, was poised to be the mother-in-law from hell.

If Meg even made it that far.

Athena and Phil stared at her, waiting for her to say something.

Do I go to the Underworld to save the soul of the woman Aegeus left me for? Or do I refuse Hera and make an enemy of one of the most powerful gods on Mount Olympus? Great options here.

"You okay there, Red?" Phil asked, looking worried.

Athena continued to stare at her. No doubt she would

report everything back to Hera. Meg could just picture the gods sitting around on a cloud laughing over her predicament. "The mortal will never survive!" they'd say. "You're so clever, Hera!"

Well, she wouldn't give them that satisfaction.

Meg had two options, and while neither sounded particularly appealing, the thought of backing down from the quest left a bad taste in her mouth. She might have been a lot of things, but she was not a coward. She thought back to something Hercules had said to her a few months earlier when they'd stolen away—her to secretly do Hades's bidding and get close to the would-be god; him from Phil.

"You know what I love about you, Meg?" Hercules had said. "You're not a quitter."

They'd been lying on a cliff overlooking the ocean for what turned out to be hours. Speaking earnestly with this sweet boy, getting caught up in his observations—she was breaking rules all over the place, but for the first time in a long time, she didn't care. There was something about this Wonder Boy, as she had grown fond of calling him, that drew her to him like a moth to a hunky flame.

"What makes you think that? You hardly know me."

He brushed a piece of hair out of her eyes. "You could have let me use my strength to get you out of that mess with

Nessus," he said, referring to the river god through whom they'd met. "But you wanted to fight your way out instead."

"I recall you calling me ma'am," she said pointedly, and his ears turned bright pink. "But you're right. I had things handled till you came along. I like a challenge."

"It's more than that, Meg," Hercules said softly. "It's the way you talk, move, act. You're a go-getter; you won't take no for an answer. Sometimes I think I need to be more like you."

Meg felt a twinge of guilt. If Hercules knew who she was working for, he'd feel differently.

Now, standing in front of Athena, Meg recalled Hercules's words in a different light. He'd said he wanted to be more like her. Did that mean she was worthy of being a god, too?

Could be.

Maybe this was her chance to finally figure out what to do with her life. She'd lost her mother, had lost Aegeus, had given up her soul, had been through hell and back . . . and yet she was still breathing. And now Hera was giving her yet another chance. She might have been less than thrilled at the idea of helping Katerina and Aegeus, but she still wanted to prove she could take whatever the gods threw at her. This quest was about more than just having an opportunity to be with Hercules. It was about proving to herself that she was strong enough to face a challenge as daunting as this one through to the end. And to see what she could become on the other side of it.

Meg could feel a new sensation coursing through her veins, one she hadn't felt in a while: determination. "Tell Hera I'll do it," she said to Athena as Phil gaped at her in surprise.

"She'd expect nothing less," Athena said simply.

"But I have a question first," Meg said. "What is it about Katerina that makes her worthy of another spin around the Earth?"

"Um, Red . . . people don't usually get to ask the gods those kind of things," Phil whispered, a bleat escaping his lips before he could stop it.

Just the sound of Katerina's name on her tongue made Meg taste bile. She might have moved on to a new and better (if complicated) relationship, but whenever Meg pictured the woman with her milky white skin, wispy blond hair, and tiny laugh, her gut still ached at the injustice of it all. "I feel like I have the right to know," Meg said, looking at Athena. "I gave up my soul for a man, which I'll admit was a dumb move. But then he fell for this woman in less time than the sun revolves around the Earth. And Hera wants me to save her? Why?"

Athena moved toward Meg, standing so close that their

noses were almost touching. Power radiated off her. "Listen to the satyr. You, mortal, have no right to ask such questions of a god," she said, her voice low and pulsing with anger.

Meg tried not to look afraid. She held her breath.

Athena's face softened ever so slightly. "But considering how you found my flute, I will forgive this one transgression. I suggest you focus on your journey. The Underworld is a large place and you don't have much time."

Meg sighed. Even if she *wanted* to save Katerina, the sheer vastness of the Underworld was a problem. It was made up of three realms, with most people resting in the vast Asphodel Meadows. The worst of the worst were in Tartarus, and the most revered were in Elysium. There was no way Katerina was living in paradise, which meant she was in one of the other two places; and they were tricky to navigate, even with a guide.

Plus, there were, of course, the relevant rules of the Underworld—that mortals couldn't enter or leave, and that Hades never gave up souls once they were there. Meg's debt to the god seemed to be a gray area that had made her exempt at the time, but Katerina was already deceased. Getting her out and back to the land of the living was impossible. Plus, Meg was supposed to pull it off on a deadline.

"How am I supposed to find someone I've never met?" Meg asked, changing tack.

"You will start your journey by visiting Aegeus and learning all you can about his wife," Athena replied.

His wife. Meg tried to brush aside a sudden chill. So the two of them had gotten married. And now she not only had to confront Aegeus, she needed to listen to him gush about Katerina, his *wife*? This seemed unusually cruel.

"You will find him in Athens near a bluff much like this one. He lives on a road anchored by an olive grove, in a humble home near the sea."

"I know the place," Meg said. The olive grove had been her and Aegeus's favorite spot in Athens. They would sit at the top of the bluff and play music and talk about the house they'd one day build there together—the one that would replace the tiny home they shared at the bottom of the hill.

"Well, now that we all know what Red here has got to do, I guess I'll be getting back to my retirement. Good luck, kid." Phil started to scoot backward toward his house.

Athena shifted her gaze, glaring while her owl hooted. "Where do you think you're going, satyr?"

Phil stopped, balancing on one hind leg. "You don't expect me to go on this quest with her, do you?" Athena didn't answer. He laughed nervously and a bleat came out. "You might have heard I've done a lot for Mount Olympus already and am now just trying to enjoy my retirement."

Meg moaned. Phil was the least of her problems. "Fine

by me! Go! I don't need you anyway. We're not exactly the closest of friends," she told Athena, who looked mildly amused. "If you'd just tell me how to get to the entrance of the Underworld, I'm sure I can get there on my own."

Phil bleated. "Oh, yeah, sure. Like you took care of that Empusa on your own."

"I did take care of the Empusa!" Meg snapped.

"You barely survived. And *I* healed your injuries," Phil said, eyeing Athena.

"Why, you arrogant little goat boy!" Meg seethed.

Phil turned bright red. "Did you just call me a goat boy? Why, I . . ."

"Stop!" Athena thundered, and they did as they were told. "Philoctetes, you are skilled in helping heroes on their journeys, so you *will* take Megara to the entrance of the Underworld via the river Acheron. Once you reach the river Styx, Charon will take Megara from the land of the living to the land of the dead. That is an order."

Phil's face drooped. "But . . ."

Athena lifted her chin. "You will leave this island together at dawn."

"Dawn? You expect me to help this one find the Underworld when she has no previous experience with quests or fighting monsters?" Phil's face was scrunched.

Athena didn't blink. "Yes."

"We're doomed," Phil said.

"Great," Meg said under her breath at the same time.

Athena strode forward, stopping to move a broken statue with her foot. "I suggest you both thank the gods for your gifts and fill your bodies with nourishment. Gather your supplies. Learn what you can from one another. This journey will not be easy."

"Tell me about it!" Phil scratched his chest and sighed. "I guess I'll start dinner." He pushed his way past some of the goats. "Coming through."

"Maybe I should help him," Meg suggested.

"No," Athena replied, surprising her. "Let us walk."

Meg stared at the god, who had turned and started heading toward the edge of the island. She quickly followed. When they reached a bluff overlooking the water, Athena stopped, holding out the double reed flute. "Play it for me."

Meg stared at the flute warily, its brass gleaming in the fading light of day. She had no desire to touch it, but was not about to further insult the god by refusing. She took the instrument from Athena's outstretched hands and felt the weight of it. Her flute was a piece of art, so carefully crafted, so different from the rusty one Meg had owned. And yet its notes would, in theory, be the same. Meg just didn't want to hear them.

"Is something the matter?" Athena asked.

"No," Meg said quickly, but the truth was she was afraid that the mere act of returning to this instrument would fill her with an aching sadness for the life she had once traded. But she couldn't deny Athena. She took a deep breath, then placed her mouth over the double opening of the reeds. Closing her eyes, she started with the first few notes of a familiar song almost instinctually—"The Plight of the Lily." The sound that emitted from the pipe was different from the one she was used to, but that seemed to be a good thing. It helped her separate the tune from her memories. When she was finished, she was relieved to hand the flute back to Athena.

Athena clapped, the wind blowing through her glowing hair. "Brava, Megara. You didn't miss a single note. And yet, I still can't help thinking something was missing from your performance."

"I'm sorry?" Meg faltered.

"Don't get me wrong. You are clearly a strong musician, child. One the Muses would be proud of, to be sure. But a true artist *feels* their notes in their soul." She looked at Meg. "You clearly have lost that desire along the way. You do not play as you once did."

Meg frowned, understanding dawning on her. "You've heard me play before?"

Athena smiled wanly. "At a concert in Athens. When true musicians play in honor of their gods, we come to listen from time to time. You were superb that night. Such a shame how lost you have become."

Meg felt her cheeks color. "Perhaps it is because this is not my flute. I'm used to my own."

Athena turned toward her. "And where is that one?"

Meg avoided eye contact. "In the Underworld." It was a half-truth, at least.

"I see." Athena turned away for a moment and looked out over the darkened sea. "Then you will take mine with you on your journey." She held the flute out to Meg again.

"I couldn't," Meg said. She didn't want to be responsible for the god's instrument, and all this talk about music had made her even warier. She had no interest in playing it again. "You've been without it for so long."

Athena smiled. "I suspect it will find its way back to me in the future. But for now, it will aid you more than it does me." She turned her head to the side. "Besides, I rather don't like to play the thing myself. It contorts my face in a way that is less than appealing."

Athena held the flute out to her again and this time Meg took it, knowing it was pointless to argue. "Thank you," she said. "I will care for it as if it is my own."

"I can see the thickness to your skin, Megara. You are tough. Courageous. Proud. I will assist you however I can."

Meg had heard tales of Athena helping those on heroic endeavors, but she'd never imagined she'd be worthy of such a thing. *"Thank you,"* she said again, with more feeling.

"But you must promise to open your mind and listen," Athena went on. "That is the best advice I can give you. You can complete your task if *you* believe you can. Don't fall victim to distractions."

Meg nodded. Athena sounded like her mother. The only person she would be able to rely on in the Underworld was herself. "Got it."

"Sometimes your head will lead, and other times it will be your heart."

An image of Hercules popped into Meg's head, her hand instinctively going to the satchel where the orchid was safely tucked away.

"Remember, the sands of time cannot be stopped," Athena warned, her voice deeper than it was before. "If you lose your way, you'll never see the light of day again."

Meg wrapped her burned arms around her chest. The wind seemed to pick up as night took hold, sending another chill through her. "Understood."

"You must ask Aegeus about Katerina," Athena insisted, and Meg felt her stomach begin to churn again. "What he knows about this woman could be the key to saving both your futures, Megara. Good luck." She squeezed her hands. "I'll be watching."

And then Athena faded away as the sun began to sink into the sea.

ELEVEN: Home Sweet Home

Meg found the ride to Athens with Phil and Pegasus uneventful. They hardly spoke, and Meg wasn't sure if that was because neither was thrilled to be together or because the howling wind made it too hard to hear anything but the whistling past their ears.

Besides, it was difficult enough to focus on not falling off the flying horse. As Peg soared over Athens, the vastness of the city rose up to greet them, homes and temples dotting the landscape like trees. How had she never realized how large this city was? Athens was the last place she had called home . . . thanks to Aegeus.

"If we want to truly make music worthy of the Muses, we have to go where the action is—and the action is in Athens," he'd told her one night after they'd raked in a few measly coins for a performance in a little village.

"I don't know." Meg had hesitated. Her mother had never been a fan of being boxed into a big city. "Athens is so vast."

"Come on, Meg." Aegeus put his arm around her. "Would I ever steer you wrong?"

Not sure, she thought. *Would you?* There was so much she wanted to ask him, but sometimes the hard questions, the ones her mother had always warned her about, felt like marbles in her mouth.

"I love you, and I want a new life for us," he said, touching her cheek.

"Me, too." He'd already hinted at marriage. Starting their new life in a big city could be just the change she needed to finally rid herself of the ghosts of the past and move on with her life.

Meg looked around the square of the small village she'd been living in since she met Aegeus. There was the butcher arguing with Mr. Kostas over the price of meat again. Two doors down, the usual group of women watched their small boys play in a fountain. If she walked a few steps farther she knew she'd find the beggar outside the agora, where all the merchants were set up with their linens, spices from Syria, and dates. The crier would be shouting about the fresh fish that had arrived that day, and Mrs. Aikos would be trying to sneak all the samples she could before having to pay for her fruit. Meg knew the market so well she could navigate the area blindfolded. She'd lived longer in this village than she had lived anywhere since her mother died.

So much of her past she kept locked away in a part of her heart that she didn't share with anyone. Aegeus knew her mother had died when she was young, but he didn't know the details. It wasn't as if she thought Aegeus would look down on her. His life had just been markedly different from hers. Yes, he lived on his own, but it was because he wanted to, not because he had no one. Somewhere out there, Aegeus still had a mother and a father that he sent money to when he could. He talked often about his brothers and sisters and how he hoped they could visit someday. Aegeus had many lifelines, while he was Meg's only one. Maybe there was still a part of her that feared telling him too much could scare him away.

"You think we'll stand out in a place with so many people?" Meg had asked him.

Aegeus spun her around. "How could anyone not notice you, my love? You're extraordinary, and in Athens, you'll be a muse to the finest scholars! Not just Mr. Kostas."

Aegeus put her down and Meg looked at Mr. Kostas, still arguing with the butcher. "You've got a point there."

"So?" Aegeus's face was so eager his smile practically overtook his face. "Shall we start our new lives together in Athens?"

Our new lives together. It sounded so appealing, Meg pushed her mother's voice out of her head. She was making the decision to be with this man. She would still look out for herself, but now she could look out for both of them. "Yes," Meg said. "Let's move to Athens!"

Aegeus had hollered so loud the butcher and Mr. Kostas stopped arguing. They were so absurdly happy.

What a fool she'd been.

Meg felt Phil's elbow nudge her. "Hey! Red! Where are we landing?"

Meg touched her stomach, which was still sore from the Empusa injuries. "I could do without you punching me in the ribs every time you want to ask a question, Phil."

"Sorry! You see Aegeus's place anywhere?" he shouted over the wind.

"Peg!" Meg tapped the horse's side with her right leg. "Can you bring us in closer so I can look around for a landmark?"

Peg neighed and swooped down through a cloud, bringing them low enough that Meg could finally get a clear view of the city and the water beyond it. She and Aegeus hadn't had enough money to move into the heart of the city, so they had lived on the outskirts, using their funds to buy a small piece of land on a bluff. As Peg flew over the Apollo coast, Meg spotted the grove.

"That's it! Peg, land near those olive trees!" Meg shouted.

The home should have been at the base of the grove, but as Peg flew closer, all Meg saw was rushing water at the bottom of the hill. *How strange,* she thought. *Where is our house?* Meg searched the area and spotted a larger home she'd never seen before. Her heart gave a lurch. Aegeus had built their dream home for Katerina.

Peg came in for a landing on the cliff near the front steps. Meg helped Phil down, then lowered herself.

"Okay, listen up, Red. You need to approach this reunion a certain way," Phil said as he rushed to give Peg water and unload some bags. "Don't scare this guy off."

Meg was only half listening. All she could do was stare at the house she and Aegeus had talked about building. The single-story clay home had the long porch she'd so badly wanted, and several windows that opened up to the sea to let in the salty air. He'd built this home to her exact specifications. Aegeus had traded in their dream for one with Katerina. And though this was no longer her dream, it still stung.

"Hey, Phil?" Meg said suddenly. "Do you think this woman is worth saving?"

Phil shrugged. "What do I know? Never met her. The gods seem to like her, though."

"Unlike me," Meg said, "who no one noticed was missing from the world. No one fought for *my* soul."

"Hercules did," Phil reminded her. "He saw something in you I sure didn't. Maybe you need to do the same with Katerina." Meg couldn't help making a face. "Look, this conversation with Aegeus is going to be no picnic. But who cares that he dumped you for another woman?" Phil wagged a hoof at her. "You're working on becoming a god now! Use him to find out what you need to know and we'll be on our way."

Meg stared at the front door warily. Maybe Aegeus wasn't even home and they'd have to come back.

Phil crossed his arms. "We haven't got all day."

"I'm going." Meg strode toward the door, leaving Phil and Peg on the grass behind her. She pushed her bangs out of her eyes and adjusted the waistband on her dress. Her arms, while still bandaged, hurt less than they had the day before. She was growing stronger. She *was* strong. She was Megara. Someone Hera thought could be a god. She could have one little conversation with a spineless former flame. Meg reached the door and knocked.

"Is there someone at the door?"

It was Aegeus's voice. Her heart started to beat faster.

"Coming! We never get visitors! Who could it be?"

Who was he talking to in such a lighthearted manner? Katerina was in the Underworld. Meg's face began to burn. Had Aegeus moved on to another already? Unbelievable! Meg tried to stop herself, but she could feel her right arm pulling back and a fist begin to form.

"Red? What are you doing?" Phil called. "Red?"

Meg felt her heart speed up as she heard the door handle turn. The door creaked open. She had visions of her fist connecting with Aegeus's lying, cheating, unfaithful chiseled face. She lifted her hand as the door swung open.

It was Aegeus. "Me—Me—Megara?" The color faded from his face.

"Aegeus?" Meg's voice shook. Her hand fell to her side in shock. There was something rather large lying in Aegeus's arms.

It was a baby girl, no more than a few months old, her face round and chubby with eyes big and dark like Aegeus's. She had rolls on her legs and thighs and a tuft of blond curls on her head. She took one look at Meg and burst into tears.

Meg understood the feeling. She wanted to cry herself, but she wouldn't.

Instead, Aegeus did it for her.

TWELVE: Hard Truths

"What did you say to him?" Phil came up behind her. "I told you to be nice!"

"Not a word," Meg insisted.

Phil covered his pointed ears with his hands as the baby's wail reached a fever pitch. That only made Aegeus cry harder. "Well, make it stop already. It's giving me a headache."

"You think I know how to make a baby stop crying? I know nothing about babies!"

"Well, you know him! Make him stop it!" Phil motioned to Aegeus, who had tears streaming down his face, his sobs so heavy his whole body was shaking.

Now she was worried he was going to drop the thing—baby—child. There was really no time for such added bumps in the road. "Aegeus?" Meg tried, but he kept crying, holding the baby to his chest as they both heaved great sobs. "Aegeus?"

He leaned back against the doorway and closed his eyes, crying harder. "Why, my gods? Why?" he railed to the heavens, and his arms looked like they might drop.

Meg swooped in and snatched the child from him just as Aegeus collapsed against the doorframe. The baby registered that Meg was holding it and started to scream louder. Meg held it under the armpits as if it might bite her.

She'd never held a baby before in her life. Aegeus had talked about his siblings' children and how much he wanted kids of his own, but truthfully, Meg had never felt that pull. Her mother's life had been hard and having a kid to provide for had made it even harder. Her own circumstances hadn't been much better. Even when she met Aegeus, they had gotten by, but they weren't wealthy by any means. She couldn't imagine bringing a kid into the mix. And now, here she was, holding Aegeus's baby in her arms—his, and, of course, Katerina's.

The child had her light hair and his eyes. As much as Meg had tried to deny it at the time, Hades had been right—Aegeus didn't love her. He hadn't mourned for her. He had moved on immediately and created a family with Katerina, forgetting she had even existed.

The truth felt as painful as the wounds still healing on both her legs. She wanted to wish the pain away, but it was currently in her arms, screaming. Could she put the baby down somewhere? Why was it crying so hard? How did she make it stop? Now its tears were plopping onto her arms. Her whole body felt numb.

Phil reached up. "Give the kid to me."

"Gladly." Meg handed Phil the baby and he cradled it in his arms, making a shushing sound as he rocked it back and forth. Amazingly, the child stopped wailing. The baby started to close its eyes, still sniffling as it was being rocked asleep. Phil marched past the sobbing Aegeus into the house. Aegeus and Meg followed.

"My child," Aegeus said through his sobs.

"Relax, Papa," Phil told him. "I have no interest in taking the kid. I just want it to be quiet. This baby needs a nap! Ah, here's what we need right now." Phil spotted a small wooden crib near the window and laid the child in it. Then he gave the cradle a rock for good measure. He looked at Aegeus. "Now you two can talk in peace."

"I need air," Aegeus said, wiping his eyes as he walked back to his front door.

Meg marveled at Phil. "How did you do that?"

"Satyr. We've got the magic touch. I was the oldest of

four; I looked after the little ones," Phil said proudly. "I've always loved babies."

Meg thought they seemed like a lot of work. "I was an only child," she said. "I looked after myself."

"Well, now you need to worry about that one." Phil motioned to Aegeus, who was walking ahead. "Go talk to him! And do it quietly so he doesn't wake the kid!"

Meg sighed and followed Aegeus out the door, watching as he moved through the gardens near the house. How was she going to get through this conversation when all she wanted to do was wring his neck?

"Aegeus?" she said as calmly as she could muster. "I need to talk to you."

"My child," he started to say, looking back at the house.

"The baby is safe with Phil," Meg said dismissively. "He's practically a nursemaid."

Her response only made Aegeus cry again. She, on the other hand, found herself growing angrier. How dare he weep at the sight of her? He was the one who had betrayed *her*, who'd repaid her biggest sacrifice for him by starting a family with another. She thought of her mother's words: *Trust yourself.* Perhaps if she had done more of that, she wouldn't be in this ridiculous mess in the first place; she would be asking some random man about his lost wife to complete Hera's quest. In any case, she would not allow him to waste the little time she had with false tears.

"Enough is enough," Meg said under her breath, spinning him around by the front of his chiton. "Aegeus! Stop it at once!" she shouted. As soon as they made eye contact, he rubbed the wetness from his eyes.

"How is this possible?" he asked, sounding shaken. "I'd say you were a ghost, but you arrived with a satyr and a winged horse. Am I dreaming this, Megara, or have you come back from the dead?"

"I'm alive," she said stonily. "No thanks to you."

Aegeus threw his hands in the air. "Thank the gods! The sacrifices and prayers I made have finally been answered! You are okay." He reached out to touch her face and she stepped back.

"What do you think you're doing?" Meg asked, outraged.

Aegeus shook his head, his eyes still brimming. "I'm sorry. I never thought I'd ever see your face again. I can't believe you've been returned to us after all this time!"

Us? Did he mean him and his *wife*, Katerina? What was Aegeus playing at? She knew Phil would tell her to stick to the script and get the goods on Katerina, but she couldn't help herself.

"Returned? Don't act as if you're happy that I've come

back. You *abandoned* me!" Meg shouted, and Aegeus winced. "The moment I was gone you moved on and got yourself a wife!" Aegeus flattened himself against an olive tree as if pushed by the force of her words. "I made a deal with Hades to save your life. You didn't wonder where I'd gone when you were suddenly well enough to rise from bed? You just followed the next woman who crossed your path? I gave up my soul for you!"

"What?" Aegeus gaped. "Meg, I—"

"And the moment I was out of the picture, you married Katerina!" Meg spat. "So much for wanting to spend your life with me. I saw it with my own eyes! Hades showed me everything!"

"Hades?" He shook his head once more and let out an anguished cry. "I don't understand."

She wouldn't be swayed by his pain. She had enough of her own to last three lifetimes. He needed to know how much he'd hurt her. She had given up everything for him. What a fool she'd been.

"And now to find you in our dream home with a child?" Meg felt hot tears touch her cheeks. "This was supposed to be *ours*! I saved every coin I had to help you buy wood and materials for this place! And the minute I was gone you went and built it for your new love? You aren't worth the dirt beneath my sandals."

"No, Meg! Please! Just listen to me," Aegeus begged. He reached for her hands, but again she pulled away.

"Why should I?" Meg snarled. "So that you can spin more lies? I'm the one doing the talking now." Meg paused, realizing she was doing the very thing Athena had warned her against—getting distracted. She took a breath, focusing. "Look, I am only here for one reason—for myself. I need you to tell me all you know about Katerina." It sounded ridiculous, even to her, but now that the true purpose of her visit was out in the open, she crossed her arms, waiting. The sooner she could get this over with, the better.

Aegeus's eyes widened. "Katerina? How do you know my wife?"

"She's the reason I'm here." Meg stood a bit taller. "Hera has sent me on a quest to retrieve her soul from the Underworld."

"You're going to bring her back?" Aegeus put his head in his hands and sobbed even harder.

She couldn't take this crying, the reminiscing, the painful reminders of her old life. She was clearly getting nowhere with Aegeus, and had no desire to comfort him. This sort of thing wasn't her bag.

She needed to think.

Before she knew it, she was racing out of the garden.

She heard Phil calling her, but she didn't care. She whistled for Pegasus and the horse landed at her side.

"Get me out of here," Meg said, climbing onto his back and taking off into the sky. She didn't look back.

THIRTEEN: I Won't Say

Meg took a deep breath and inhaled the salty air as they took flight, letting it fill her lungs. The sound of the wind helped her heart slow, and for the first time she could remember, she wasn't squeezing Pegasus's neck. *Maybe this flying thing isn't so bad after all,* she thought. *Maybe I just needed to be in a panicked rage to enjoy it.* Of course, Meg was not about to look down, but she certainly felt calmer and more in control than she had on the ground. The farther they flew away from Aegeus and her old life on that cliff, the more she felt something else: freedom. With Pegasus, she could go anywhere her heart desired and no one could follow. Meg felt a primal roar rise up from inside her.

"YESSSSSS!" she shouted into the clouds.

Peg neighed nervously.

"I'm fine!" Meg patted his mane. "Better than fine!" She started to laugh. She'd never felt more free. She could kind of see why Hercules liked riding Pegasus.

Hercules. Her hand went to the satchel and the orchid tucked inside it. *It would be nice to hear his voice right about now,* she thought. *He is so much better at tapping into emotions than I am.* Maybe he'd know how to handle the conversation she still had to finish with Aegeus.

"Peg, can you land somewhere Phil and Aegeus can't find us?" The horse neighed again. "Not for good," she clarified. "Just so I can take a breath. All this feelings stuff is exhausting."

Pegasus seemed to understand, because he came in for a landing in a meadow blooming with hyacinth, orchids, and myriad other colorful blooms. The meadow was gorgeous and completely private. She didn't see another soul around. Carefully, Meg removed her orchid and held it up to the sun.

"Ready to see your friend?" she asked Peg, and he launched back on his hind legs in excitement. "Here goes nothing." Meg ripped the petal in half and watched as it blew away.

Seconds later, she saw a bright flash. She shielded her

eyes as a glowing ball started to form in the air. In a moment, Hercules was standing in front of her.

"Meg!" He ran to her, scooping her up in his arms and swinging her around before pulling her in for a kiss. "Are you all right? What's happened? Do you need my help?" He put her down and pulled out his sword in one swift move, his face darkening as he spun around.

She couldn't help laughing. "I don't *need* anything." The lug was cute when he was in protective mode. It suddenly struck her that she'd not even thought to call upon him during her battle with the Empusa. "Well, that's not exactly true. I could use your advice." She touched his blond curls. "Plus, I just wanted to see you. Is that enough of a reason to call?"

"More than enough!" He pulled her into his arms again. "I've missed you."

"I've missed you, too." She sank into his large glowing arms. She was still getting used to his being a god. They stood there for a moment, listening to the sound of the flowers rustling in the breeze and each other's hearts. Then she heard a neigh.

Hercules turned around. "Pegasus?" Peg jumped around. "Hi, boy! Have you been taking good care of Meg?" He patted the horse's side and saw the healing scar. "Whoa, what happened to you?" He noticed the bandage on Meg's arm. "And you!"

"You've missed a few things while you've been upstairs," she said, nodding to the heavens before quickly filling him in on their fight with the Empusa, finding Phil, meeting Athena, and her insistence that Meg talk to Aegeus. It was draining, rehashing it all. Maybe that's why she left the most important part of the story out.

"Meg . . . wow, I'm so sorry you had to go through all that alone." He held her even tighter. "Seeing Aegeus must have been rough."

"Brutal." She buried her head in his chest and wished she could just forget about the whole journey.

"Why did Athena want you to talk to him, anyway?" Hercules pressed. "Does he have anything to do with the rest of your quest? Which is what, actually? You never said what Athena told you my mother wants you to do now that you've found Athena's flute."

Meg sighed. There was no prolonging the inevitable. "You might want to take a seat for this next part." She patted the lush grass beneath their feet and Hercules looked worried as he settled in next to her. Meg sat up straighter. She wanted to appear strong. She *was* strong. Still, her lower lip trembled. "I am supposed to retrieve a soul from the Underworld—the soul of Aegeus's wife, Katerina, to be exact."

Hercules jumped up. "Meg, no, she can't make you go back there!" He tumbled over his own words. "Hades won't let you go again! It's impossible! And to save your former flame's new wife? That's mad!" Meg felt her heart warm. He really was something—immediately taking her side, not showing a shred of jealousy, even when they were talking about her ex. Then Hercules started to stride away. "I need to talk to my mother."

"No!" Meg grabbed his hand and pulled him back down. "You know you can't do that. This deal is between me and her, and besides, I'm not telling you all this so you can try to sweet-talk her on my behalf. I think I just needed to hear myself say the plan out loud." She snuck a glance at him. "It's as bad as it sounds, though, isn't it?"

Hercules didn't speak right away. "It's . . . well . . . it's not easy, but this is *you* we're talking about. You can do anything you set your mind to. I'll help you any way I can. Just say the word."

This was why she liked this boy—er, *god*. She squeezed his hand. "Thanks."

He leaned in and kissed her softly. "So what's your next move?" he asked, his lips still close to hers. "Did you talk to Aegeus about Katerina? Maybe he can tell you a bit about her that would be helpful in tracking her down in the Underworld. It's kind of a large place."

"Oh, I remember." She plucked a poppy growing near their feet. "I tried to talk to Aegeus, but our conversation didn't go well." She looked at Hercules. "I kind of bit his head off." Hercules's eyes widened. "I know! You don't have to say it. I need his help. But just seeing his stupid face again got me so fired up! You don't know what it's like to stand in front of someone you thought you loved who betrayed you. . . ." Her voice died out and they looked at one another. Hercules couldn't help a small smirk. Her cheeks began to burn. "Okay, I'm going to eat my own words now. It was just hard, okay?" She ripped the poppy into pieces that blew away in the wind.

"Of course it was," he said gently. "But you still have to face him if you want to learn about Katerina. And who knows? Maybe he'll surprise you." He touched her hand. "People can do that, you know."

Wonder Boy really was too good for this world. "True. But I'm not holding out hope for Aegeus. I was gone one measly week when he recovered from his illness, met Katerina, and completely forgot I existed."

"A week? How is that possible?" Hercules plucked a new poppy and held it out to her. "I can't imagine anyone forgetting someone like you, especially not in a week."

"You should see him now," she grumbled. "He's married with a kid and everything." She looked at him. "Not that I want those things with him, of course. It just sort of, well, *stings*."

But Hercules seemed distracted. "A week . . ." he whispered to himself, shaking his head. "It doesn't make sense." Meg looked at him. "I'm not defending the guy or anything, but a *week*? Meg, are you sure?"

"Yes!" She took her anger out on the flower again, ripping apart its petals as well. "Hades showed me them together seven days after I got to the Underworld. After that, he'd make me watch scenes of Aegeus and Katerina together at night, like it was some sort of performance."

Hercules sat up straighter. "Hades did that?" He looked out across the meadow. "Huh."

Meg sat up taller too. "What do you mean, 'Huh'?"

"I just mean, you believe him? It is Hades, after all, and he is the god of the Underworld. He's played some pretty dirty tricks on both of us. What if he was lying?"

"Lying?" Meg dropped the flower stem. "But he *showed* me them getting close, falling for one another. And they did end up getting married."

Hercules nodded. "I'm not saying they didn't end up together, but Hades has his ways of distorting the truth.

If you had to pick one person to trust, would it be him or Aegeus?"

"Neither!" Meg said, but she knew he was right. She hadn't even really questioned the tricky god of the Underworld. She threw herself back on the grass and looked up at the clouds in the sky and groaned. "My gods. Now I don't know what to think. Also, I pretty much just ripped Aegeus's head off. Like clear off, as if he were Medusa and I had a sharp blade."

Hercules lay down next to her. "I'm just saying, give Aegeus a chance to explain. Like I gave *you*." He squeezed her hand and she laughed.

"Okay, yes, you've made your point. I'll talk to Aegeus again." She ruffled his hair. "Thanks for the pep talk. This is why I keep you around," she teased.

He leaned his chin on her hand. "I'm glad you do. And just think: when you finish this quest, we get to be together for eternity."

Meg's smile fell slightly. There was that word again: eternity. That was a *long* time. But, she reminded herself, there was still a quest and a week left before she had to think about it. One thing at a time. "I'm glad you're here."

"Me, too." He kissed her again. "I know this task isn't as fun as mine was—beating up monsters and all that. But my mother must trust you if she gave you a quest as major as this one. There's a reason she wants you to save Katerina. The gods don't tell us everything. Or at least, that's what they're telling me in my Olympus training classes." He rolled his eyes. "There are so many dos and don'ts and rules to this god thing. I had no idea."

Meg put a hand to his lips. "Wait. Back up. What did you say about a reason?"

"You mean, the 'the gods must have their reason' part?" Hercules repeated.

"Yes!" Meg tapped her chin. "They must need Katerina for something. Do you know why?" He hesitated. "You *do* know!" She waved a finger at him. "Tell me!"

"All I know is what I overheard my mother telling Athena," Hercules admitted. "They mentioned the name Katerina the other day after you left. It sounds like she's important, but I'm not sure why. All I know is Father feels guilty about her death. I don't think they intended for it to happen. Mother said something about a flood."

Meg thought for a moment. "Flood, huh? Gods know, Greece has had a lot of those."

"Maybe that's how you handle helping Aegeus's wife," he suggested. "Keep thinking about how she wasn't meant to die."

"True." Meg ran a hand through her red hair and thought of that wailing baby. She was so young to be without her mother. Even younger than Meg was when she had lost hers. She closed her eyes and let the sun warm her face, then opened her eyes to look at him for as long as she could. A field of hyacinths swayed behind him. "I wish I could live here in this meadow. It's gorgeous."

"Yeah, it is," Hercules agreed. "That's Persephone's handiwork," he explained. "She's the god of vegetation."

"Demeter's daughter, right?" Meg said. "I heard Demeter talking when I was on Olympus. Something about not knowing where the girl had run off to."

Hercules nodded. "Yeah, Demeter keeps appealing to my father to find her. No one has seen her in months, and harvest will be coming before long." He touched one of the hyacinths with his finger. "Every flower has its season."

Suddenly Meg heard the distinctive chime of bells. She looked at Hercules.

He smiled sheepishly. "Uh . . . they're ringing for me upstairs."

Poof! Hermes popped up in front of them carrying a clipboard and a writing utensil. He stared at Hercules over the top of his glasses as his winged hat fluttered fast. "Hercules, your father wants you home immediately. Helios is threatening to walk off the job and refuses to race his chariot across the sky tomorrow. Something about lack of vacation time. Zeus wants you there to facilitate the argument."

"Okay, I'm coming. Let me just say goodbye to Meg." Wonder Boy turned to look at her. "Are you okay getting back on your own?"

"Of course," she said, sitting up and wrapping her arms around him one more time. "I should get back, too."

Hercules leaned in for one more kiss as his whole body started to waver. "Be safe, Meg! I love—" He disappeared before he could finish the sentence.

FOURTEEN: Ugly Truths

Pegasus and Meg landed softly outside Aegeus's house as night began to fall. There seemed to be a fire glowing behind the house, creating shadows along the ground, but all was quiet except for the sound of the ocean in the distance. She'd been gone longer than she intended, but she felt much more prepared now. *Time to face the music,* she thought as she patted Pegasus and headed to the door. Before she could knock, she felt a tug on her skirt. She turned to find Phil holding a hand up.

"You stay right there!" he hissed.

"Phil, I—" Meg started.

"Shhh!" Phil shushed her. "Cassia is asleep!"

"Cassia?"

Phil rolled his eyes. "The baby? Took me an hour to get her to nod off." He grabbed her by the arm. "We're sitting out back so we don't wake her. Come on. You two still need to talk."

"I know," Meg said with a sigh.

"You don't have the whole story, okay?"

"I am starting to see that," Meg told him.

"Now don't clobber me for saying this, but Aegeus seems like a good guy, and that baby . . ." Phil got a goofy look on his face. "She's a cutie." His face hardened again. "I think you have to put your history aside and help the kid."

"That's why I'm back, Phil—to talk to Aegeus. Alone."

"Finally! Go, and make it snappy, okay? You only have seven days left."

"No need to remind me."

Phil motioned to the garden, where Aegeus was sitting on a log, staring into the flames. Meg hesitated. "What are you waiting for? Talk to the guy."

Meg cocked her head to one side. "Were you this bossy with Hercules?"

"Worse," Phil said. "Go! I need to wash a few of Cassia's things and clean up inside. That kid can make a real mess." Phil shook his head, a little grin playing on his lips, and walked off.

Squaring her shoulders, Meg walked toward the garden.

A soft hum of music reached her ears and she realized Aegeus had his lute. Hearing the melody gave her pause. Perhaps sensing her presence, Aegeus lowered the instrument and looked up. He didn't burst into tears, so that was an improvement.

"Don't stop playing on my account," she said, walking closer.

He smiled softly. "It would sound better if I had a partner. You have a new flute, I hear."

The satyr had been doing some talking, it seemed. "It's not mine. It's on loan."

"Would you consider playing something together?"

The thought was too painful to even entertain. Meg shook her head. "We still need to talk about your wife."

"Of course," Aegeus said, sounding sad. "And we will, but first, I think I must explain myself."

"Aegeus—" she said, attempting to cut him off.

"No, please." He put the lute on the grass beside him. "I need to understand what happened with us. Did you really make a deal with Hades to save my life?"

In the distance, Meg thought she heard Phil puttering about inside the house. "Yes. I gave up my soul for you."

His face twisted with anguish. "Why?"

"I couldn't let you die," she said, her voice breaking as she sat down on the log beside him. "You were so ill, and I couldn't imagine a world without you in it. I prayed to many gods while you were sick. Hades was the one who answered and made a deal with me. I just didn't realize he'd come to collect my soul immediately."

"Megara . . . I can't believe . . ." Aegeus's voice was so low she could hardly hear him. He fiddled with his hands. "Well, this explains why you were gone when I woke up."

She closed her eyes, reliving the moment despite herself. "Yes. I was gone, and you were free to move on with your life," she added bitterly, despite herself. "Which you did immediately."

He turned to her. "That is where you are wrong. When you disappeared, I searched for you everywhere. I assumed you had journeyed somewhere to get help, and when you didn't return, I feared the worst. I knocked on doors and put up notices for months. I couldn't sleep. Couldn't eat. I was desperate to find you." He looked at her sadly. "Megara, I searched for you for almost two years."

Meg's head whipped around. His words made her feel like she was in a free fall. "Two years? But . . ."

"Two years," he repeated. "When there was no sign of you after that time, I knew I had to accept the fact you were truly gone."

Meg felt a lump form in her throat. Had she lost more time than she'd realized? The Underworld was a place where that happened. She'd seen many a soul come through Hades's door, imagining they'd been dead mere moments when it had, in fact, been years. Was that what had happened to her as well—did the "days" that had passed actually equate to months? Years? Her hands were shaking. It all made sense now. For Hades to allow her back on Earth to do his dirty work, he had to be sure she wouldn't run to find Aegeus, and the only way to ensure she wouldn't search for her love was to keep her there for as long as it took for Aegeus to believe she was gone. And then to make sure she hated him, to make her think he'd committed the ultimate betrayal.

Oh, Wonder Boy, you were right.

"I was so consumed with grief that I built this house to stay sane, hoping you'd return to me," he said sadly. "This wasn't built for my new family. I built it as a memorial to you."

"I didn't know." Meg was still stunned. "I thought you moved on to Katerina in less than a week."

"I swear to you, I tried to find you," Aegeus said. "Finally I realized I had to stop living in sorrow, because you wouldn't want me to do that. I stopped working on the empty house. And then I met Katerina. Even after we married, I couldn't imagine living here. This home was your dream, and Katerina understood. I fixed up the house at the base of the hill instead and we started our new life together there."

"You did?" Meg felt her voice shake.

He closed his eyes for a moment. "I only moved in after Katerina died and our house was destroyed. The baby and I needed somewhere else to live." His eyes brimmed with tears again.

"I'm sorry. How did she die?" Meg asked as gently as she could.

"There was a storm unlike anything I had ever seen. The rain pounded the roof like Titans' fists. The wind was so fierce I thought Zeus himself was blowing on the house, ready to make it cave in. I feared the house wouldn't make it through the night, so I told Katerina we needed to get to the newer one. I knew that its framing was strong enough to sustain such conditions. Katerina handed me the baby and sent me out first, staying back to collect as many of our things as she could." Tears began to trickle down his face. "I had only started to head up the hill when . . . the house was swept away by rising waters." He let out a sob. "Katerina was gone."

Aegeus looked completely broken.

A flood. Wasn't that what Hercules had mentioned?

"And now there is suddenly a river where the house

stood. An actual river! It's a constant reminder of what I lost. It's like the gods themselves put it there."

The gods themselves. A rain pounding like the Titans' fists. Meg thought for a moment. "When did you say the river appeared?"

Aegeus's throat seemed to clench. "Only a few days ago."

Meg looked at the dancing flames as the facts started to click into place. The flood had occurred during the Titans' return, when the world had been thrown into chaos . . . before Hercules had saved it, of course. It was the Titans and the gods that had caused the disaster that took Katerina's life. *Maybe if I can save her, we can all finally find peace.*

"Do you really think you can bring Katerina back?" Aegeus's soft voice interrupted her thoughts.

Meg set her jaw. "I'm going to try." She shifted her attention back to him. "What can you tell me about her that could help me find her in the afterlife?"

"She was a lot like you, actually," Aegeus told her. "She didn't have much in the way of family nearby, so she did everything on her own."

I can admire that, Meg thought. "What else?"

"Her birth name was Katerina Aikos, but she took my last name when we married."

Dimas, Meg thought. She'd often wondered how

Megara Dimas would sound, but she'd never said the name aloud. Katerina Dimas actually had a better ring to it, anyway. "And?"

"Her parents live on the other side of Greece. She hadn't seen them in years, which sounds strange, I know, but she said it was too painful to visit them."

"Why is that?"

"Katerina had a younger sister. Layla. She died of illness when she was only seven. They were very close. Katerina always blamed herself for Layla's death."

"But if she was ill . . ."

Aegeus shook his head. "Like you, she couldn't accept that her loved one was dying. She begged the gods for help to cure the child of her illness, but they didn't hear her prayers. She didn't like to talk about Layla's death itself, so I mostly know how the girl lived. She was pure joy, Katerina always said. She was always making up stories as big as myths. And she loved to gather poppies, which she placed all over their home. Katerina loved them as well."

Layla Aikos. Tall tales. Poppies. Meg tried to commit the details to memory.

Aegeus smiled to himself. "I never saw Katerina without a poppy tucked into her hair. That's how I spotted her that day in the market—I saw the red flower. I must have looked haggard, because she took it out and gave it to me, saying something about how I needed a spot of sunshine more than she did. After that, we started talking every day that I came to the market. I started to make daily trips in the hopes I'd run into her. I felt we had something in common—we both had lost someone we loved, and that connected us. At first, all we talked about was the two of you."

Meg startled. "Me?"

"Yes." Aegeus looked at her. "Katerina wanted to know about the woman who captured my heart. She encouraged me to talk about you often, as if you were still around us in the very air we breathed. She talked of Layla the same way. She said, 'We imprint the lost on our hearts.'"

Mother, Meg thought. Katerina was right—while Meg's mother was gone, she knew she always carried her with her.

"Katerina was the one who actually inspired me to pick up my lute again," Aegeus went on. "She wanted to hear the songs we had created. She encouraged me to play for the public again in your honor."

"She did?" This Katerina was making Meg feel horrible for thinking so ill of her before. And slightly jealous. She just seemed so . . . perfect. *What is wrong with me?* "This is a lot to swallow," Meg admitted.

"I know," Aegeus said. "I guess I just wanted you to know you will always hold a place in my heart, Megara, even if the Fates led us in different directions."

Meg knew the end to their love affair was tragic, but it hadn't ended because they stopped loving each other. The Fates—or in her case, Hades—had intervened. She'd channeled her rage and hatred toward a woman she'd never met and a man who had truly cared about her. And yet, now that she knew the truth, that anger dissipated as quickly as a summer storm. As awful as that period of her life had been, the path had led her to Wonder Boy and given her the opportunity to truly find out where she belonged in this world. How could she be mad about that?

The sound of wailing wrested Meg away from her thoughts.

"Cassia is awake again," Aegeus said, standing. "She is not the best sleeper, I'm afraid. I should go to her. Phil has been a godsend, but he needs rest for your journey. He said you must leave in the morning."

Meg followed Aegeus into the house, where they found a bleary-eyed Phil rocking the crib.

"Why don't you two get some shut-eye and I'll sit with the kid?" Meg said, lifting the child from the cradle. This time the baby stopped crying, almost in surprise. She looked up at Meg with her big, dark eyes, seemingly wondering the same thing Meg was: *Are we going to get along or not?*

"You?" Phil sputtered.

"Why not?" Meg hoisted the child on her hip, straining a bit. Babies were heavy.

Aegeus and Phil looked at one another. "I won't break her, if that's what you're worried about. Get some sleep. Us girls will be fine on our own." Maybe the night air would soothe her. On her way out, Meg spotted a small wooden platagi and took that with her.

Meg walked back out to the fire and looked around for something suitable to sit on. Holding a baby on a log would probably not be the most comfortable. Then she spotted a *klismos* nestled in the trees. The chair had a curved back-rest and tapered legs with a woven seat. Meg brought Cassia over to it and bounced her on her knee. The two stared at one another.

"Well, it's you and me, kid, for the next few hours at least."

At these words, Cassia started to whimper. Meg bounced her quicker.

"No, no—no tears. We've had enough of those today. Any more and this house will float away like your last one."

Cassia started to cry a bit then.

"Sorry. Okay, cry if you need to. I just mean we need some quiet. There's been a lot of heavy talk about things you'll never have to deal with. Hopefully. Unlike your father, mother, and me, maybe you'll meet someone nice and settle down without the Fates or the god of the Underworld pulling the strings."

Cassia began to cry harder.

"All right, no more talk of the Underworld or tragedy." Meg shook the rattle, hearing the beads move around inside. The baby saw it and her wailing stopped for a moment. She reached out with chubby hands and clutched the rattle clumsily in her fingers. Cassia shook the rattle so hard it hit Meg in the nose.

"A little less enthusiasm, please." Meg gently pushed the rattle down so that it wouldn't keep hitting her in the face. "But the sound is nice." When Meg had been young, her father had never let her use her rattle—he'd said it made too much noise. But Meg found she actually enjoyed the sound. *Shake it, kid,* she thought.

Meg started to hum along with the shaking rattle, rocking Cassia at the same time. The two of them stayed like that for a while. Eventually Meg saw the child's eyes slowly closing. She took the rattle from the little hands and rocked the chair as long as she could. Meg had never been happier for the quiet. She'd never been a fan of cryfests. Her mother wouldn't allow them.

Meg couldn't have been more than six or seven at the time, but she remembered tears coming hard and fast. She had found her mother just coming out of the forest with her bow and arrow and a sack, most likely full of birds or hares, fresh kill for supper. Meg raced into her mother's arms.

"Shush now, Megara. It's all right," her mother had said, placing her bow and arrow on the ground and hugging the child. But Meg had just kept crying. "What have I said about wasted tears? They don't help us. What is the problem? Together we will fix it. Now what's wrong?"

Meg had looked up at her mother with her slightly sunburned cheeks and the dark circles under her eyes that came from working the olive groves for hours. Her mother didn't have much, but she fought hard for everything they did have. Even at a young age, Meg knew telling her the truth would break her heart, but she'd already learned fighting her mother was pointless.

"They said I couldn't play with them," Meg said softly. "They said they don't play with beggars."

Her mother had held her close then. "You are no beggar, Megara. You are strong. You are clever and you are brave. You know friends like those aren't worth your time. Trust your instincts." Gently, she placed the bow and quiver of arrows in Meg's hands, urging her to try them on her own. "They won't steer you wrong. Remember that."

Trust yourself; trust your instincts. It was something her mother said to her over and over. She didn't need anyone but herself. And her mother had been right, of course, but Meg still couldn't help wishing the woman were still on this Earth to help her navigate this world. She held Cassia tighter, feeling tense as she looked down at her small pink face, hearing the tiny baby breathing. Cassia was so young. She hadn't even had a chance to know her mother like Meg had. Did she have any clue what she'd already lost at such a young age? How different would this child's life look if Meg could bring Katerina back to her?

You can save her.

Meg heard the words inside her head as clearly as if they'd been spoken aloud, and she knew then they were true. She would rise to this challenge and help this innocent child. Cassia didn't have to grow up as Meg had, feeling lost. Cassia deserved to see the world differently than she did. Tears sprang to Meg's eyes.

Cassia stirred slightly, her arms twitching in her sleep. Meg rubbed them gently and the child's right hand closed over her finger and held on tight. Meg didn't move.

Who are you? Meg wondered as she stared at the child's dreaming face. *Who will you become? You must be someone important for Hera to take interest. But even if you're not, I will help you,* Meg thought. "I won't let you grow up without a mother like I did, Cassia," she whispered. "I promise I will bring Katerina back to you."

At some point, Meg fell asleep, too. When she awoke, purple and pink swirls were racing across the sky and Helios was getting ready to start their day. Hercules had obviously worked his magic and figured out Helios's vacation time in some other way.

Aegeus and Phil appeared looking slightly in awe that all was still quiet.

Meg stood up with the baby still asleep in her arms. "We bonded." She placed Cassia in Aegeus's arms. "Tell her I'll be back soon and next time I'll have her mother with me."

Phil beamed. "Attagirl. One question: where are we headed next? We still have no clue where an entrance to the Underworld might be from here."

"I wish I could help you search," Aegeus said. "I barely leave the cliff. The new rapids at the bottom of the hill make it impossible to travel with Cassia."

Rapids. The new river—the flood that had been caused by the Titans and their war with the gods. Meg rushed to the edge of the cliff and looked down. The water below was rushing swiftly, debris and twigs floating past at a high speed. Meg's eyes followed the trail of the water, which headed in the opposite direction of the ocean. It seemed to move inland and then disappear near a mountain range. Her instincts told her this was the way.

"I think we should follow this strange new river," she said, turning to Phil and Aegeus. "My gut tells me this was made by the gods. Pegasus can help us sail over it until we get to the Underworld's entrance."

Phil walked over to the hill to look down at the water with her. "For mortals, the Underworld is only accessible by boat. If you think it's this river, we're going to need some sort of vessel."

Aegeus's eyes brightened. "That I can help you with! It isn't much. I only use it for fishing in the ocean, but it should take you where you need to go."

Aegeus and Phil trotted down to collect his boat while Meg continued to hold Cassia. She was determined to memorize every detail of the child's face so that she could tell Katerina about her. She walked around bouncing the baby and felt something hit her foot. She looked down. Cassia's rattle had rolled away when they'd fallen asleep. Meg picked it up, staring at Aegeus's woodwork, listening to the beads move. There was something about the sound that was very soothing. Meg wasn't sure why, but she opened her satchel and tucked the rattle inside it.

FIFTEEN: Rising Water

Aegeus's caïque was a small, bright orange fishing vessel with a long, sharp bow and a sail that pulled taut in the light breeze. Pegasus was the first on board, stepping gingerly onto the wooden planks, which immediately began to rock.

Meg came right behind him. She handed Cassia back to Aegeus, then glanced at the hourglass before returning it safely to her pouch. She was alarmed to see it was more than a quarter filled with sand. Six days left. It was not a lot of time. "Coming, Phil?"

"I'm coming, hold your feta," Phil said, and she thought she heard him sniffle as he touched Cassia's cheek. "Bye, kid. You're going to miss Uncle Phil, aren't ya?"

"*Uncle* Phil?" Meg repeated, and she and Peg snorted.

Phil shot them both a look. "What can I say? Babies are cute and much easier to deal with than stubborn heroes-in-training."

Meg rolled her eyes.

"We will miss you, Philoctetes," Aegeus said. "If you ever travel this way again, please know you are always welcome here."

Phil looked like he might cry. "Maybe I'll drop in on my way home and see how you guys are doing."

"Please do." Aegeus's eyes moved to Meg. "You are welcome as well. I still don't know how to thank you."

"You can thank me when I've returned with your wife." Meg looked at the baby, who was reaching for her, and longed to say something she'd understand, but knew she couldn't. Instead, she silently appraised her. *Hang on, Cassia. I'm going to find her and bring her back for you.*

"We will be praying for your safe return, Megara," Aegeus said as he shifted the baby on his hip. "May the gods show you favor."

"They already have," said Phil proudly as he stepped aboard and cut the line holding them to shore.

They drifted away so fast Meg barely had time to turn and see Aegeus lift his hand and wave goodbye before the boat rounded a bend, rocking and swaying as it moved faster downstream. Meg felt her heart rate quicken. They were on their way.

"Buckle up, kid," Phil said as the boat jostled over a rock. "If you're right and this river leads to Acheron, this is going to be a bumpy ride, especially since you've never sailed before."

"Says who?" Meg asked as she dipped her oar in and steered them around a cluster of rocks ahead. Phil looked at her in surprise. *You can thank your boy Hercules for that.*

Months earlier, Hercules had gone from zero to hero practically overnight. He destroyed the most infamous monsters in Thebes day after day. Hades, on the other hand, was practically molten with frustration, and he was coming down on her and his other minions hard to try to figure out how to stop the Wonder Boy. Could she help it if she seemed anxious when Hercules showed up one afternoon wanting to see her?

"Let's go do something," she recalled him begging. "Anything you want! Maybe a ride over the sea on Pegasus?"

"No rides on that thing," she'd said quickly. "Look, I appreciate you coming by and all, but I'm not exactly in a sightseeing mood."

"Come on, Meg," he'd insisted. "We can do nothing but sit quietly and stare at our sandals if that's what you want. Let's just take a teeny-tiny break to spend some time together. Please?"

She knew she should say no, to protect his heart as well as her own; but he had that adorably goofy grin that was almost too big for his face and that earnest look in his eye. He'd even shown up with a bouquet of flowers, for gods' sake. How could she turn him down? "I guess I could slip away for an hour, but nothing more."

His smile grew even wider. "That's great! An hour is all we need. We can . . . well, let's see; flying is out, and we can't go anywhere Phil can find us," he rambled. "Ah! I've got an idea. Follow me!" He grabbed her hand and led her to a nearby lake.

"You want to go swimming?" she had asked, the disdain probably written all over her face.

"No, no, of course not." He ran behind some brush and pulled something large out from within it with ease. It was a small fishing boat. "We're going sailing!"

Meg remembered scoffing. "I don't sail."

"Why not? It's fun! My father used to take me." He pushed the boat into the water, then put one foot up on the bench to hold it steady and held out his hand. "I'll teach you."

She'd stared at his hand apprehensively.

"Come on, Meg! No one will find us out on the water. Don't you ever want to escape?"

"Always," she'd said without hesitation, and before she knew it, she was climbing aboard.

He rowed them effortlessly over a light chop to the center of the lake, his biceps bulging as he paddled with both oars. Then he handed her one. She looked at it for a moment. "I can row on my own, of course, but usually when two people each take an oar, it's a smoother ride."

"Why don't I just take a turn driving us?" she'd asked, grabbing the second oar from his hands and attempting to use both oars at the same time. Okay, it was way harder than it looked. She nearly lost one oar in the water as she dipped it into a wave. Hercules reached out and grabbed it.

"Here, let me show you." He carefully moved to the back of the boat and sat behind her so he could guide her arms with the oars. She was well aware of his body being so close, but she tried not to seem ruffled as he placed his hands on her arms and gently guided her through the circular motion. "Like that. You've got it!"

She could feel his breath on her neck. *How does he smell as sweet as nectar in this heat? Do I smell?* she found herself wondering. *Why do I care?* Their close proximity was definitely doing something to her.

"Okay, now you try it on your own."

He let go of her arms to let her paddle both oars, and instantly she felt the difference. Churning the oars through the water was tough, not that she wanted to let on, and the only motion she could make was turning them in circles.

"You sure I can't do one and you do one? There's nothing wrong with teamwork," he'd said.

"Fine." She passed him an oar. "But only because I don't want us stuck out here in the middle of the lake forever."

As soon as Hercules had taken an oar, they were able to paddle in tandem, and the boat began to glide over the chop, sailing at a clip across the lake.

"Nice, Meg! You're doing it!" he'd yelled as they moved faster and faster. "Isn't this great?"

It kind of was, though she hesitated to admit it. What wasn't to like about the sun warming her face, the breeze blowing through her hair, and the fact that she was alone on a lake with a guy who seemed to want nothing more from her than her company?

"You're a good boating partner, Meg," Hercules had said with a laugh.

"So are you, Wonder Boy," she'd told him.

Partners. She'd never been around a man who didn't

seem to have an ulterior motive. Her father had left when she and her mother got in his way. Hades owned her. Aegeus had turned out to care only about himself and the next woman on deck. With Hercules, things felt right.

Hercules was someone who challenged her to see the good in the world, while accepting her as she was. He was someone who never stopped surprising her, who could make her heart race with a mere look. But did that mean they'd work well together for eternity? How did she know for sure she was even in love with the guy? There was no guide for these things. It was a feeling, but what if she was wrong? Or what if she made a bad decision like she had in the past, one that would wreck them? Eternity was a long time to not screw things up.

Aegeus's boat lurched sideways, almost tipping them over, and Meg grabbed the oar and righted the boat. "Don't worry, Phil. I know what I'm doing here. This river will be the easy part of this gig."

"I don't know about that." But Phil moved to the left side with his oar while Meg navigated the right. Within minutes, they were steering in tandem without arguing. They were somehow making it work, jumping in to balance the ship, and maybe that was the point.

The same could be said for her and Hercules, couldn't

it? When the two of them worked together, each of them picking up slack and lifting the other one up, things felt right. Maybe there would never be some huge sign that he was the one. Perhaps it was a bunch of little signs, and she just had to decide once and for all to take that leap.

They hit a rock and the boat lifted off the water, then dropped fast and hit a sudden dip. Meg kept her oar steady as the river kept winding and turning. The dense vegetation along the sides of the river was so thick she couldn't get her bearings. All she knew was that she didn't want to fall overboard. That dark churning water beneath them felt uncomfortably familiar; it reminded her of the haunted streams in the Underworld—the ones teeming with lost, anguished souls. Her gut said they were on the right path, at least.

"Pegasus," Meg called out to him. "Grab an oar. We could use your help." The horse took one with his mouth as they all leaned to the left, hoping the boat would turn away from a tree trunk jutting out into the water. They narrowly made their way around it.

"Red, we're nowhere near the entrance," Phil yelled as he paddled faster around a floating branch rushing alongside them. "We'll never get there at this rate."

"How do you know?" Meg called. "Have you been to the entrance before?"

"No, but I . . . *rock*!" They leaned to the left and paddled to avoid it. "If it was that easy to find, don't you think everyone would be banging down the door to the Underworld to go get their loved ones back?"

Meg hadn't thought about it that way before. "Only if they've forgotten about Cerberus!" Pegasus snorted in agreement. "How will we know when we're getting close?"

Phil looked back at her for a second. "Believe me, we will know because . . . *tree*!"

They navigated the boat around the stump sticking out into the rapids.

"Because what?" she pushed. "I didn't arrive in the Underworld by boat before. Last time I was just dropped in Hades's lair." They hit another bump and both she and Phil fell backward. They scrambled to get up again.

"Really?" Phil momentarily turned to look at her. "Huh. Didn't think humans were allowed to chill in the Underworld. Chill. Ha! Get it?"

"Yeah, and they're not," Meg said as water splashed over the side of the boat. "Hades hid me, I guess."

Phil wiped water off his nose. The boat righted itself and started to move along more steadily, giving them all the opportunity to catch their breath. "They say the Underworld messes with your bearings. You sort of lose track of things—sense of place, time . . ."

"Yeah, figured that last one out. How does everyone seem to know all of this except me?" Meg asked.

Phil shrugged. "All I'm saying is hang on tight to that hourglass down there," he said as they began to round another bend. "That will help you remember, and—hey . . ." Phil stopped rowing. "You hear that?"

"Hear what?" Meg used the back of her hand to keep the ongoing spray of water out of her eyes. Peg neighed nervously as Meg tried to see what was up ahead. The river seemed to just end right beyond a row of trees. But that didn't make sense. The water was still rushing forward, almost as if . . .

She and Phil looked at one another at the same time. "Waterfall!"

"Hang on!" Meg shouted as she leaned back, pulling the oar's flat side through the water trying to slow them down. The boat kept barreling forward. Meg pictured a hundred-foot drop ahead of them. If that were the case, they would be done for. "We have to bail!" she said. "Pegasus, let's fly!"

"NO! You can only find the entrance on water!" Phil argued. "If we lose this boat, we're finished."

"Are you mad? If we stay here, we'll be smashed to smithereens!" Meg cried, her fingers itching to drop the oar and rush to Pegasus's side. "There's no way we'll make it!"

They were nearing the edge now. She could see the spot where the river just dropped off.

"We will!" Phil countered. "Trust me!"

I don't trust anyone but myself, Meg wanted to say. But she had little choice. "Fine!" she yelled as the front of the boat neared the edge and Peg started to whine. "If we die, don't expect me to play chess with you in the Underworld!"

"Deal!" Phil shouted. "Now lean back! Everyone! One, two, threeeeeeeeeee!"

The boat hit the edge and fell forward so fast, Meg thought they were going to plummet ahead of the boat to their deaths. Water rushed over them, making it impossible to scream. Meg felt Pegasus come flying toward her. She grabbed hold of the mast at the same time Phil did, and Pegasus wedged his body behind it. Meg held her breath, waiting for impact. The boat finally slammed into a wall of water, then bounced for a moment, water spilling into it, and righted itself again.

Pegasus collapsed on the deck of the boat in exhaustion. Phil fell over, clutching his oar. Meg sank to the floor and found a fish flopping on the deck next to her. She picked it up, disgusted, and threw it back in the river.

"Look! I can't believe we made it!" Phil looked back at the waterfall gushing behind them. "Yowza! That had to be a hundred feet!"

"What do you mean, you 'can't believe we made it'?" Meg said, trying to catch her breath. "You said we'd be fine."

"Well, we were, weren't we?" Phil spat more water out of his mouth. "You got to learn to trust people, Red."

"Yeah, because that always works out so well," she said under her breath.

"I mean it! Once you learn that the horse and I are on your side, we'll have you to the entrance of the Underworld and back with Hercules in no time. And then I can get back to relaxing." He wrung water out of his furry tail.

"Oh, sure. This has been a piece of baklava so far. What more could go wrong?" Meg pushed her wet bangs behind her right ear and looked away.

"Hey now, don't do *that*."

"Do what?"

"Doubt yourself." Phil stomped over to her, climbing onto the boat bench to look her in the eye. "I've had heroes-in-training do that before, and they are the ones who don't make it. It takes guts and faith to do what you're about to do."

The satyr sounded so smug she wanted to take his small body and throw him overboard. But then, who would help her steer?

"I know, Phil," she said with an involuntary eye roll.

"Do you?" he protested. "You've got to believe you can

take anything this quest throws at you, whether it's a waterfall or a harpy."

"Harpy?" Meg asked. "Why would we run into harpies?"

He sighed. "I'm just saying you've got to believe in yourself." Phil jumped down and grabbed a bucket to try to get some of the water out of the boat.

Believe in yourself. There it was again. But did that contradict what Phil had just said about trusting others? Her mother had thought so. . . .

"I believe, okay?" Meg fixed her ponytail. "If I didn't, I wouldn't be here risking my life."

The tingling of bells made them stop arguing.

"Hi there!" Hermes hovered above the back of the boat, his winged hat helping him navigate closer. He seemed out of breath, and his brow was sweaty. A handkerchief appeared suddenly in his right hand and he used it to wipe his face. "Wow, were you two hard to find! I was flying on and on and on! She said you'd be on the river Acheron and to bring you this gift, but then you weren't there yet, even though you don't have a lot of time left on your hourglass. So I thought, they can't still be back at Aegeus's, can they? But I made a pit stop there, popped into his house, and woke the baby. Whoa, can she cry."

"You woke the baby?" Phil groaned.

"Kid has some lungs! Boy!" Hermes held his head. "Aegeus said I should follow the river at the bottom of the hill, so I did, and then I saw the waterfall and thought, they're goners! But she said to keep looking, and I did, and found you down here." Hermes flew around the boat and then shot up high into the sky and came back down again. "Wow, you haven't made it that far, have you?"

Meg tried to be patient. "Hermes, you said you had a gift?" She hoped it wasn't that they got to keep the messenger for the rest of the journey.

"Yes, from her!" he said, his winged hat fluttering fast.

"What her?" Meg asked impatiently. "Hera?"

"Oh, no!" Hermes laughed. "She's not getting in the middle of your quest. You're on your own when it comes to her."

"Hit her where it hurts, why don't ya?" Phil muttered under his breath.

"This is from Athena." Hermes snapped his fingers and two sacks appeared on a seat of the boat. Meg opened the first sack and found a bow and arrow. "Ever use one of those before?" he asked.

Meg expertly nocked the arrow and pulled the bowstring back, then spun around, targeting Phil.

"Not funny!" He jumped out of the way and she laughed.

She used to practice archery with her mother. Her mom

had expert aim, and she'd caught them many a dinner this way. Meg hadn't held a bow and arrow in her hands in years, but the sensation came right back to her. "Yes. My mother taught me how to use one of these." She placed both items on the bench again and opened the second sack. Inside were two long pieces of metal held together with leather straps. "Is this an instrument?" she asked quizzically.

"A special kind of instrument," Hermes said. "Listen to the sound it makes."

Meg clapped the two pieces of metal together, and a terrible, high-pitched shriek emitted from them. Everyone held their ears. She could still hear a ringing even when the clapper was silent. Pegasus neighed miserably.

"Pretty dreadful, right?" Hermes asked. "Athena had Hephaestus make it for you. Said it might come in handy if you're reckless."

Phil snorted. "Reckless is her middle name." Meg shot him a look.

"Please thank Athena for me," Meg said.

Hermes looked farther down the river and whistled. "Will do. Looks like you'll need those gifts if you're headed that way."

"Why? What's up ahead?" Meg asked worriedly.

There was a chiming of bells again.

"I'm late!" Hermes cried and, poof, he was gone.

SIXTEEN: Leverage

Meg stared at the bow and arrow and clapper worriedly. If Athena was suddenly granting gifts for her journey, there had to be a reason. Meg looked ahead at the newly calm waters and endless miles of trees and wondered, *What out there would cause me to be reckless?*

"I've seen that thing before," Phil said as she placed the instrument carefully inside her satchel. "I think it has a name. Rota? Rata? No. That's not it. Tala?"

"It's called a clapper," Meg said.

Phil scratched his left ear. "No, it's got an official name, I tell ya. It's on the tip of my tongue. It's a krotala!"

"What's a krotala?"

Phil's smile faded. "I forget. It's important, though. I think."

"Well, it looks like you have time to remember." Meg stared at the waterway. "We're barely moving." The water was almost stagnant now, the breeze nonexistent. Up ahead, the river grew narrower and the waters became almost turquoise blue. It was so shallow that she could see white sands at the bottom. Rocks rose to greet them on one side while thick vegetation and trees were on the other. There was no sign of life on the riverbeds nor another boat to be found. Eerily, she didn't even hear wildlife. For such a serene spot, it was completely deserted. Meg looked at the mast and saw it was split in half. "So much for this sail."

"Wouldn't work if it was whole anyway," Phil said, putting his hand on the split mast. "No wind, no current. Even the water doesn't want to go where we're headed. But at least we are moving in the right direction. If your instincts were correct, we've finally made it to the river Acheron. When we cross with the Kokytos and the Pyriphlegethon rivers, we should find your entrance."

"And Charon will be waiting," Meg said almost to herself. She'd ridden with the ferryman to the Underworld numerous times; Hades always traveled to and from the Underworld with the chauffeur, but she'd never ridden with Charon by herself before. She shuddered at the thought.

Phil did the same, though his chill seemed to be from

sticking a hoof in the water. "You feel this river? It's dead already. As cold as ice."

Meg dipped her fingertips off the side of the boat, and they grew numb after a few seconds. No wonder she saw no wildlife or other people here. Acheron might have *looked* beautiful, but it truly was the gateway to hell. She stretched her legs out on a bench and leaned back, her face to the sun. "So now what do we do? I don't have time to just sit here and wait for a breeze."

"Relax, Red! I'm sure a breeze will pick up at some point. In the meantime, we row."

Phil picked up an oar and Meg did the same. For some reason, as clear and pristine as the water looked, moving the oar through the river felt like pushing through sludge.

"It's not working," Meg said in frustration and put down her oar. She pulled out her hourglass. It was almost halfway empty. "I've got less than six days and the Underworld is a labyrinth. How am I going to find Katerina and get her out of there before the sand runs out?"

"You've got to be smart!" Phil said as he continued to row. "We both know Hades ain't going to be happy to see you again, so avoid him as long as you can. You said the place is a labyrinth, but you should know your way around there more than the average soul, no?"

"Kind of," Meg admitted.

"Good! Stick to the shadows and avoid Hades's minions. You've got to find Katerina before he finds you. Did Aegeus give you any clues that will help you find her down there?"

"Aegeus made her sound like a saint, so she's certainly not in Tartarus, but Elysium sounds like a long shot, too. My guess is she's in Asphodel Meadows, like most."

Phil scratched his chin. "That's still a large place. How are you going to narrow things down?"

Meg thought for a moment. "Aegeus said she has a younger sister, Layla, who died when Katerina was young. I'm sure she's with her."

"Good!" Phil's face lit up. "I mean, not that the kid's dead, but it's a clue to finding Katerina. What else?"

"I know Layla loved poppy fields—so did Katerina—and telling tall tales." Meg yawned. Suddenly she was quite tired. Were the events of the last couple of days finally catching up to her? "That's about all I know. We had a lot of ground to cover in a short amount of time."

"Yeah, yeah. Tragic love affair. I know. Stay focused and find that kid," Phil said, his eyes looking as heavy as hers felt. "We may have a plan to get you *in* the joint, but how are you going to get out?"

"I'm not sure," Meg realized as she settled down on the bench again. The boat was barely moving. "But Hercules did give me this." She pulled the orchid out of her satchel. "It allows me to call for him three times. Well, two, since I already used it once." Her cheeks burned.

"Then that's your ticket out of hell! Literally!" Phil said. "Don't waste those petals. Use them to have Herc get you out of there once you find her."

"Maybe." Meg stared at the flower. She wasn't the rescuee type. Maybe she could get out on her own.

Phil shook his head. "You really are stubborn, Red. You know that?" He yawned again.

It made her yawn once more, too. She tucked the orchid back in her satchel and stretched. Would it be so wrong to take a nap? Meg started to lie down on the bench opposite Phil, who was already drifting off. She sat up with a start. "Phil, I think this river is putting us to sleep!"

"Sleep?" he murmured. "Why would a river do that?" He curled up in a ball and started to snore.

"Phil? Peg . . . ?" She looked around to see that the horse was curled up on the deck, already fast asleep.

Meg's heart quickened. *Stay awake!* she told herself, but her eyes were closing almost of their own volition. This river had somehow taken hold, as if it didn't want them to see exactly where they were going or how to ever get back there again. And no matter how hard she fought it, within minutes, she had drifted right with it.

When Meg awoke some time later, she noticed the sun straightaway. It had moved.

No longer was it high overhead. It was now halfway across the sky, and shadows were stretching from the trees. It had to be late afternoon already, and it looked like they had barely moved. She looked over at Phil and found him still snoring away, along with Pegasus. She hurried over to wake them.

"Phil! Pegasus!" she said, and the satyr stirred. "The river put us to sleep."

Pegasus flapped his wings and blinked rapidly as if rising from a long slumber.

Phil rubbed his eyes. "What? No. How?" He yawned, stretched his hooves, and looked around. "How long were we out?"

"A while," Meg said with a groan. "And we haven't moved at all."

"No!" Phil rushed to the side of the boat and looked around. "These trees definitely look different. I think." He stood on the boat bench. "And look, up ahead. There's a meadow. We haven't seen a meadow yet."

"A meadow?" Meg joined him at the front of the boat to look. Something gold glinted in the distance and made her blink. What was that? The boat drifted closer, and suddenly a clearing appeared. Phil was right. The boat had moved toward a meadow dotted with trees full of low-hanging fruit. Were those golden apples?

You haven't lived till you've had one of these, Nut-Meg, she heard a voice in her head say. *They're to die for! As a matter of fact, many a man has! Ha!*

Hades. She remembered seeing him eating one once or twice, savoring every last bite down to the core. It might have been one of the few occasions she'd seen the god happy. Usually the only thing that did that was talking about his Titan takeover, or a large group of souls showing up to his realm at once. Those golden apples were an elusive bright spot in his life. If she could get her hand on just one of those pieces of fruit, maybe she'd have some leverage with Hades if they crossed paths.

Her eyes moved to the shoreline, where a short gate was all that stood between the apples and the river. There was even a group of baskets sitting on the ground near the gate, just begging to be used to collect fruit.

"Phil," Meg said excitedly. "We've got to steer this boat over to the shore. Those apples are Hades's favorite. If I bring some with me, I might be able to barter with the hellion."

Phil moved to the right side of the ship and frowned. "Yeah, no can do. That orchard looks like it could be on the Hesperides' land."

"The Hesperides . . . *hmmm* . . ."

Her mother had told her legends about the Hesperides, who guarded fruit said to give people immortality. No wonder Hades enjoyed eating them—he was already immortal, so taking that gift away from a human would be something he would relish. But this couldn't be the nymphs' orchard. The legend said nothing about it being near the entrance to the Underworld, did it? Why did she think there was a piece of this story she was forgetting?

"I don't like this, Red," Phil said. "Those apples are not meant for human consumption."

"Good! I don't plan on eating one," said Meg, rowing closer to the side. "They're for Hades if I run into him."

"See that gate? It means stay out. We can't trespass."

"No one is even going to know we're there!" Meg argued. "The orchard is deserted."

"Unless there's some sleeping dragon around there somewhere just waiting to eat us. I wouldn't put it past those nymphs to have an extra layer of protection around apples so rare." Phil tried to rush in front of her. "Don't do anything rash. Let's call on Athena, or Hercules if you want. I'm sure they'd tell you this isn't a good idea."

Meg snorted. Phil was being ridiculous. She gently went around him. "I'm not wasting their time on something like this. We don't need their help. Phil, I'm telling you, dragons are massive. If one was there, we'd see it." She pulled her oar through the water, turning the boat toward shore. "I'll be quick. I promise you." Meg jumped out of the boat as soon as she was close enough. That way Phil couldn't stop her. "I'll be back quicker than your hooves can get you off this boat."

"Red!" Phil growled. "You're being reckless! Remember what Athena said? Don't be a fool!"

Meg ignored him, stepping onto land and walking swiftly to the gate. It was unlocked. *Ha!* she wanted to say. *This was meant to be!* She pushed the gate open and walked a few yards to the first tree she found, her eyes darting back and forth for any sign of movement. There was none. *Phil is such a worrier,* she thought.

The trees were so full, the golden apples were hanging as low as Meg's head. They were practically begging to be picked. She reached up for the first shiny gold apple she saw and gave it a quick twist from the branch, hearing the small snap as it broke free.

She turned to Phil and Peg triumphantly. "See? No problem."

She'd barely gotten the words out of her mouth when she heard an ear-piercing screech. Meg turned and saw countless birds swooping over the orchard, angrily heading straight toward her.

SEVENTEEN: Rash Doesn't Look Good on You

It took Meg a moment to comprehend what she was seeing. At first glance the birds looked like nothing more than tiny, tan specks on the horizon line, but as they flew closer, their size grew apparent. They were as large as humans, with sharp metallic feathers and bronze beaks, and there were hundreds of them all heading her way. She noticed something drop from the sky. Was that dung? The dark-colored substance hit the top of a tree and the branches surrounding it withered on contact, the whole tree starting to smoke. Poison!

Their ear-piercing squawking on approach made her instantly cover her ears, but the move did nothing. The sound was making her dizzy. She needed to get out of that orchard, but she was suddenly unsure of her surroundings. She turned toward the river and saw the boat.

"Red! Back to the boat! Red!" Phil called.

Meg dropped the precious apple and started to run, going no more than a few feet before she tripped over a root she'd failed to notice in the ground. She stumbled, but kept going, her eyes on the gate a few yards away. *Bang!* She was down again, her toes catching on a large root that seemed to appear out of nowhere, which was impossible, and yet . . . Meg sat up and spun around. Roots were growing up out of the ground all around her. She scrambled to get up again and felt a sharp root pierce her right sandal.

"Ouch!" she cried, dragging her right foot behind her as she kept moving toward that gate. Suddenly a root broke out of the ground right in front of her, rising like a tree. Meg stopped short, trying to change direction, but the vines whipped around her ankles, tightening and holding her firm. "Phil! I'm stuck!"

"Bat them away with anything you can find!" Phil shouted.

Meg spotted a large rock. She reached down and began bashing the roots with it. They recoiled, loosening their grip, and Meg burst forward, throwing herself at the fence.

"It's locked!" Meg cried.

"Pegasus, go get her!" Phil yelled.

Why didn't she think these things through first? Now she'd put the three of them in danger.

The horse took off from the boat, flying straight toward the gate, and Meg held her arms up, ready to grab whatever part of him that she could. Pegasus reached the fence and—*BOOM!* He bounced back as if he'd been struck.

"Peg!" Meg screamed in horror as the stunned horse flew through the air.

Phil saw what was happening and used an oar to turn the boat around just in time. Pegasus landed with a thud, half in, half out of the back of the boat, sending wood flying and breaking the sail completely off. Phil struggled to pull him back in.

WHIZ! BAM! The birds' feathers were launching off their wings into the air and hitting targets. Several feathers pelted the tree closest to her, slicing it in half. The tree fell to the ground, apples rolling toward the gate.

"Phil! Their feathers kill!"

"I know that!" Phil shouted. "Those are Stymphalian birds, Red! They aren't here for a picnic!"

"What do I do?" Meg cried as she pulled harder on the gate. She tried to get a foothold in the bottom and pull herself up and over it, but her sandals kept sliding. The fence was as slick as ice.

"Oh, now you want to listen—RED! Behind you!"

Meg dove to the ground as one of the birds attempted to hook its talons in her shoulders. It kept coming, Meg rolling out of the way before it could land. The bird hit the gate, denting it and stunning itself in the process. It shook its beak, trying to get its bearings, and Meg jumped up and ran farther down the fence line looking for an opening she could squeeze through. Feathers pelted the ground around her. A huge dung ball splattered the nearest tree and poisoned it on contact. The tree slammed to the ground, narrowly missing her.

Meg dove for cover, hiding herself in its branches. She gathered as many apples as she could around her to shade her from sight.

Phil saw what was happening and rowed in her direction. "I'm coming toward you!" he called from the boat, swatting at incoming birds with his oar. He batted one away and it landed in the river. "You need a weapon! Those birds can't pierce cork. If you can find some, it would protect you."

Meg could hear feathers slicing the ground around her as the birds squawked angrily. They were looking for her. She pulled herself in tighter, trying not to be seen, but the birds spotted her anyway, landing on the downed tree, pecking away. One pierced the fabric of her dress and slid right through. Meg screamed. She was a goner if she didn't find a weapon soon.

Weapons. Athena's gifts in case she was *reckless*. How did that god know her so well? If only she hadn't left the bow and arrow on the boat.

"Red, use the krotala!" Phil cried.

"What?" Meg pulled her legs tighter to her chest.

"The clapper! Use the instrument!"

The clapper? she wondered as a bird grabbed hold of her dress hem and started to pull. *What is that thing going to do? Do I throw it at them?* Meg pulled the instrument out of her sack and looked at it skeptically, ready to question Phil, but then she thought better of it. She had to have faith he knew what he was talking about. She clapped both pieces together, hearing the sharp sound it made. Several birds shrieked in agony and flew off. *I can't believe it!* she thought with glee and struck it again. The birds on the tree disappeared and Meg crawled out. "Phil, it works."

"Good job, Red! Take that, you bronze metalheads!" Phil reached the shore and was holding her bow and arrow.

"Phil, watch out!" she screamed.

A bird swooped in low on the boat from out of nowhere, lifting Phil and the bow and arrow into the air. Meg ran out into the open and threw a golden apple, trying to strike the bird down, but missed.

"Aaah! Red!" Phil cried, trying to kick out from the bird's grasp as he was pulled higher and higher.

You are not taking my satyr. She picked up another apple and threw it as hard as she could. She hit the bow and arrow, which dropped from Phil's hands. Meg bolted out into the opening, placed the krotala in her satchel again, and grabbed the weapon, quickly placing the arrow in the bow and aiming at the bird's wing as it climbed higher. She had only seconds before Phil's height would be too great to let him fall. She squinted into the sunlight and aimed, then let the arrow go. It pierced the bird's wing and Phil fell, screaming, into the top of a tree.

"Phil, stay hidden in that tree or the birds will—aaaah!" Meg felt the back of her dress lift as she was hoisted in the air by one of the birds. She could see other birds headed her way to get their piece. With no arrows left to nock, she used the bow the only way she could—to whack the bird holding her. The bird instantly let go, and Meg went tumbling several feet to the ground. Vines instantly wrapped around her legs and arms and slammed her face into the dirt. She tried to kick herself free and felt something grab her by the shoulders again. That gods-forsaken bird was back and tugging on her upper body while the vines tried to claim her lower half. She felt like she was being split in two.

She punched the bird's talon with her right fist and its grip loosened just enough for her to reach in her satchel for the krotala again. She clapped it fiercely and the bird immediately let go of her. Then Meg used the krotala to bash the vines till they receded. She kicked out of the vines and threw herself forward, the krotala slipping from her fingers in the process. Her reaching hand had just grazed the instrument when she felt herself being lifted in the air again.

"Nooo!" Meg cried and turned and punched the bird again. It dropped her and she started running.

"Red, it has Pegasus!" Phil cried as he started climbing down from the tree.

"Phil, stay there!" she shouted. "I'll—aaah!" Two new vines tightened around her legs, winding higher and higher around her body till they squeezed her chest so tight she was afraid she'd pass out. She felt her eyes start to close. She had lost the bow and arrow. She'd misplaced the krotala. Pegasus was just a dot in the sky. She didn't have much time to save him or herself. And what about Phil? *Stay awake!* she told herself. *Fight!*

Phil appeared out of nowhere, running as fast as his hooves would take him as he hurled apple after apple at the vines. He didn't see the bird come up behind him till he was hoisted in the air again.

No! She tried to cry out, but her voice was gone. She was being squeezed tighter and tighter. With the only thing free being her hands, she dug her nails into one of the vines and it recoiled. Meg did it again and again till they retreated enough for her to get her arms free. She reached out to grab the leather straps of the krotala and felt a bird yank her back, lifting her body off the ground again.

Concentrate, Meg, she told herself. *You're a big, tough girl. . . .* Meg kicked out hard and felt a vine holding her leg tear away. Arms flailing, she wound back with her free hand and socked the bird in its chest. *You . . . can . . . do . . . this.* The bird shrieked and instantly let go.

It would be back in moments, but a moment was all she needed to kick-start her plan. Meg launched herself forward again, trying to reach the krotala. If she could just reach it, she could scare the birds, then run for the bow, find the fallen arrow and aim it in the sky to make the birds drop Peg and Phil, and then . . . and then . . . okay, she'd have to figure out how to catch them, but she had the start of a plan. Plans were good. She needed to remember to make more of those before she sprang into action. But the point was, she was fixing things on her own.

Meg reached for the clapper again and her fingers closed around it just as the bird landed on her back and two more vines latched onto her arms. There was a loud snap and Meg was able to see a cluster of the birds breaking the bow with their razor-sharp beaks before the vines wove around her chest and squeezed. Meg felt herself start to lose consciousness. *You can do this, Meg! Fight!* she told herself. She had started to tap the clapper ever so slightly when there was a sound like thunder, followed by a crackle of lightning. Hercules burst from the sky dressed in what looked like a suit of armor made of cork.

It all happened so fast. Hercules landed two punches on the birds holding Pegasus and held on to another for dear life so that he didn't plummet to the ground. The bird released Pegasus and the horse began to fall, waking just before he hit the ground. With a giant flap, he tore up to the heavens and Hercules leaped for him, climbing onto his back and racing toward the bird carrying Phil. Pulling up alongside him, he punched the bird in the chest and it let go of Phil, who fell onto Pegasus's back. The three quickly descended, heading straight toward her. Meg barely had time to inhale before Hercules had jumped from Pegasus's back and landed on the bird holding Meg. He picked it up and launched it into the river with a flick of his wrist, then picked up the krotala and clapped it together so hard, every bird around took flight, flying away till they were nothing more than specks on the horizon.

EIGHTEEN: Control

"Meg!" Hercules ran toward her, ripping off the vines still wrapped around her with his bare hands. "Are you okay?"

Meg rubbed her arms, staring at the rope burns from the vines that had replaced the burns lingering from the Empusa. Her ears were still ringing from the sound of the krotala, so his voice sounded muffled, and her legs were weak from being stretched and pulled, but the birds were gone. She tried to stand and Hercules offered her his arm. She didn't take it.

"How did you know I was here?" she said, her voice hoarse from all the yelling.

Phil and Peg were racing toward her.

"I heard you were in trouble." Hercules fixed his headband, which was askew and covering his right eye.

She bristled. "And you thought I needed rescuing?" Meg leaned against a tree to catch her breath. She was covered in grass stains, had cuts from the branches and vines and possibly a gash in her back from all that pecking, but she was still in one piece. "You didn't think I could take care of myself?"

Phil interrupted them, practically jumping on Hercules in his attempt to reach up and rub his golden hair. Pegasus hopped along excitedly beside them. "Am I glad you showed up, kid! I thought we were goners!" He hung onto Hercules's massive biceps, sitting on it like a chair.

"I saw my mother and Athena looking toward Earth from their cloud, and when I heard them mention Meg's name, I rushed over to see what was going on." He looked at her sheepishly. "As soon as I saw you were in trouble, I came running."

"Good thing you did," Phil agreed.

Meg's cheeks warmed with embarrassment at the thought of Athena and Hera watching her mess up. "This is just swell. Athena is probably furious with me."

"Actually, I think she's mad at *me*," Hercules admitted with wide eyes. "She said to let you handle things on your own, but I couldn't just stand there when those birds were trying to tear you apart."

His confession made her bristle once more. "I had it

under control," Meg said, hearing the edge in her voice. The men looked at her skeptically. "I did!"

Phil turned to Pegasus, who snorted, then back to Meg. "You're delusional. The birds had us, vines were pinning you to the ground, and there was a bird on your back. If Hercules hadn't been here to save our butts, your quest would be over! All because you wanted to bring Hades an apple."

Hercules did a double take. "You wanted to bring Hades an apple?"

"No! I mean, yes. I mean, it's hard to explain," Meg said, getting frustrated. "It doesn't matter now!"

"Wait, Meg, are you angry with me?" Hercules looked confused.

Meg tried to bite her tongue, but she couldn't hold back. "Yes! I was this close to using the krotala and finishing off the birds myself when you swooped in to do the whole hero thing. Athena gave *me* these gifts to use, not you."

"You wouldn't even have needed that krotala if you had just stayed on the boat and listened to reason in the first place!" Phil chimed in. "Now you've cost yourself even more time!" Phil bleated, and it set her off.

"This is my quest, remember? Not his." She pointed to Hercules. "And not yours. It's mine to do what I want with or screw up. I didn't ask anyone to butt in."

"I wanted to lend a hand," Hercules said. "I thought you needed me."

"I can take care of myself! Why can't any of you see that?" Meg stormed off toward the fence.

"Meg." Hercules ran after her. "I really didn't mean to step on your toes. I was just trying to help you."

The whole innocent farm boy routine was too much for her to handle at the moment. "I don't need your help. I do things on my own. Always have, always will," she said, thinking of her mother. "This is my quest, and it will only work if I rely on myself."

He looked unsure. "But why? You can count on me. I thought you knew that. When you called for me last time, you wanted my help figuring things out. Didn't you?"

"Yes! I mean, no. I just wanted to hear myself think!" she cried, starting to get confused herself. "I wanted you to be there for me. Not take over. There's a difference." Thea had taught her never to be indebted to anyone, and she'd already screwed up once when she went to Hades for help. She wasn't about to do it again.

"I thought we were a team," he said.

"Team?" She didn't like feeling helpless, and for some reason, that's how he was making her feel. "We're not a team! You're a god and I'm a mortal. How can we be a team if I only earn my own spot on Mount Olympus if I complete this quest? Your life isn't on the line here."

"Meg." He tried reaching for her and she stepped back.

Angry tears sprang to her eyes. She didn't want to hear what he had to say. "No. When this boat finally reaches the entrance to the Underworld, it won't be you or Phil or Pegasus who has to keep going. It will be me. I'm the one that has to convince Hades to let me take Katerina back to the land of the living. I'm the one who has to survive another brush with death." She was shaking. "How am I supposed to face Hades and whatever beasts await me down there if every time I'm in trouble, the mighty Hercules swoops in to save me?" For the first time, he didn't contradict her, and for some reason, that made her realize something. "You don't think I can do this, do you?"

"Meg, no . . . that's not true!" Hercules said, but she could see the fear written all over his face. "I just want you to know I'm here when you need me."

"Well, I don't." She just wanted to put an end to this ridiculous argument. "I can do this on my own, and I'll prove it." She pulled the orchid out of her satchel.

"Meg, what are you doing?" Hercules looked panicked.

"Red!" Phil's voice sounded like a warning. "Think about this! Red!"

But she didn't want to think. She hurled the orchid into the water. It floated for a few moments before sinking in front of their eyes.

"Meg . . ." Hercules looked forlorn. "I can't get another one of those. I . . ."

Bells chimed, and Hermes appeared. "Hercules, your mother wants to see you."

Of course, Meg thought.

"Can you tell her I just need a moment?" Hercules started to say.

"Nope! You're needed now. Something about a bird? Let's go, lover boy!" He grabbed Hercules's right biceps.

"Meg, I . . ." Hercules's face was pained.

She turned away. This part she was familiar with—he was going to leave her like everyone else did. "Just go."

Hercules stared sadly at her as he started to glow brighter.

"Goodbye, Wonder Boy," Meg whispered as he disappeared from sight.

NINETEEN: Second Thoughts

"Are you nuts?" Phil cried, rushing to the edge of the boat to look for the orchid, which had disappeared below the surface. "You needed that flower!"

"I don't need anything," Meg said defiantly, but inside she was already regretting her impulsiveness. *What did I just do?*

"Not to mention letting him leave without having him get us down the river," Phil continued to rant. "We've got no sail at all, if you haven't noticed, and there is still no wind! We're basically stuck here!"

Meg hadn't thought about that. She stared at where the mast used to be and then looked around for the paddles. In the chaos, they, too, had been lost. The air was sickeningly hot and sticky and completely stagnant. Meg looked up, hopeful for signs of an impending late afternoon storm, but there wasn't a cloud in the sky. She sat down on the cracked bench and stared miserably at the spot in the water where she had hurled the flower. That was not smart. She'd really laid into Hercules, too. Also not smart. This wasn't really his fault. She'd just gotten so mad. She placed her head in her hands. "This is a mess."

"Yep," said Phil, sitting down next to her. Pegasus looked at them, forlorn.

"I'm sorry, Phil," Meg said, patting his hand. "I've doomed us, haven't I?"

"Pretty much. The day is almost done and you'll have one less day in the Underworld, *if* we can even get you there at this point." He gave her a look. "What were you thinking?"

"I don't know!" Meg groaned. "I started thinking about Hera and Athena watching me screw things up and laughing about it, and I got *so* angry. I hate the idea of them thinking I can't do this quest without Hercules's help. What god can't get things done on their own?"

"A lot, actually," Phil admitted. "Why do you think they're always teaming up on things or looking to mortals for help?" Meg paled. "It's okay to not always have all the answers on your own, you know."

The oars. Teamwork. *Right.* "Oh, Phil," Meg groaned. "I just imploded the best relationship I ever had."

He patted her back. "Chin up. You can't scare that kid away. He loves you."

"Sounds like a bad decision on his part."

"Is it?" said a voice.

Meg and Phil turned around. Pegasus jumped.

A god was standing on the ship, aglow in magenta, with rosy pink lips, long lashes, and the bluest of eyes. She wore a single-shouldered gown held together by a heart-shaped pin. Meg instantly remembered where she'd seen her before—on Mount Olympus talking to Demeter.

"Aphrodite," Meg said in surprise. "What are you doing here?"

Aphrodite smiled from ear to ear. "Athena sent me, of course, and it looks like I'm just in time if you were about to give up on love after one argument." She looked at Meg pointedly. "I didn't think a girl as tough as you would be willing to throw it all away so easily."

Meg stared at the god, flabbergasted. How did she know that? "Are *all* of you on Mount Olympus watching me screw things up down here?"

"No," Aphrodite said with a laugh, but the glint in her eyes said otherwise. "Let's just say many of us are invested in you, Megara, and we want to see you succeed, which is why aid is given when needed. Athena has declared herself your guide and as such, she's sent me to help you get past this unfortunate bump in the river, so to speak." Aphrodite looked out over the bow of the boat. "Such a beautiful river to lead to such a sad place. What a shame." She turned around. "And it's unfortunate that your mast is broken and there is no wind to move you along. How are we going to fix that?"

"We?" Meg repeated and looked sideways at Phil. "I guess we could start by patching the sail, but I can't do anything about the lack of wind. That's Notus's territory." Her mother always prayed to Notus in the hot summer months, hoping the god of the south wind would bring along a thunderstorm to cool things down. Hades had always commended the god's penchant for hurricanes.

Aphrodite's sparkling eyes seemed to cut right through her. "Oh, dear. Athena was right to send me. Of course we can do something about this wind—by working *together*, as this satyr was so right to point out." Phil puffed up his chest. "Gods and mortals do so all the time. There is nothing weak about that."

Meg felt her cheeks flush. "It's just not the way I was taught to do things."

Aphrodite sat down on the boat bench. "I know. Your mother did the best she could, but her life was hard. Thea taught you to use your instincts and rely on yourself to get by, and there isn't anything wrong with that. But don't you see? When you find someone worthy of your love, letting them help you is also powerful. Just as you, in turn, have helped him. It doesn't have to be all or nothing. You have found a true partner in Hercules. Love means it's okay to lean on one another."

Meg recalled something Athena had said. *Sometimes your head will lead, and other times it will be your heart.* "I just don't want him to think I can't handle this quest on my own."

"He doesn't think that!" Aphrodite sounded surprised. "Hercules knows you are a strong, confident woman. It's one of the things he loves about you, just like you relish his big heart and ability to see the world in a bright way. You've opened yourselves up to each other, which is a beautiful thing! But it's important to remember that when you let someone into your heart, you allow them to see all sides of you—even the vulnerable side. Loving someone does not make you any less strong. It means you trust in another and they trust in you—that you can give and you can take. No one is keeping count," she said softly. "When you love someone, you want to give them the world."

Meg placed a hand over her eyes. How could she have been so narrow-minded? Aphrodite was right. Wonder

Boy wasn't trying to take away her power; he was just trying to be there when she clearly could have used a hand. "Great. Now what? I tossed the orchid in the river, and I can't even call on him to say I'm sorry." He had given her a one-of-a-kind gift and she'd thrown it away so cavalierly.

Aphrodite smiled. "I have a feeling you two will be just fine—*if* you complete your quest on time. So why don't we focus on that? Put your faith in the journey and the rest will follow."

"Trust in the journey. I can do that." Meg rubbed her hands together, happy to move forward. Maybe she could fix things, one step at a time, starting with the boat. "First, we need to fix this mast." Using every bit of strength she possessed, Meg pulled it out of the water and drenched Pegasus in the process. "Maybe if we anchor some more wood to it, we can hold it together to get down the river." She grabbed some of the debris from the boat. "Phil, do you know if Aegeus left any supplies on the boat?"

Phil reached below a floorboard and pulled out a small box. "He left some fishing things."

Meg opened the box and pulled out the fishing wire. "This should work."

Within a half hour, they had fixed the mast, anchoring it with an assortment of fishing wire and fabric that had been ripped off the sail. They'd fashioned new oars out of driftwood, and Meg had used the wood carving skills she'd once seen Aegeus use on their instruments to smooth the edges of the wood that would pull them through the water. There were still holes in the sail of the ship, but enough was intact that the sail could still catch wind, if there was any.

"Ship is ready again. Now what?"

Aphrodite handed Meg a daisy that appeared in a trail behind her. "We trust Notus will answer our prayers."

Meg's stomach gave a lurch. Trust in prayers? They hadn't worked when she'd tried to save Aegeus. That's why she had called on Hades.

"Sometimes we must take a leap of faith," Aphrodite said kindly.

She'd never get used to the gods reading her thoughts. *A leap of faith.* Just like the one she'd taken when Wonder Boy wanted to slip away with her to row on that lake, or when Phil wanted to go over the falls. She had to open up and learn to just jump. "Okay. Let's call on Notus."

Phil grabbed a giant palm leaf and placed it over his head. "That god is brutal. How do we know he won't send a storm that will blow us all away? Notus destroys crops all the time."

"Yes, but this time, Meg is asking to return somewhere

Notus finds favorable—to the Underworld." Aphrodite looked deep into Meg's eyes. "Concentrate and believe he'll hear you, and I know he will."

Maybe Aphrodite was right. In addition to hurricanes, Hades was always singing Notus's praises for causing famines in the heat of the summer or wiping out an entire field of grain. If anyone would help a boat reach the Underworld, it would be him. "Let's think positive, Phil. At least the rain will cool us off." Meg closed her eyes and channeled all her energy into connecting with Notus.

If you can hear me, God of Wind, the Great Notus, send your rain and wind down on the river Acheron so that this boat can move swiftly to the entrance of the Underworld. She opened her eyes.

Phil frowned. "Still sunny."

"Keep going," Aphrodite encouraged.

Meg thought for a moment. What would Notus respond to? What would he want that she could offer him?

Notus, I promise you, the passenger on this boat is one that will win you favor with Hades. Send your rain down on us and you will be rewarded.

She paused. The gods seemed to like being in favor with one another, especially the powerful ones. Maybe Notus would appreciate the chance to show off for Hades.

Bring all you have! Wind! Rain! Thunder! Shake the

heavens with your storm! We can take it! We need it and want it now! I beg you, Notus!

She wrung her hands, trying to channel all the blind faith she could that this would work. And that's when she heard it—a low rumble of thunder.

"Red, I see clouds ahead! *Big* clouds! Look!" Phil jumped up and down and pointed to the dark clouds moving in fast, much as they had that day on Mount Olympus when she had incited the wrath of Zeus. Within seconds, she felt drops of rain, and there was a rustle through the trees as the wind picked up. The boat started to rock. Pegasus neighed with excitement.

"How can I ever repay you?" Meg asked Aphrodite.

"I knew you could do it." The god smiled. "Continue to open your heart to help and to new possibilities, Megara. It won't lead you astray." Her body started to glow brighter. "We are watching over you from above, praying for your safety, and guiding you on this next chapter."

There was a huge clap of thunder and then gigantic drops of rain began to fall. The boat took a fast dip and lurched forward.

"I should go," Aphrodite said and started to evaporate. "Be well, Megara."

Meg reached for her suddenly. "Please, tell Hercules I'm sorry."

"Tell him yourself when you see him," Aphrodite said, and she reached into the water and swirled her fingers around. "Oh, and watch the waves," she said as the water grew choppier and lightning flashed. "You never know what the water will dredge up."

As if in answer, the newly churning river splashed over the side of the boat, and Megara saw a flash of something bright white—the orchid! She reached out and snatched it before it drifted away again.

"Holy Hera," Phil whispered.

"Look at that," Aphrodite said as she started to fade away once more. "A flower as rare as this deserves to be cherished, don't you think?"

"Thank you," Meg said, trying not to get emotional. The rain was coming down in sheets as she quickly placed the flower in her satchel.

There was a huge clap of thunder that seemed to shake the boat loose. The rain was coming down so hard Meg and Phil had to squint to see as they both grabbed paddles and took their positions. Then the boat began to move at top speed.

We're on our own again, Meg thought. *But not really.* Then she stuck her oar in the water and plowed onward.

TWENTY: The Unknown

The storm raged for what felt like hours, lightning crackling across the sky and wind rampaging. The thunder was so loud, the trio didn't speak. They just rowed and continued looking at that mended sail, wondering if or when it would crack under the strain of the wind.

It will hold, Meg told herself, trying her best to believe. *This boat will get us where we need to go.*

When their arms had begun to ache terribly from continuous rowing and their bodies started to shiver from being so wet, the storm stopped and the boat began to slow down. The sky was still dark and gray and thunder rumbled in the distance, but the storm was pulling away. In its place, a low-lying fog began to roll in, blanketing much of the landscape. Phil and Meg wiped the water from their eyes and looked at one another.

"We're alive!" Phil said as he wrung water out of his fur. "I'm not sure if we'll ever dry out after that storm, but look!" He pointed off the bow of the ship. "The river seems to be widening again. That must mean we're close to the crossing of the three rivers and the entrance to the Underworld." He looked at Meg in awe. "You did it, Red. You got Notus to bring a storm, and it carried us the rest of the way here!"

"I did, didn't I?" Meg said, feeling pleased with herself as she squeezed the water from her ponytail. The river definitely looked like it widened up ahead, but it was hard to see much of anything in this thickening fog. *Notus,* she thought. His sometimes-wicked storms seemed to also bring in a lot of fog, shrouding the river completely in mystery.

Meg pulled the hourglass out of the satchel and Phil peered over her shoulder. The glowing pink sands in the lower chamber had climbed higher since she'd last checked.

"Halfway full," Phil said somewhat glumly. "Looks like we lost about half a day between the birds and the lack of wind pushing our sails."

Meg tucked the hourglass away again and tried to think

positively. "Five days is still a lot of time to find Katerina . . . right?" She looked at him.

"Oh, yeah," Phil agreed quickly. "Think of all you've done in five days already!"

It was true. How had it only been five days since this journey started? In that time she'd been to hell and back, left Wonder Boy on Mount Olympus, fought an Empusa for Athena's flute, gained the god of war and wisdom's trust, made peace with Aegeus, almost killed them all with her jaunt to get a golden apple, and gotten a pep talk from Aphrodite. *And* she'd fought with Hercules. Meg closed her eyes, wishing to block that last bit out. What she wouldn't give to tell him how sorry she was for the way she treated him.

She had to believe she would see him again. But for now, she had to concentrate on the journey ahead. This next part was going to be the hardest of all.

"We should see Charon any second now," Phil said, sounding anxious. "Sorry. Just the thought of that guy gives me the creeps. But it's going to be fine," he added quickly. "Are you ready?"

Meg patted her satchel and motioned to Athena's flute, which was hanging from her waist. "As ready as I'll ever be, I guess. I know what I have to do. First step is getting past that three-headed mutt."

Phil nodded. "Steer clear of Hades as long as you can and get to Asphodel Meadows."

"Got it!" Meg repeated, taking deep breaths.

The current beneath them was starting to pick up, bringing her closer and closer to the river Styx. The end of their time together was fast approaching, which meant that soon she'd be alone. Meg's heart started to beat more quickly. The only time she'd traveled the river Styx before was with Hades. She'd never been in Charon's boat by herself. She and Phil looked at one another. She had a feeling they were thinking the same thing.

"Phil, I don't know how to thank you for getting me this far." There was so much she wanted to say, and not much time to do it. "I know I'm not your favorite person . . ."

"You weren't," Phil admitted, "but you are now. What you did back there with the birds to save me—that took guts." He swallowed hard. "You're going to do this thing, Red. I can feel it."

"Thanks, Phil," Meg said, feeling her throat tighten.

They looked at one another as the fog overtook them. Meg could hardly see the hand in front of her face. The air grew cold; the sound of the birds on the river disappeared. The boat seemed to stop moving, and then it started to spin.

"Hang on!" Meg said as the boat moved faster and

faster, twirling round and round till she couldn't tell which way was north and which was south.

Finally, the boat shot forward, gliding through the mist and coming to another halt in the middle of a lake where the fog began to fade. A charred wall of rock began to appear in front of her. The mountainside was dotted with dead trees that looked like they had been destroyed by fire. Near the base of the mountain was a cave with a river running through it. The entrance to the Underworld.

A small boat emerged and moved slowly toward them. It was ferried by a skeleton-like creature. Hades's minion who ferried the dead to the Underworld made her anxious. Meg placed one hand on Athena's flute to steady herself. *You can do this,* she told herself, standing quietly as the boat approached. *Trust yourself.*

Charon paused and sniffed the air as he approached. "Mortals, you may not enter here."

"We can pay, Charon," Meg said quickly, and he glanced at her curiously.

"We can?" Phil repeated.

"Yes, give him a drachma," Meg instructed.

He looked at her blankly. "I don't have any drachmas."

"What do you mean you have no drachmas?" she hissed. "You knew you were getting me to the entrance to the Underworld. Everyone needs a drachma to get there!"

"Right." Phil scratched one of his horns. "I forgot about that part."

"How could you forget?"

"Hey, Red, we had some other pressing things to worry about, like getting you here in the first place, and in one piece."

Meg groaned, unable to believe they hadn't discussed this before. "Well, what do we do now?" she asked.

"I don't know!" Phil started to pace. "If you don't have one, they say Charon makes you wait, and we don't have a day to spare! Where am I going to find a coin?" Phil started overturning everything on the boat in his search, but Meg knew he wouldn't find one. Aegeus would never be as careless as to leave a coin behind.

Where could she get a drachma fast? *Think, Meg.* She didn't feel right calling on Hercules for this. But she could call on her guide, couldn't she?

Meg looked up. "Athena, god of war and wisdom, guide to heroes and caretaker of those on journeys, if you can see us or hear me now, we could really use your help here," she whispered. "I need a drachma." Nothing happened.

A low growl emerged from Charon's mouth. "Do

you have payment or not? I have many souls to transport today."

"Please, Athena." Meg tried again. "I will take your knowledge and your gifts with me to the other side, but this I can't do without help." Meg thought for a moment about what might sway her. "Someday I will thank you in person and play your flute, and when I do, you'll feel my music with your heart. I promise."

Meg and Phil looked to the sky, both imagining a coin falling from the clouds. Nothing happened. Meg was starting to join Phil in his panic when she felt something cool appear in her right hand. She opened her palm. It was a silver drachma.

"Smart move, kid!" Phil cried. "We have a drachma!"

"Yesssss?" Charon hissed, reaching a skeletal hand out for payment.

"Thank you, Athena," Meg said solemnly to the sky. "I guess it's time for me to go."

"Wait," Phil said quickly. "What if you asked Athena for two more coins?" He eyed the cave ahead of them. "We could go with you, you know. Maybe we could be of some help down there."

Meg smiled wanly. She couldn't believe what Phil was offering. Even though they both knew that he couldn't follow, it was a touching offer nonetheless. The fact that she was heading back into the Underworld, a place mortals did not leave, let alone escape twice, was starting to feel ever more real. "You're going to miss me that much, huh?"

He rolled his eyes. "No. I just don't want you getting yourself in trouble without me."

They looked at one another, and Meg hesitated. "Phil, if I don't make it back . . . tell Hercules—"

"No," Phil cut her off. "I'm not giving any messages. Tell him yourself when you get back."

"But if I don't," Meg insisted, "promise me you'll tell Hercules that I . . ." She swallowed, still unsure of the right words. "Let him know that I . . . Just tell him I'm sorry."

Phil met her gaze, his face as serious as she'd ever seen it. "Okay."

Meg moved toward the edge of the boat. She felt her satchel for the krotala, and her waist to make sure the flute was still attached. She rubbed Pegasus's nose and he neighed sadly. Meg felt a tug on her heart. "And Phil, one more thing?"

"Anything," he said.

"If I don't return, make sure Hercules moves on from all of this," Meg said.

"Meg . . ." Phil swallowed hard.

It was the first time he'd called her by her actual name.

She tried to put her spinning thoughts into words. "I don't want him wasting his immortality on me. He's a good guy who gives so much of himself. He deserves to have someone do that for him in return. Got it?"

Phil looked at her. "Wow, you really do love the guy, don't you?"

Meg didn't answer. She handed the coin to Charon, and he motioned for her to step onto his boat. Then she turned around and looked at Phil and Peg again one more time. "See you on the other side," she said, hoping she sounded surer than she felt.

"You will!" Phil said, but tears were streaming down his face. Even Peg looked upset. "I know it. I'll see you in a few days. Hey . . . you know what? I'll wait for you at Aegeus's. Gods know he could use some help. I'll meet you there."

"Deal," Meg said. Charon immediately started to row away. She held up her hand in a wave.

Phil did the same, and they silently watched one another for as long as they could. Then a shadow crossed Meg's face. They had entered the cave.

A low moan came from somewhere in the darkness, and then another. Meg felt a bump underneath the boat and a tug on her dress. She jumped back. Something had just reached up and grabbed her. No matter how many times she rode in this boat, it was a feeling she couldn't get used to.

"Keep your limbs inside the boat, mortal, or they'll pull you down with them," Charon said in a gravelly voice.

Meg swallowed hard and tried not to imagine the river beneath them filled with thousands of lost souls who would do anything to get out. She pulled her arms and legs in and sat down on the narrow bench, peering into the darkness surrounding her. The moaning continued, as did the boat's swaying while the dead tried to climb aboard. "How long is this going to take?" Hades had always been too busy talking her ear off for her to pay attention to how much time passed, but she didn't remember the ride being this long.

Charon slowly but surely steered them forward. "The land of the dead is a large place and not a quick journey. It's meant to give you time to process all you've lost."

Meg closed her eyes, trying to block out the cries, but it was near impossible. *Don't look at the water. Don't look at the water!* She thought about how she had lost track of time in the Underworld before, about Phil's warning not to lose her bearings. It would be so easy to get pulled into the darkness, to give up hope as those shrieking beneath her were demanding she do. *Think of something happy,* Meg told herself. *Think of something good so you aren't pulled under.*

Wonder Boy. Meg smiled to herself as she recalled the one and only chance she'd had to cook for him.

"You did all this?" he'd asked when she'd convinced him to meet her one afternoon at the lake where they'd gone rowing. She was supposed to be scouting a Minotaur to add to Hades's cause, while Hercules was supposed to be throwing discuses to keep his hero skills sharp. But she figured they needed to eat anyway; no one would miss them for one measly hour.

"What do you think?" she'd asked, motioning to the blanket on the grass and the assortment of foods. There were nuts and dates, warm bread and cheese that she'd gotten at the market, and center stage was a fish roasting over a small fire.

"No one's ever cooked for me before," Hercules said, heading over to admire the blackening trout. He looked at her sheepishly. "Except my mother. And actually, Phil, but he's terrible. Don't tell him I said that," he added quickly and she laughed.

"Your secret's safe with me, Wonder Boy." She motioned to the blanket. "Sit down. Eat something. We'll have to get back before long."

Hercules seemed like a kid with a new toy as he ripped off a piece of bread, pairing it with a hunk of cheese and some dates. "The fish smells delicious. I didn't know you could cook."

"There's a lot you don't know about me," she'd said lightly. "I taught myself, actually. My mother was always working and exhausted when she came home at night, so I helped by making our meals. I'd spend hours in the market talking to the different vendors and pestering them with questions about cooking fish and what cheeses to pair with what meats and how to roll grape leaves and . . . by the time my mother got home she had a full spread waiting." She checked the fish again. "It was the one time of day she didn't look tired." She stopped herself when she heard her admission and glanced over at Hercules. He was listening with rapt attention. "I'm boring you, aren't I? I don't usually tell anyone my life's story." She'd never told anyone that particular anecdote, actually. Not even Aegeus.

What was she doing? Cooking for the man that Hades wanted to take down?

She felt Wonder Boy's hand on her shoulder. "You can tell me anything, Meg. I want to hear it all. I want to know everything about you."

"Are you sure about that?" she couldn't help saying.

"I'm sure," he'd said, and then he'd leaned down and kissed her. His lips tasted sweet like the dates he'd just eaten. She'd kissed him right back.

———

Meg saw a flash and looked up. Torches were coming alive along the cave's path, and she suddenly remembered where she was again.

"Get ready, mortal," Charon said. "You may have gotten by me, but Cerberus won't be so forgiving."

TWENTY-ONE: Cerberus's Lullaby

The end of the cave suddenly opened, pulling apart like someone was parting overgrown vines. Quickly Meg saw what was on the other side: Cerberus.

The massive three-headed creature was as black as coal, and as large as the first monster she had lured Hercules to fight when she was still working for Hades. She watched as one of the heads snored, its mouth opening and closing, revealing teeth as large as the columns on a building. Drool puddled around its massive mouth and oozed into the river. The creature was collared and tethered to something on the ground, but it could certainly move its heads. There was no sailing past the thing without being swallowed whole. To make matters worse, the area around the animal was littered with hundreds of bones and skulls that she could only assume were the remains of other foolish mortals who had tried to enter the Underworld with their lives intact.

She needed to get ready to face it. She quickly began unhooking Athena's flute.

"Could you slow this boat down?" Meg said, but Charon kept his steady rowing pace. She cursed herself for not using her time on the boat more wisely. She had mere seconds to prepare, and she wasn't even sure what tune she was going to attempt with Athena's flute, let alone if she could remember how to play it. Athena had sensed her heart was not in it. Would Cerberus be the same? If she couldn't produce a solid melody for the beast, she was done for.

A low howl rocked the cavern and Meg looked up. Cerberus's right head was fully awake and alerting the other two of the mortal before them. The three heads sprang up and the creature lurched forward, filling up every available space in the cave. Its eyes were bloodred and its snouts were as large as Stymphalian birds. Spit flew from each mouth, landing inches from the boat as the dog chomped at the air. The sound reminded her of bones being snapped. She tried hard to ignore it.

You play so well you could put Cerberus to sleep, she thought. But the phrase didn't make her think of Aegeus this time. It made her think of the challenge at hand

and what it would take to return to Hercules. *Put this beast to sleep and get Katerina so you can leave this dreary place,* she told herself. She was about to play for her life. Literally.

"Goodbye, mortal," Charon said with an air of glee as the boat neared the creature. He'd clearly seen how this story typically ended.

He won't see it again today, Meg vowed.

She lifted Athena's flute to her lips and blew a few quick notes to get the beast's attention.

The right head immediately snapped to attention while the other two looked around.

Good. Meg blew into the flute again, hitting several high notes in a row that even made her wince.

The other two heads stirred and sniffed the air. Their growls momentarily stopped.

Now I have your attention, she thought. Her hands were slippery from sweat, but she held them steady and placed her lips on the reed. Once again, she returned to "The Plight of the Lily."

The left head spotted the boat approaching and started to growl, and the center head roared in response. It wasn't working. Meg removed her lips from the reed and exhaled slowly. Her hands were shaking. *Concentrate,* she reminded herself. *Remember why you used to play.* Meg started the melody again.

This time she noticed the change right away. The second head snapped back, listening, then the third, and then the first. She focused on each note, her fingers running along the reed as the notes came to her from the stores of her mind. She tried to forget about the creature and just focus on giving her best performance. *Forget he's there,* she told herself. *Just play.*

After a few seconds, Meg felt a thick stillness. She opened her eyes ever so slightly. The boat had moved closer to the creature, but its heads weren't moving. Its eyes had drifted shut and the creature was slowly sitting back. It lowered itself to the floor. She heard the first head snore and her stomach began to relax. She kept playing as Charon passed by, not stopping her tune until Cerberus disappeared and the cavern closed behind them.

"Impressive, mortal," Charon said as he rounded a corner and the cave opened up again, revealing a massive structure in front of her. "You've earned passage to the Underworld."

She breathed a sigh of relief. She'd passed her first test!

The Underworld rose to greet them, the landscape in front of the boat looking like a howling tree with a city atop it. Building after gray-stoned building was piled on top of each other, climbing haphazardly into the sky. Below them were two cavernous eyes that seemed to lead in different directions. And below that were two bone-like columns holding the whole thing up. Meg knew what she'd find between them—Hades's lair.

"Stop!" Meg said quickly.

For the first time, Charon stopped rowing. "Yesssss?" he questioned, an eerie grin on his skeletal lips.

"I . . ." Where did she want to go? Which way was Asphodel Meadows? She stared again at the large structure that led to each realm of the Underworld. The fire of Tartarus was a dead giveaway as to which way *not* to go. But which part held Elysium and which one contained Asphodel Meadows? How was she going to find Katerina there? And without being seen? "I want to get off," Meg said suddenly. "Please pull over."

"At the end," he said and started to row again. "There is only one way in and one way out."

"But I want to go to Asphodel Meadows," Meg protested as the boat neared a familiar spiral staircase leading to the structure above it. It was lit by flaming blue torches. Meg had taken those steps many times before. Her eyes darted around for a sign of Hades. She needed to get off this boat before he knew she was there.

"Don't they all?" Charon said, steering to a platform near the stairs and stopping. "There is only one way to reach all paths of the Underworld, and this is it. The end of the line, so to speak."

Meg sighed and stepped off. She approached the stairs. "Thanks for the ride. Any chance you know which floor to get off on?"

Charon looked at her. "No." Then he turned the boat around and headed back down the river, lost souls nipping at his bony heels.

"Helpful. Thanks." Meg looked around. The cave was eerily quiet except for the sound of licking flames. Meg took a deep breath and began to climb, rushing past the first two floors she knew to be Hades's home. She'd never had a need to go above them before. All her work for Hades had taken place on Earth, so most of the Underworld outside his lair was a complete mystery. Meg took the steps two at a time, staying close to the wall to avoid falling off the other side. When she reached the first landing, she was relieved to see signs chiseled into the stone walls.

TARTARUS–DOWN

ELYSIUM–UP

ASPHODEL MEADOWS–MIDDLE GROUND

Beneath the signs was a ticker that read: OVER 5,000,000,001 SERVED (AND COUNTING!)

"The Underworld, helpful as always." Meg looked around.

Well, she knew which general direction she wanted to head, anyway—up. Out of the darkness sounded like a good idea. Meg started climbing the never-ending staircase. She felt like she was walking forever. She wound around bend after bend looking for an exit to Asphodel Meadows, but there were no off-ramps. After ten flights, her legs were burning and her breath was ragged, giving her no choice but to stop for a moment. And just a moment. The fear of Hades appearing was enough to make her push on. She leaned against the wall for a second and looked up. She was high enough now that she could actually see a light among the stacked towers. Was that blue sky she saw, or an illusion? Could that be the land of the living or Elysium? She wasn't sure, but she knew she had to keep moving . . . so long as she didn't have a heart attack from all these stairs.

Ping!

Meg peered at the peculiar object that made the noise. Chiseled into the rocky wall were hand-carved double doors. They were so seamlessly part of the rock, she would have walked right past them if they hadn't chimed. As she stared, the doors opened. Meg ran down a few steps to hide.

"Going up?" asked a droll voice.

Meg peeked around the corner. The space behind the doors was empty. Who was the voice talking to?

"Asphodel Meadows on level two!"

Asphodel Meadows? Meg tentatively approached the open doors. Could this contraption take her up faster than the stairs? She peered into the small space. It was empty.

"Going up?" the bodiless voice prodded again.

Meg looked inside. There were four buttons: ELYSIUM, ASPHODEL MEADOWS, TARTARUS, and HADES'S PALACE. If this thing meant she could avoid more stairs and slip by Hades, it was worth trying. "Oh, what the hell." She stepped in and pressed the button.

Maybe using the word *hell* was her mistake. The doors closed and then opened again, filling with smoke that wound its way around her shoulders and down her body before she could react. She found herself being pulled forward.

Hades's face suddenly appeared inches from her own. "Hello there, Meg-let. Miss me?"

TWENTY-TWO: Hades

As god of the Underworld, there was one thing Hades was not—a fool.

He knew Meg was back the second Charon rowed into the cave.

Scratch that.

He knew his little Nut-Meg had returned the moment Notus came calling about a redheaded mortal begging for some wind to get her boat to the entrance of the Underworld. She wasn't the first one to try that move, and usually he said no to these types of requests. Or, if he was in a generous mood, he'd let Notus do his thing, and the boat would be knocked around so badly, everyone aboard would perish and he'd get a few new souls without having to work for it. And they'd get what they'd wanted anyway—passage to the Underworld, just not quite the way they had pictured. Either way, it was a win-win.

But while the thought of Meg trying to sneak back into the Underworld made his blood boil, he was also intrigued. His most prized servant had betrayed him and run off with that beefy half-brained god, ruining everything he had spent the last eighteen years working for. For a move like that, it should have been *her* soul floating in the river Styx for eternity. Instead he'd had to climb his way out of the swirling river as those nasty beasts clung to him, begging for second chances.

He didn't give second chances, of course. Didn't they know that by now? He'd only given a mortal a second chance once, and look where it had gotten him. Meg had traded up, literally, and gotten out of her contract with him in the process.

Which was why payback was in order.

"So, Meggie, what brings you back to this neck of the woods?" Hades asked as he pulled her back out of the elevator, his smoke winding around her body and squeezing.

She managed to choke out a simple sentence. "I thought I smelled a rat in this dump."

Hades shot her into the air and let her hang there in his smoky cuffs. "My little flower, my little bird, my little

Nut-Meg, as lovely as it is to see you again, I have to wonder what brought you back so quickly. Did things go south with your muscleman already?"

Meg struggled against the smoky bonds. "Hercules is fine—no thanks to you."

"Hmm . . . then what brings you here?" he wondered, enjoying this a tad more than he thought he would. "You're not dead, sadly, so you're trespassing, which means you want something. What else is new?"

"I don't want anything," she said, her voice weakening as the smoke tightened.

"Are you sure?" Hades picked at the skull clip on his chiton, refusing to make eye contact with the temptress. "Kind of feels like you do, or you wouldn't have dared show your face here, since"—his body erupted in blue flames as his rage took hold—"you tricked me out of keeping your soul and helped Hercules defeat me!"

"How is that any different from how you tricked me?" Meg snapped.

"*I* tricked *you*?" This was an interesting development. His smoke disappeared. Meg started to free-fall as he walked away to think about what her statement meant. Then he heard her scream. If she died so quickly, this would be far less interesting. He snapped his fingers and his smoke caught her inches from the ground. He used it to bring her straight back to him.

His face came close to hers again. "Care to explain?"

Meg grit her teeth. "You lied to me."

"Me? Lie?" Hades asked, and his smoke disappeared. "Does that sound like me?"

Meg fell a few feet and hit the landing. She quickly jumped up and dusted herself off. "You made me think Aegeus moved on after I'd been gone days. I was here for *two years*!"

She'd caught on to that trick, had she? Hades scratched his chin. "Who? Sorry. Name doesn't ring a bell."

"You made me think he left me for someone else right away so I'd forget him and do your dirty work for eternity."

"Really? That cannot be true," he said, feigning innocence. "I am burning up at the thought."

"I paid my debt." She shook her head, her ridiculous hair bouncing about. "*You* made the deal with Hercules to change that. So actually, you should have no beef with me."

"True. True. True. But guess what?" He bared his teeth. "I am mad!" His whole body erupted in flames again. "So are you going to tell me why you're here or are you going to make me dump you into the river Styx with all those other useless souls?" He sent his smoke slowly toward her again.

Meg backed away as the smoke started to wind its way around her feet, then her lower body, and lifted her up again. "Fine! I'll tell you, okay?" she said hoarsely. "Just put me down."

He waved his hand and she landed on her hands and knees. "Go ahead. Spill your sob story. I could use a good one. There hasn't been anything good to watch down here in weeks."

"I've been sent on a quest to retrieve a lost soul."

Hades looked at her and blinked twice slowly. Then he dissolved into laughter, the flames on his head nearly reaching the next landing. "You're kidding me, right? This has to be a prank!" He looked around. "Who put you up to this? Hercules? Athena? Poseidon? He loves a good fish tale. Who?"

"Hera," Meg said calmly.

He laughed harder. "Zeus's little wifey-poo? Hilarious! No one leaves the Underworld once they arrive. No one!" His laughter died out. Smoke shot out of his hands and wound around Meg's waist. "Especially not with you." The smoke carried her over to the side of the stairs again as she struggled.

Ping!

"Uh, Magnanimous Lord of the Underworld?" The little demons Pain and Panic nervously shuffled out of the elevator. "The Fates are here to see you, Your Darkness."

"They can wait!" Hades roared as he prepared to toss Meg over the side.

Panic cleared his throat. "They said it's about the Underworld stowaway."

Hades dropped Meg without thinking and heard her scream as she disappeared over the side of the staircase. "Stowaway? Tell them I'll be right there." Hades joined them on the elevator, which shot down at breakneck speed and opened on the first floor. He strolled out, leaving Pain and Panic to go on ahead and deliver his message. He waited till the doors closed to exhale.

It was a pity not to hear Meg explain more about this Hera thing, but a fall like the one he'd just sent her on would kill her instantly. He supposed he could learn the details about her failed journey once her soul settled into one of his realms. He had bigger issues to deal with at the moment.

"Per? You can come out now."

A figure slowly emerged from the shadows. "Are they gone?"

"No one is here," he reassured her, his voice dropping to a new calm at the sight of her.

She was exquisite. He loved everything about her, from the crown of silver flowers she wore in her black hair to the dark eyes that offset her tan skin. For the first time ever, he even noticed clothing. He couldn't help admiring how she favored cobalt blue for her gowns over drab browns. Today's dress was clipped at her waist with a floral silver belt.

"What did the Fates say?" she asked, sounding timid for the first time since he'd met her. She was anything but a wallflower. She was fiery. He loved that about her most of all.

He glided over and put his arms around her. "I'm on my way in to see them right now. I don't want you to worry. I thought you were going to go do that thing to take your mind off all that."

"I am," she said with a smile. "You're going to love it."

He doubted that, but he wanted her to be happy. "In any case, we'll make sure the future is in our favor. Even if we have to burn the whole world to the ground."

She nodded and wound her arms as far as she could around his ample waist. "I'm not going back, Hades."

He had a fire coursing through him now that was different from anything he'd ever experienced before. He couldn't put his finger on what the feeling was. It wasn't anger, it wasn't hate, it wasn't even envy. Was this what all those lovesick souls were always talking about? Was he in love? It sure felt like it, and if that were true . . .

He was done for. And yet—he could not deny how nice it was to have someone to talk to after all these years, someone besides his ridiculous minions or the sniveling souls or the needlessly confusing Fates. She was interesting and lively. She went toe-to-toe with him when she disagreed on something, which was fun. And she made his future seem brighter, which he thought would have been impossible after the Titan plan failed.

"I know," he said, his hand caressing her cheek. "I won't let anyone come between us. That is a promise."

TWENTY-THREE: Asphodel Meadows

She was falling. *Again*. Meg had her arms out in front of her, flailing as she struggled to grab hold of anything to keep her from plummeting dozens of stories to her death. She felt her hand hit something hard and she grabbed on, her body slamming against the rocky surface.

Ow, she thought, all the wind knocked out of her as she dangled by one arm off the edge of the staircase. She looked up, half expecting Hades to come roaring after her. Strangely, the god didn't appear, but she wasn't about to complain.

Panting, she grabbed hold of the ledge with her other hand and winced through the pain, pulling herself up to the steps to shimmy back onto the stairs. She needed to get going before Hades realized his mistake.

Taking the stairs two at a time again, Meg rounded corners fast, not paying attention to the number of levels she was ascending. She passed the floor with the bizarre lift contraption, bypassed the hot-zone turnoff to Tartarus with its unbearable screams, and kept moving, praying Hades was so busy with the Fates he'd forgotten all about her. Where was Asphodel Meadows already? She needed to get lost in that level fast.

She'd never been to that part of the Underworld before. No one went to Tartarus by choice, but she had visited Elysium one time when Hades made her deliver a message to Achilles for him. Elysium was like one large party—the finest food, the perfect weather, homes as large as Greek temples, and endless laughter. All they seemed to do was sit around all day and tell their hero war stories. Meg almost had to wonder if they remembered they were dead.

She had caught sight of Asphodel Meadows once, and at the time it had reminded her a lot of Earth—on the outside it was perfectly lovely, but upon closer inspection, things were definitely flawed. Maybe that's why Hades barely bothered with the souls there. If there was ever a place to get lost, it was in the Meadows.

Meg took another turn, and that was when she finally saw the sign carved into the rock:

THE MIDDLE: ASPHODEL MEADOWS

Meg moved to the door fast and turned the knob. It was unlocked. She took a deep breath and slipped inside.

At first glance, it looked like she'd stepped into the village where she'd spent the first few years of her life before her father had left. There was a square surrounded by small buildings, all quite plain, but nicely kept. Small flower boxes dotted the windows, each box containing strangely just one flower. There were the sounds of hammering in the distance and of birds chirping incessantly, even though none were in sight.

Meg tugged at her dress. The air was muggier here than it had been in the stairwell—not hot, not exactly cold, just a bit warm. The sky was filled with a smattering of clouds that kept passing the sun, as if the weather couldn't decide what it wanted to do for the day. She moved into the village, walking over patches of green grass that had a few dead spots in it. Other than the hammering and the birds, she didn't hear anything, and she didn't see a soul.

Is this the right place? she wondered. *Souls do live here, don't they?*

Finally, she heard talking and turned around. A group of women was walking toward her dressed in chitons and robes in various shades of tan. One wore a wrap on her head, reminding Meg of someone.

She felt a sudden pang. *Mother.*

Thea had to be here somewhere. Meg knew that from her digging last time she was in the Underworld. Of course, back then Hades had blocked Meg's mother from knowing Meg was there so Thea wouldn't try to find her daughter. But this time, she wasn't sure if Hades had thought to place a veil over Thea. Did that mean Thea had been able to learn of her arrival like other next of kin souls did when someone entered the Underworld? Would she look for the daughter she hadn't seen in almost two decades? Meg's heart gave a lurch. Was there time to even try to . . . *No.* Phil had been clear—stick to the quest. That being said, if Meg and her mother crossed paths in Asphodel Meadows, she knew she wouldn't be able to just walk away. There was so much she wanted to say.

If only she had more time. The breeze picked up and Meg felt her hand go to the satchel. She pulled out the hourglass and looked at it with dismay. It was almost two-thirds full. How could that be? Hadn't she just arrived in the Underworld hours ago?

Time moves differently down here, she reminded herself. *And I'm running out of it.* She had to focus on the task at hand.

Meg looked at the women again, their nameless faces coming straight toward her. She stepped into their path.

They were talking hurriedly, and one was laughing. It was good to know people in the Underworld still smiled.

"Excuse me," Meg interrupted them. "Do any of you know Katerina?"

They stopped short. "I'm sorry, love. Katerina who?" one asked.

How silly of me. There must be thousands of Katerinas here. "Katerina Dimas," Meg clarified.

The women looked at one another and shrugged. "Sorry, dear. We don't know anyone with that name," said one with gray eyes.

"Are you new here, dear?" asked one with a scarf wrapped around her head. "You speak rather loud for the dead."

"And your gown is purple," said the shortest, sounding wistful. "Oh, how I miss wearing vibrant colors. These tan gowns are quite dull."

"And never fit exactly right," said the first woman. "Mine is just an inch too long."

"While mine is a bit loose around the waist," said the one in the scarf.

"That's from a lack of overeating," said the short one. She looked at Meg. "We eat well here, not to worry, but it always feels as if we could go for one more bite, you know?"

"Or an extra sip of wine," said the gray-eyed one with a sigh. "The glass is never entirely full."

"But it could be worse," the short one reminded her. "We could be roasting."

"So true," they all agreed.

"You look lively, dear," said the one with the scarf. "Your skin is still glowing."

Meg knew she couldn't say she was alive. That would certainly cause a commotion in the Underworld that she didn't need. Hades would find her in seconds. "That's because you're right. I'm new."

"That explains it," said the tallest to the others. "Then you're in the wrong place, dear. You'd be with the new recruits. That's in the Evergreen, south of here."

"What?" Meg asked as the sound of hammering increased.

The one in a scarf huffed. "I swear, that construction is around the clock! I'm so tired of hammering!"

"And birds!" said the first woman.

"And bees," said the second. "But they beat the hammering. So many people moving in, the construction is never-ending. Such a headache."

"I said, go south to the Evergreen," the tallest repeated, speaking loudly and enunciating to be heard over the hammering.

"How do I get there?" Meg shouted.

"Follow the path," said the shortest. "But hurry. The

welcome party is only a few hours a day, and you don't want to miss it—all your relatives are usually there waiting."

"It's so much fun!" said the short one.

"And the one time you'll find the wine flowing freely," said the one with gray eyes wistfully.

"What is your name, in case anyone we know inquires about your whereabouts?" asked the tallest woman. "Word travels fast when a loved one arrives."

Meg hesitated as the clouds passed over the sun again. "Megara Egan," she said softly. "Daughter of Thea."

"Thea," one said, her eyes widening. "I think I once met a Thea with a daughter. If I see her, I will let her know where to find you!"

"Thank you!" Meg said, wishing more than anything she could stay and look for her mother herself. *That's not why you're here,* she reminded herself. *Keep to the quest.*

She hurried down the path, walking for what felt like an eternity, passing village after village that looked identical to the first she'd arrived in. They all had various names that sounded vaguely alike with buildings labeled things like ASPHODEL B-1,000. She wondered yet again which one could possibly be her mother's.

At least now she saw people outside. Some were sitting on blankets chatting. Others were taking walks or playing musical instruments. She heard laughter and singing.

People genuinely seemed content, although there was the occasional complaint to be heard about the mugginess of the air, or the hammering, or even the abundant bird population.

"What lovely coloring you have!" remarked a woman on a walk with her husband. "It's almost as if you're still alive!"

"Don't be silly," snapped her husband, giving Meg a look. "Why would the living want to come here?"

Meg smiled uneasily. It wouldn't be long before someone alerted the powers that be that a mortal was in their midst. Meg quickened her pace when she saw a meadow peek out over the next hilltop. As she got closer, the sun seemed to pull away from the clouds and the grass under her feet turned a bright green. She heard definite sounds of a party in the distance and quickened her pace. The air started to smell sweeter. Were those apricots she smelled? Or figs?

And there were trees again! She hadn't realized how much she missed them till she saw them growing there along the path. They had perfect little green leaves and flowers budding on branches. And at the side of the road was a woman kneeling over a garden tending to a bed of hydrangeas blooming in rich fuchsias, blues, and whites.

"Those are gorgeous!" Meg said in surprise. They

were the most colorful things she'd seen in the Underworld and the vibrancy warmed her heart for a moment. "I can't believe anything like that grows down here!"

The woman looked up at her and smiled, her eyes dark yet warm. "Thanks. I wasn't sure if it was possible myself, but with deep rooting and some good soil, it seems anything is."

"You planted these?" Meg said in awe.

The woman looked pleased as she glanced at the colorful beds of blooms in the nearby meadows. "You could say that. I love the *drama* of it all—the seeds being sown, the elements working for and against them, the flower erupting against all odds, then the death of the bloom. *So* much more exciting than my old life." She looked at Meg as though just remembering she were there. "But it's probably best if you don't tell anyone you saw me here."

"Oh." Meg made a motion to seal her lips. "No problem there. I'd rather you not tell anyone you saw me, either." She briefly wondered about the Underworld rules for changing the landscape—Hades probably would not take kindly to that.

"You've got a deal," Meg said.

"I didn't even expect to be here this long," the woman admitted, wiping her tan hands on her cobalt blue dress. "But time moves fast."

"Too fast," Meg agreed, taking another admiring look at the garden the woman had cultivated.

"And I refuse to let anyone control what I do," she said, a new fire in her voice. She ran a hand through her black hair. "I'm not sure why I'm telling you any of this."

"It's nice to have someone to talk to," Meg said. She never would have thought she'd miss Phil, but she did. Not to mention Wonder Boy . . . "It gets me out of my head."

"Exactly," the woman agreed. "As does gardening." She frowned. "Except this batch is extremely frustrating. This is my third time tending to these hydrangeas this week and the leaves are still dying out." She held out a yellowed stem for Meg to see. "I've never had this problem before."

Meg leaned down for a moment, taken by the sweet scent and the beauty of the blossoms. "Does this area get enough sun? Kind of feels like nothing in this place gets enough, but this spot in particular is kind of especially shady, don't you think? Hydrangeas do best in full sun in the early part of the day and then partial sun the rest." Meg looked around the area for a moment. "This bed might need to be moved farther down the road, where the sun is brighter."

The woman rocked back on her heels. She looked at Meg with interest as she pushed her black curly hair to the right side of her neck. "You really know your hydrangeas."

"My mother loved them," Meg recalled. "No matter

where we moved, she always splurged on flowers to spruce up the joint." Her heart tugged at the thought of Thea being so near. "She taught me how to prune them and make them grow."

"They are one of my favorites," the woman admitted and stared at Meg again. "What is your mother's name?"

"Thea," Meg said, realizing it felt good to say her name aloud again. It suddenly occurred to her that she should say it more often. *We imprint the lost on our hearts,* she thought. Aegeus said Katerina had liked to say that.

"Thea," the woman repeated, inhaling deeply as she said the name. "She will be happy to see you, I'm sure. You're new, I take it?"

"Yes," Meg said quickly, and felt a wave of panic. "Which is why I should probably go. You know, to go find her."

"You're lucky," the woman said wistfully, seemingly not wanting their conversation to end, "that you can be with the person you love. That's why I'm here, too, but it's not easy."

"No, it's not," Meg agreed. "Love is complicated."

"Exactly!" The woman shook her head. She sighed and plucked one of the flowers at her feet. "Living in shadows is exhausting, isn't it?"

Meg nodded. Then she heard the music growing louder in the distance and knew she'd already been there too long. "It was nice meeting you."

"Good luck with your mother!" the woman said.

Meg continued down the path, the flowers growing almost fluorescent, they were so bright and plentiful. Buildings came into view next, and Meg immediately noticed they were as vibrant and varied as a rainbow. In the middle of a large courtyard were several fountains spraying full streams of water high into the sky. And that was before she noticed the people.

Unlike the other villages, this square was flooded with people dancing, hugging, and crying happy tears. People were dressed in radiantly colored chitons (that appeared to fit perfectly) and still looked almost rosy in appearance as if they were still alive, even though they weren't. Meg didn't hear the incessant chirping of birds or hammering. She only heard the sound of laughter and light. Meg felt her stomach relax for a moment, reinvigorated by their joy. The Underworld could make a person feel like the weight of the world was on their shoulders.

It could also make people think no time had passed, when it clearly passed much quicker down here. It had been less than a week since the Titans' attack, but who knew how long that time had felt to Katerina? Would she still be partying and rejoicing at connecting with her family again? How long did people live in this in-between? There was only one way to find out: she would need to ask for help. *What would*

Aphrodite say about this development? Meg wondered with a small smile. Then, *What would my mother say?*

Meg hurried forward, joining the crowd of people who still looked a lot like her. The sound of the flute made her turn around. A group of men had gathered to play music while others danced, reuniting with some who were wearing tan and were grayer in appearance. A woman danced by her and Meg touched her arm gently. "Excuse me. I'm looking for someone."

"Sure! Who can we help you find, dear?" The woman's smile was still bright, her eyes still flecked with color.

"Katerina Dimas."

The woman thought for a moment. "I don't recognize the name, dear. When did she arrive? Was she on the ship that sank off the Greek isles today? There's a large group in the south of town from there."

"No." Meg shook her head. "She would be here a few days. She died during the Titans' attack last week."

"Last week?" the woman said in surprise. "That occurred a few months ago."

"No, it was only a few days ago," Meg started to say and stopped herself. But of course. If time moved differently down here, then the normal rules wouldn't apply. Katerina definitely would have moved on if she'd been here a few months. Where could she be? "I'm sorry. You're right.

Where would she move to after the Evergreen, then? Is there a directory I could look at to see where she lives now?"

"Directory!" The woman laughed. "Oh no, dear. Can you imagine how big it would be and how often we'd have to update it? I'm afraid not. You'll have to ask around, unless one of her relatives is here among the newly departed. Or she signed on to be a guide, like me. I get to stay here for eternity—and keep my rosy, alive glow, which is lovely." She looked at Meg again. "But you *do* look familiar." Her eyes opened wide as she scanned her up and down. "Are you Megara?"

Meg looked at her in surprise. "Why, yes."

"Your mother was just here looking for you!" the woman said. "She was told you arrived today and gave me your description, but I hadn't seen anyone with hair as bright as yours, so I sent her to Asphodel Unit A-6,985. That is where most of the new recruits were sent in the past few days. Maybe you can catch her."

Meg felt a deep pang of longing. Her mother was looking for her. "I wish I could, but I have to find Katerina first. Are you sure you don't have any suggestions about where I might find someone who has been here a few months?"

The woman pursed her lips. "I wish I knew. The only people that stick around the Evergreen for any length of time are children, and the adults looking after them tend to stay, too. Hades never bothers to make them move on. Someone has to take care of the young'uns, after all."

Meg felt a flicker of hope. *Layla*. "All children? What if they're here alone and later reunited with an adult?"

The woman thought for a moment. "We always send the adults to them there—they have the most beautiful seascape and mountains and glorious weather. It's gorgeous! The adults always fall in love with the area when they see it. Aside from Elysium, it's the nicest place in the Underworld to be."

"Where is it?" Meg asked eagerly.

The woman pointed toward the sun beginning to lower on the horizon. "The fields near the water. Sometimes you can also find them at the poppy fields."

Meg felt her heart begin to rev. "The poppy fields? Where are they?"

"Same direction, dear," the woman said, and Meg was already pushing past the dancers moving by her. "Good luck!"

"Thank you!" She was finally getting somewhere, and a lot quicker than if she had not bothered to ask. *Thanks for the tip, Aphrodite.*

Meg ran toward the water in the distance. As she ran, she noticed the path widen, and flowers sprang up from the cracks in the road. Trees grew fuller and flowers more colorful than she ever remembered them on Earth. Even the air felt different in the Evergreen. The mugginess was gone, replaced with a comfortable temperature and a sun that shone brighter. And that was all before she heard the wonderful sound of children laughing.

As she crested the next hill, she could see them. There were kids of all ages running and playing in the massive poppy fields along the rocky shoreline. Meg stepped onto a rock to get a better look at them. Some children were alone and some with adults. The question was, which one was Layla? Meg had to hope she looked something like Katerina, whom she'd seen in Hades's flames.

Meg jumped off the rocks, wincing in pain, and started searching, but it was like looking for the ripest grape in a huge vat. Children were running in every direction, playing, and picking poppies that seemed to grow back instantly. From a distance, they looked identical. Every one of them was dressed in beautiful vibrant colors and was carrying baskets of poppies. Some had flowers in their hair, while others walked hand in hand with parents who watched them play; but still, this offered her no clue to finding the girl.

Meg pulled the hourglass out of her satchel and sighed. The bottom of the jar was now more than three-quarters full. Somehow walking through Asphodel Meadows had cost her almost a day, which meant she had only two left. If it took her just as long to locate the pair in the poppy fields, she was doomed.

Please let Katerina and Layla be here, Meg prayed to the gods as she walked among families young and old, searching for anyone who might have Katerina's golden hair, pale skin, and dark eyes. *Please. I'm running out of time.*

The field seemed to go on for miles. Many women she came across had blond hair, but were older or younger than she imagined Katerina to be. Others had longer hair, or hair so short Meg knew they couldn't be her, and after a while, Meg wondered if she'd ever find the woman at all. At last, Meg saw someone who fit Katerina's description exactly. She was standing with a small child about Layla's age. Meg touched her arm.

"Katerina?" Meg asked hopefully, and the woman turned around.

A woman with green eyes stared back at Meg in confusion. It wasn't her.

"Sorry." Meg moved on.

The same thing happened over and over again to the point where Meg thought she'd never find her. It was if she could hear the grains of sand in the hourglass falling. *There's almost no time left!* they'd say. *Move faster! Faster! Find Katerina!* She spun around in desperation, her eyes searching the large field of poppies again. And that's when she heard a familiar melody.

Aegeus, she thought immediately.

The tune drifting across the meadow was one he had played for her the first night they met, and then a hundred times more over the course of their courtship. She knew the chords and notes as well as if she'd written them herself. Meg rushed toward the sound, trying to find who was humming the melody. She moved between children and mothers and babes in fathers' arms and whirled around, hearing the melody play on the wind, but still she saw no one. How was she going to find them?

What if she played the same tune on the flute? Yes. If she did that, maybe the person would come directly to her. Her hand went to Athena's instrument.

If she played, would she give her location away to Hades?

She had no choice. She had to risk it.

Hands shaking, Meg took Athena's double flute from the strap around her waist, put it to her lips, and started to play Aegeus's song. Two notes in, she hit a wrong note and then one way too high. It was as if the past was rising up to meet her, and she didn't like the memory. The tune made her feel restless and uneasy and she had to fight the urge to put the flute down and forget the song even existed; but she knew she had to keep trying. She took a deep breath and rushed through the notes, trying not to link the music with memory. When she was finished, a small girl with dark brown hair, holding a basket of poppies, was standing in front of her.

"I know that song!" said the girl with a laugh.

Meg held her breath. "You do?"

"Yes. I once heard Medusa play it to her snakes, and they all fell fast asleep," the child said with wide eyes. "All of them! At the same time!"

"Really?" said a small boy, listening to the story.

"Yes," the girl said solemnly. "I was secretly watching, but when Medusa caught me, she woke her snakes up, and that's how I wound up down here."

Layla likes to tell tall tales, Meg reminded herself.

"Layla?" Meg whispered.

"Yes." The child smiled. "How do you know my name?"

TWENTY-FOUR: Lost and Found

Meg inhaled sharply. She didn't want to scare the girl away. "I know your sister. Is she here?"

"She's sitting right over there. Katerina!" Layla called and skipped a few feet away to approach a woman sitting quietly with her legs outstretched and her head facing the warm sun.

Katerina.

Meg paused. This was the person Meg had spent so much time thinking about: first, in anger and bitterness, watching her and Aegeus's love story in Hades's fire. Then, as the object of this quest, learning more about a woman who was not all that different from herself, someone who seemed to have been caught in the cross fire of the gods' affairs. It was strange to finally see her in the flesh (so to speak), sitting and drumming her fingers casually against her leg.

She had hair the color of wheat and skin as pale as the sand. Her eyes, Meg noticed, were deep brown, and there was no mistaking that distinct round nose. The baby had one just like it. As she drew closer, Meg could hear Katerina was humming Aegeus's song. She took a deep breath. This was it.

"This woman was looking for you," Layla said, bounding ahead. "She was playing that song you like to hum."

"Layla," the woman warned, giving Meg an apologetic look.

Layla turned to Meg. "Sorry! I meant to say, 'What is your name? Are you new here?' My sister says we should always help new souls."

The woman smiled, the corners of her mouth producing dimples in both cheeks. Cassia had them, too. "Much better."

"My name is Meg." She looked at the woman again, unsure how to explain everything succinctly. The faster she could impress upon Katerina that she was her ticket out of there, the better. "I'm looking for Katerina Dimas. Is that you?"

"I'm Katerina." Katerina's smile faded slightly. She

sat up on her elbows and stared at her. "But my last name is Aikos."

"You mean your maiden name was Aikos, right?"

"Maiden?" Katerina looked confused. "Oh, I am not married."

"Katerina!" Layla admonished, giggling. "That's not true! When you arrived, you said your new last name was Dimas. Remember?"

"I . . . Did I? I don't remember." Katerina reached for the child's hand and smiled up at her. "All I know is I belong with you." Layla leaned over and nestled into her sister's shoulder. Katerina looked up at Meg again and shook her head. "I'm sorry I'm so distracted! Forgive me. Do we know one another?"

"That's a complicated question," Meg admitted, "and it's not one I have time to explain in too much detail, unfortunately." She eyed Layla. "Do you think we could talk in private? It's important."

Katerina gently whispered something in Layla's ear. The child beamed at Meg, then took off racing across the meadow with her basket in hand. Katerina kept smiling till Layla disappeared from sight. Then she looked at Meg and her face hardened.

"If this is about my leaving the Evergreen, I'm not going," Katerina said, her eyes suddenly burning with a fire

Meg could respect. "I won't leave my sister here alone, and from what I hear, she'll be happier here than she'd be anywhere else. The two of us are staying."

"This isn't about the Evergreen—" Meg tried to interrupt, but Katerina kept going.

"She's been on her own far too long already," Katerina said firmly. "If you have a problem with it, then bring me to Hades and I'll take it up with him. I won't leave this child again."

Meg held her hands up to surrender. "No one is going to see Hades. At least I hope not. This isn't about Layla. It's about you. I'm here to take you home."

Katerina blinked. "Home?"

"Yes," Meg said breathlessly. "I'm here on direct order of Hera to get you out of the Underworld," she whispered. "Your husband, Aegeus, and daughter, Cassia, need you in the land of the living."

Katerina ran a hand through her hair, clearly flustered. "Daughter?"

"Yes! And your husband, Aegeus," Meg repeated, her voice rising with excitement. "You weren't meant to get caught up in that flood."

"Flood?" Katerina echoed again.

Meg stared, wondering if she wasn't being clear enough. "The one that you were lost in. I believe the gods didn't mean for you to die. In any case, they've sent me here to retrieve your soul. I'm to bring you back to your family, but if that's going to happen, we have to move quickly before Hades finds us."

Meg couldn't blame her for being overwhelmed. No one got an offer like this. Meg took Katerina's hand, finding eye contact to make sure the woman was registering what she was saying. "Do you understand? You can leave the Underworld!" A shadow fell across Katerina's face and Meg noticed eerie dark clouds start to gather in the sky. "But we have to go immediately."

Katerina pulled her hand away. She started to breathe more heavily. "I think you have the wrong person. I don't know an Aegeus or a Cassia. I don't have a child! I'm sorry. Good luck in your search." She stood up and started to hurry away.

Meg was dumbfounded. *How can Katerina not remember her own daughter?* Did the dead forget the living when they crossed to the other side? No. That couldn't be possible. If it were, the families around her wouldn't have been reunited. The people celebrating at the Evergreen village wouldn't have been reconnecting. So why didn't Katerina remember Aegeus or Cassia? Of all the problems she'd imagined having in the Underworld, Katerina not wanting to live was not one of them.

"Katerina," Meg started again, following her. "That song I heard you humming when I found you—it's Aegeus's tune. Your husband wrote it. You must remember him."

For a split second, Meg thought she saw Katerina's face flicker with some sort of recognition. But in an instant, it was gone.

"I don't remember where I learned that, actually. All I know is Layla likes it."

Meg stumbled over a rock, panic rising in her throat. She reached toward the retreating woman. "I know this must be confusing. But you have to understand: this is a once in a, well, *never* offer. You'd be a fool not to take it. Don't you want to live again?"

Katerina spun around. "I am living! In a way—with my sister here in the Underworld." Her voice was sad, but her eyes were firm. "She's who I choose to spend eternity with. Please respect that and just leave us alone."

Katerina hurried over to Layla, who was picking more poppies. Meg felt her heart stir at the sight of the two of them together. It was only then that she realized what she was asking this woman to leave behind.

Don't leave me, Mother! She heard her own voice in her head and winced at the memory. *Stay with me!*

You're a big, tough girl. You tie your own sandals and everything.

Thea and Meg's time together had been too short and much of it was difficult, but Meg still wouldn't trade it for the world. She couldn't begin to imagine what it would be like to say goodbye to a younger sibling. No wonder Katerina felt so conflicted.

"I lost someone I loved when I was young," Meg said, approaching the pair carefully. Both Katerina and Layla turned to her. "My mother." She looked at Layla. "She died when I was just a girl, and then I was on my own. Life was never the same after that. I miss her terribly every day."

"I miss mine, too. Missing is a part of living and dying," Layla said quietly. Katerina took her hand and Layla perked up. "Do you look like your mother?" she asked Meg.

It struck Meg that a child this young seemed comfortable talking about death. "Yes," Meg said, leaning down to her level. "We had the same red hair and we both loved music. My mother liked to listen to it, and I loved to play it. She taught me to trust my instincts and be strong. I am all that I am because of her."

"She sounds nice," Layla said wistfully. "Is she here, too?"

"Yes," Meg said, and her heart twisted at the thought.

"I'm sure she misses you," Layla added thoughtfully. "She'll be happy to see you when you find each other again.

And in the meantime, I'm sure she is okay. We're okay here, you know."

"Thank you." Meg gave her a soft smile. What an extraordinary child Layla was. She wondered if it was an effect of being in the Underworld so long, or if that was just who she had always been. She looked up at Katerina. "My mother had a tough life, and raising a kid on her own was difficult. I'm sure if she had the chance to be a mother again, she'd wish things were different."

Katerina said nothing.

Meg smiled at Layla. "Even now, though we're apart, I carry her with me." Meg looked at Katerina and repeated the words Aegeus told her Katerina favored. "Someone once told me we imprint the lost on our hearts."

Something flashed across Katerina's face again. It quickly disappeared. "Layla, look! A butterfly!" she cried. "Why don't you see if you can catch it?" The child grinned, then dashed into the field to chase it. "I'm sorry about your mother," Katerina said. "But that means you must understand my feelings on the matter."

"I do." Meg nodded and looked at Layla a few feet away. "No child deserves this fate."

"No, they don't. That's why I can't leave her," Katerina whispered. "I don't remember a lot from my recent life, but I remember my early memories. Layla's passing always haunted me. My parents never said it, but I always felt like her death was my fault." She closed her eyes and Meg saw her pink lips start to tremble. "I turned my head for a moment at her bedside and then she was gone." She covered her face with her hands.

Meg put her arm on Katerina's. "Aegeus told me that Layla was very ill. There is nothing you could have done to save her." She paused. "But you do still have a chance to be there for Cassia." Katerina opened her eyes and looked at her curiously. "Your daughter. The one you had with Aegeus," Meg tried again. "I've seen her, and she's a wonderful baby. She has the same color hair as you, and dimples in her cheeks."

Katerina seemed to be concentrating on something—maybe even a memory the corners of her mind wouldn't let her reach. Finally, she shook her head. "I'm sorry. I know I would remember my own child."

Meg furrowed her brow. She had to get through. "She has the sweetest laugh when she's not crying, and wow, can the kid eat! Layla didn't get a chance to grow up and experience the world, but Cassia will. Don't let her do it without you."

Tears began to stream down Katerina's face. "Please stop. I don't remember her. . . ."

But Meg couldn't stop now. She was close to getting

through to Katerina. She could feel it. "Cassia will miss so much," Meg continued as the wind picked up and the clouds gathered. In the distance, she saw a flash of lightning. "She needs you, and I'm here because Hera has given me a chance to bring you home to her."

Katerina put her hands to her head and started to pull at her hair. Was she finally remembering?

Meg felt her own buried regrets bubbling up inside her. "You've been given a gift that no one receives. Ever. I wish my own mother had once been in your shoes. Come back with me while you have the chance."

Katerina shook her head. "I don't remember . . . but . . ." She hesitated.

"Yes?" Meg leaned in, holding her breath.

Katerina bit her lip as a gust of wind blew through the fields, tilting the poppies sideways. "If what you say is true, will Hera let Layla return, too?"

Meg looked at the innocent child playing and felt her heart break all over again. "I'm sorry. That wasn't part of their offer."

"But you could ask," Katerina pushed as thunder rumbled again, sounding closer than it had before.

"I don't think . . ." Meg wasn't sure what to say. Layla had been gone a long time. The gods could do some miraculous things, but bringing someone back from the dead so many years later seemed impossible, even for them. "I don't think they can do that."

The anguish written on Katerina's face was almost too much for Meg to take. "Then I'm staying here." She turned to leave just as a blaring roll of thunder sounded.

Meg felt her heart stop. "Wait!"

"No!" Katerina snapped, and children everywhere looked up, worried. "I'm sorry." She lowered her voice. "I don't mean to be ungrateful. This is a generous offer from Hera, but without Layla, I can't accept. Please leave us in peace."

She hurried after Layla and Meg stood there for a moment, stunned. She was losing her. Meg racked her brain. *What convinced me Aegeus had moved on?* And then she realized: *Seeing him with Katerina! That's it! I need Katerina to* see *what she's missing. For it to be in front of her, undeniable.* But how could she do that?

The orchid.

Meg reached for the flower in her satchel. It was a tad crushed, but it was still there, just waiting for a moment to help. Her heart started to beat rapidly again.

"Wait! Please! I know how I can help you reclaim the memories you've lost!"

Katerina turned around. Layla stared at the two adults curiously as she swung Katerina's hand.

"This flower was a gift from a god," Meg explained, holding the orchid carefully in her outstretched hand. "I can use it to call for help. Perhaps if you are able to see the family you left behind when you came to the Underworld, you'll realize what you're giving up."

"You have a family?" Layla said excitedly.

"No," Katerina said quickly, glancing at the flower. "Don't listen to her, Layla."

"Please," Meg begged. "Give me a chance to show you what you lost." Meg took a deep breath and pulled off the second petal.

Katerina snatched the petal from Meg's hands. "Enough!" She ripped it into pieces before it could start to glow.

"No!" Meg cried, dropping to the ground to try to catch the fragments.

"I don't want to remember what I lost!" Katerina said angrily. "Please." Her voice broke as tears streamed down her face. "Just leave us alone! I'm begging you! Come on, Layla."

The child looked back at Meg sadly. "Good luck finding your mother."

Raindrops began to fall and children began running in different directions, laughing and screaming with delight as the orchid pieces blew away. She'd wasted a petal for nothing. There was only one left now.

Don't lose them! a voice in her head instructed, but Meg ignored it. She sank into the grass, ready to give up. Even if she caught up with Katerina again, what could she say to convince her? If she tried to use the last petal, Katerina would just tear it up again. She pulled out the hourglass. The sand was higher than ever. By her calculations, she had a day and a half left at most. She was running out of time.

Clink! Meg felt something hot clamp down on her arm. It was a glowing red cuff. She looked up in horror.

"Gotcha!" said Panic excitedly as he stood alongside Pain. "Hades wants to see you."

Then Pain snapped his fingers and the three of them disappeared.

TWENTY-FIVE: Ultimatums

Meg reappeared seconds later in Hades's throne room. An extra-large furnace—a gateway to Tartarus—was pumping off heat while Hades's music of choice—low sounds of moaning and wails—created an ambience of gloom. Pain and Panic deposited her in the center of the room, where she found Hades sitting on his usual throne of bones. He pointed to her.

"You're alive."

"Appears that way," Meg said. Her foot twitched. She needed to find Katerina before time ran out.

"My mistake." Hades snapped his fingers and smoke unfurled toward her. "But that can be easily fixed."

Meg needed to think fast. "Don't you want to know why Hera sent me here?" The smoke stopped in midair.

"Let me think about that a second. Nope!" The smoke started winding its way around her legs. "Just like I could care less about your mother."

"My mother?" Meg looked at him as the smoke tightened and lifted her into the air.

Hades rolled his eyes, and with a flick of his wrist, Meg flew toward the furnace. "Came by when I was with the Fates—interrupting my meeting, by the way—crying about how she needed to see you this time. Blah, blah, blah."

"This time?" Meg repeated. "You always said my mother didn't know I was here last time!" Being so close yet far from Thea had been torture when she had been in the Underworld doing Hades's bidding. "She knew the whole time?"

"Maybe I forgot to actually place a veil and she was alerted, okay? Big deal!" Hades huffed. "You didn't stick around anyway, so what was the use in telling you she lived in Asphodel Unit C-23,762?"

Meg's jaw dropped. Had she passed that building today?

The yellow of Hades's eyes blazed. "Hey, it's all good. Now you can bunk next to her! Have a good reunion, Nut-Meg!"

The smoke pulled her to the door of the furnace. It opened on its own and Meg could feel heat licking at her heels. She was toast unless she did something. "I told Katerina everything!" she blurted out.

The smoke paused. "And who is Katerina?"

Meg gritted her teeth as flames singed the hair on her legs. "She's Aegeus's wife!" Hades didn't say anything. "My former . . . er . . . *flame*?"

"Former flame . . . former flame . . ." Hades muttered. "Knowing you, you have a lot of exes out there . . ."

"You know which one I mean! Katerina's death was an accident; not part of the cosmic plan. Hera wants her back. If you don't do as they ask, you'll . . . you'll . . ." What could she threaten him with? "There will be consequences!"

"Consequences, huh?" Hades zipped to her in seconds, his sinister face inches from her own. "I've already faced consequences! That's how I wound up *running* this place. And now that I am, there is nothing *they* can do to me down here. I literally let the Titans out to wreak havoc and run amok, and look who's back wheeling and dealing in the Underworld. *I'm* in charge of the souls that come here," he roared. "Not my brother or his wife!"

"Why doesn't Katerina remember her old life, then?" Meg tried a new tack. "Did you make her forget?"

"Forget?" Hades's smoke loosened slightly. "Why would I do that? Because her life was abysmally boring? I don't make people forget the past. Their pain feeds me, babe."

Meg didn't understand. "Why doesn't she remember her family, then?"

"Who knows?" Hades said. "I'm not a therapist! Maybe she was so upset her brain blocked it out? Or maybe it was a divine mistake. It happens."

A divine mistake. If Katerina had been killed in a flood created by the gods' battle, maybe her memory loss was an inadvertent side effect. That could be another reason why the gods wanted to undo their mistake.

"Either way, I don't go around erasing people's memories, kid. I am a nice guy when I want to be."

"Nice?" Meg spat. "You refuse to let go of her soul so she can reunite with her loved ones."

Hades shrugged. "Yeah, well, love is a fickle thing, isn't it? One minute you have it, the next it's gone . . . or someone is trying to say you can't be together because you live in different zip codes." He bared his teeth. "No one said life or death is fair!" The furnace roared bloodred, as did Hades's head. "Bye, Meg-let!" The smoke prepared to drop her into the flames just as the doors to Hades's throne room flew open.

A woman with dark hair came running into the room. "I couldn't stay away any longer! What did they say? Did you convince them to—Hey." She noticed Meg about to be thrown in the furnace and stopped talking. "It's *you!*"

Meg did a double take. "And you!"

"Do you two know each other?" Hades cut in. "My

love, I was just about to burn Meggie-kins at the stake. Can this wait?"

"Burn who?" The woman put her hands on her hips. "Her? No! You put her down this instant."

Hades looked from Meg to the woman in surprise, and Meg noticed the flames on his head flicker. "No, Per, you don't understand."

"I don't care if I understand! Put her down. She saved my whole bed of hydrangeas this afternoon. You're not tossing her in the furnace."

Hades hesitated. "But, Per . . ."

Meg stared. She had never heard him this docile before.

The woman pursed her lips. "Put her down, Hades, and just talk to me."

Hades sighed. "Fine." He flicked his wrist and the smoke uncoiled. The furnace's flames dropped to barely a flicker. "Just know she had it coming."

Meg fell to the ground with a painful thump. She really hated when he did that.

The woman walked over and offered her a hand. "Thank you for the help earlier," she said with a smile. "I'm Persephone. And you are?"

Meg accepted her help. "Persephone . . . you're Demeter's daughter!" she realized. "You're the one the gods on Mount Olympus are looking for!"

A look of panic came over Persephone's face. "Who are you?" She looked to Hades. "Who is she?" she asked, her voice rising.

Hades smiled smugly. "*This* is who you just interrupted me from roasting: Megara. You know—the one who ruined my plan to overthrow Zeus?"

Persephone spun around and stared at Meg. *"Her?"* She started to back up. "That means you're with Hercules, and you're alive. Which means when you leave here, you could tell the other gods where I am." She moved farther away. "My mother will find me and take me away!" With that, she ran to Hades and grabbed his hands. "We'll be done for."

"Hey now, it's all right," said Hades as he brought her in close. "We won't let her."

Meg gaped. This wasn't like Hades at all. Sure, he was still threatening her life, but he seemed to actually be concerned for someone who wasn't himself.

"What did the Fates have to say?" Persephone whispered.

Hades's face was grim. "I don't want you getting upset."

"I'm already upset!"

"They don't know *everything*."

"They *do* know everything. What did they say?" Hades hesitated, and Persephone put her hands on his cheeks. "Tell me."

Hades sighed. "We're not exactly seeing eye to eye on things. In fact, I thought about making sure they never saw anything again."

"Hades . . ."

"I know. I didn't. I'm just saying I thought about it."

"So what was their prediction?" Persephone searched Hades's face. "Is there a future for us or not?" Her lower lip quivered.

"They said some riddle about the Earth being the only hope for you." Persephone gasped. "But who cares what they think!" Hades said, his voice rising. "No one knows you're here. We're safe." He looked at Meg, a smile spreading across his gray lips. "At least we were before Meg here showed up."

Persephone looked at her, and Meg started to back away. Whatever bond they had formed in the meadows was clearly not enough to save her now.

"Why do you think I was about to get rid of her?" Hades asked. Persephone folded her arms. "Your mother is part of the Olympus crew! If we let Meg out, she's going to go running to that beefy boyfriend of hers, and Papa Zeus and Demeter and everyone else will show up to take you away."

"No," Persephone whispered, eyeing Meg worriedly.

"I wouldn't tell anyone," Meg swore.

"Who are you going to believe, Per?"

Persephone looked intently at Meg. "Toss her in the fire."

Hades grinned and smoke began to seep out of his hands again. "With pleasure, my love."

Meg had only seconds to make a decision. "I can help you stay together!" The moment the words left her lips, she knew the cost might be too high, but it was her only move left to play.

"Stop!" Persephone said and Hades's smoke disappeared.

"She's just stalling," he complained. "How could she help us?"

"I heard Aphrodite and Demeter talking about you when I was on Mount Olympus," Meg appealed to Persephone. "Your mother is desperate to find you. She's worried."

"Yes, because she doesn't understand my love for Hades. She wants me harvesting solely on Earth, and I want to be here with him." Persephone put a hand on his fleshy gray arm. "If she finds me, she'll take me away."

Meg licked her lips, which felt dry in all this heat, and thought fast. Persephone had been *gardening* in the Underworld. She clearly missed at least a portion of her old life, even if, for some unfathomable reason, she wanted to be with Hades. What if there was a way for her to have it all? "What if you compromised? Offered to spend half of the year tending to the gardens on Earth, and the other half here in the Underworld with Hades?"

Persephone and Hades looked at one another.

"Why would Demeter agree to that?" Hades asked.

"Because she wants her daughter to be happy," Meg said. "Demeter would still get to see Persephone, Persephone would still get to be with you, and Persephone could have everything she loves. It's a win-win-win . . . if the gods agree, that is."

"So, what? You want me to pray?" Persephone rolled her eyes. "Prayers don't always work—especially when it's one god praying to another god."

"Maybe not, but what if I could make a god appear here so we could appeal to them in person?" Meg pulled the orchid out of her satchel. "This orchid makes whatever god I call on appear. There's one last petal, which I can use to call upon Mount Olympus and appeal on your behalf."

Persephone's gaze flickered to the flower. "And what do you get in return for doing this for us?"

"She wants to bring a soul back to the land of the living," Hades explained, looking troubled. "As if I'd ever let *that* happen."

"Who is it?" Persephone asked, curious. "Which soul?"

Meg took a deep breath. "Her name is Katerina Dimas. She's the woman my first love left me for."

Persephone's eyes flashed. "Tell me everything."

TWENTY-SIX: Wheeling and Dealing

Meg didn't waste time. "She died in a flood created by the gods in their battle with the Titans, but it seems she wasn't meant to perish. She has an infant daughter on Earth. Hera asked me to bring her back to her child."

Persephone glanced at Hades. "Can you do what she's asking—allow a soul to live again?"

"It's a gray area," Hades said, sounding uncomfortable. "She hasn't been gone long, so it's technically possible, but if I do it for Meg here and word gets out, every soul will want a get-out-of-hell-free card."

"He has a point," Persephone said.

"No one has to know," Meg replied quickly. "Just give me a chance to convince her to come back with me."

Now Hades grinned. "*Convince*? You mean she doesn't want to go?"

Meg paled. Why had she let that slip? "She will. She just doesn't remember her family on Earth at the moment. But I can fix that and get her back to Hera on time."

Hades's grin widened. "Hmm . . . interesting. You're on a quest, so you must have some sort of deadline. When does your time run out?"

The heat in this place was making her sloppy. But it was too late to backpedal. Meg pulled the hourglass out of her satchel. The sight made her stomach drop. The sands were almost to the top. "About a day."

Hades laughed. "You'll never make it!"

"Then what do you have to lose?" Persephone's eyes flickered to Meg's for half a second. "Let her help us, and then Megara can try to help this woman before her quest is done." She took Hades's hand. "I want to be with you forever, but we can't keep hiding. We should be free to enjoy our lives here without fear of losing one another." She paused. "What was it the Fates told you? The riddle?"

Hades sighed. "Something about the Earth being your only hope. I don't know, it's hard to get a straight answer from the all-knowing. They talk in circles."

"But she's technically from the Earth," Persephone continued, pointing to Meg. "What if they mean *her*?"

Meg leaped at the opening. "The Fates are never wrong. And I'm offering help. Let me at least try."

Hades looked at Persephone and put both hands in hers as he stared into her eyes. They stood that way for a while. Then he sighed, lowering his voice. "Make the call."

Persephone nodded once.

Inhaling slowly, Meg tore the petal in half. As she did, it and the stem disintegrated and drifted off into the air. She absently wondered if it would actually work to call a god other than Hercules, her stomach twisting at the thought of losing out on a chance to talk to him. Meg shook her head, trying to stay focused. There was only one god who could make her suggestion for Persephone happen. Someone who not only believed in marriage, but who could talk the All-father into going for such an unusual arrangement. "I wish to speak with Hera, please."

A warm orange and pink ball began to form in the center of the room. It grew larger and larger till it burst into a ray as bright as the sun. Hades and Persephone shielded themselves from the bright light. Slowly, the outline of the god began to appear. She was dressed in the same magenta gown Meg had seen her in atop Mount Olympus and wore the same crown, which was glistening despite the dreary room. Hera spotted her and looked around at her surroundings in surprise.

"Megara?" Then she did a double take. "Hades." Her eyes narrowed when her gaze found the woman standing next to him. "And Persephone! So *this* is where you've been hiding. Your mother has been looking for you everywhere!" She looked at Meg again. "What is the meaning of this? Why have you summoned me? *How* have you summoned me?"

"I apologize for being so bold," Meg said as Hades and Persephone watched the exchange. "Hercules gave me an orchid that allowed me to call on him if I was in need."

Hera pursed her lips. "I see. And yet you call on me instead of him?"

Her tone was frosty at best. This was not the way to win over one's potential mother-in-law.

"Only *you* can help with what needs to be done . . . and that is to allow Hades and Persephone to stay together," Meg said. Hera stared. "I know it may sound strange, but these two . . . well, they are in love." She looked back at the pair. "I've seen them together, and they actually seem to suit one another. When he's burning, she cools him down. And she has added much-needed beauty to the Underworld that Hades never would have allowed before." She paused, thinking out loud now. "I think that's because she's inspired down here with him. Maybe they're inspired by each other. In any case, they wish to be together. And besides," Meg realized, "it couldn't hurt to have a happy god of the Underworld, could it?"

"That would be a plus," Hera admitted. "But Persephone has responsibilities. The Earth's harvest, for instance . . ."

"That's why I'm asking you to appeal to Zeus and Demeter to let Persephone stay with Hades in the Underworld for half the year. She would spend the other half on Earth for the harvest. Everyone wins." *Including me,* Meg thought. She thought of Layla and her heart began to ache. *Maybe not everyone.* Though they would all be reunited again someday, she knew it wouldn't lessen the blow of Katerina leaving Layla now.

Hera looked at her sharply. "*This* is your request, then—what you really want your last appeal to the gods to be?"

"Yes," Meg said firmly. "I believe helping *this* love will help others."

Hera seemed to consider this. "Then I will grant your request, Megara, and I will talk to Zeus and Demeter." She looked at Persephone. "You will be the first god allowed to travel back and forth regularly from the Underworld."

"Really? Thank you, Hera! Thank you!" Persephone cried. She and Hades held on to one another.

Meg almost couldn't believe it herself. She'd done it! She'd negotiated with Hera! Maybe she could go toe-to-toe with a god after all.

"There are stipulations, of course," Hera continued. "Spring is upon us, and the grains of the land must be replenished. Persephone, you will come back and do your duties to the Earth now, and when the summer has faded, you will return to Hades for the fall and the winter."

Hades and Persephone looked at one another.

"We'll make it work," Hades said as much to Persephone as he did Hera.

Hera went on. "A boat will arrive in the next few hours to take you back to the world of the living. But know this: once you board, you cannot look back at the Underworld or at Hades. You should concentrate on your work on Earth and trust you will be returned to Hades when your time is over," Hera stressed. "If you turn back for any reason, the deal will be broken. No one is meant to travel back and forth between worlds. This is an exception made only for your . . . unique situation."

"Thank you, Hera," Persephone said. "I won't let you down."

Hera's eyes flickered to Meg's. "You've done well,

child. I do not say that lightly." Then Hera faded away as quickly as she'd come, the glow from her lingering embers drifting up into the cavernous ceiling. Meg was on her own once more.

As Hades and Persephone embraced again, Meg looked back at the hourglass clutched in her hand. There were only a few grains left, and she still had to convince Katerina to come with her as well as figure out their own way home. As Hera had said, no one was meant to travel between worlds.

"I need to find Katerina," Meg blurted out. "What's the quickest way to Asphodel Meadows?"

"The stairs," Hades retorted, not taking his eyes off Persephone. "And don't forget—I will only turn the other cheek until your time runs out."

Meg groaned. She'd climbed almost a hundred staircases and walked for miles to reach Katerina the first time. She'd never make it.

"Hades, a deal's a deal," Persephone chimed in. "At least give her a shot." She snapped her fingers and Meg's feet flamed, shooting her straight up the stairs at lightning speed.

She could still hear Hades shouting as she zipped around staircases faster than light: "Good luck, babe! You're going to need it."

TWENTY-SEVEN: One More Song

Meg was moving so fast, all she saw were greens, golds, and yellows as she whizzed through Asphodel Meadows. Finally, the sky in front of her started to come into focus and she saw a welcome sight: poppies. She wasn't sure how the flames knew where to stop, but she was grateful they dropped her in the familiar field. By her calculations, she had less than a day, but in the Underworld, that might feel like an hour.

The grass was still damp from the recent storm, but people were out in droves again, already laughing and playing once more. Meg searched the field frantically for Katerina, silently praying she'd still be there. She felt a tap on her back and heard a child's familiar giggle. She turned around.

"You're back!" Layla held her hand out to Meg. "Are you looking for my sister again?"

Meg nodded, a lump forming in her throat as she thought about how she was trying to take Katerina away from her. "Yes."

Layla's small face clouded over slightly. "Did you find your mom? Thea?"

"Wow, you've got some memory," Meg said admiringly. "But no, sadly, I keep missing her."

Layla plucked a poppy and handed it to Meg. "That's too bad. I'm sure she misses you, since you're her child. Even though you're no longer a child." She laughed. "Everyone likes kids."

"Sure." Meg never thought she'd agree with that statement, but she had been taken with Cassia, and Layla was pretty special herself. "I lost her pretty young, though."

Layla's face scrunched up. "My mother didn't get to be mine too long either." She concentrated on the poppy in her hand and plucked off a few of the petals. The motion immediately made Meg think of the orchid again.

"It's not fair," Meg said softly.

"No," Layla agreed and looked up at her with big, round eyes. "Did you come back to try to bring Katerina home to her baby?"

Meg knelt down. She couldn't lie to her. "I'm going to try."

"You should. She would be a good mother, and I know we'll see each other again one day."

"Yes." The kid was wiser than her seven earthly years. Maybe that came from having been around so much longer than that. "But I don't want *you* to be alone, either."

"It would be nice to have someone," Layla said thoughtfully. She broke into a grin. "But maybe I can."

The child whispered something so quickly in her ear that Meg asked Layla to repeat it, just to be sure. She could feel her heart drumming and vibrating with anticipation, and unbelievably, *hope.* She leaned down and whispered back. Layla nodded.

Now she just had to convince Katerina to go. This time, she had to get this right.

Layla held tight to Meg's hand. "Here comes my sister."

She saw the woman rushing across the field toward them and steadied herself.

"You!" Katerina looked upset. "I told you not to bother us! Layla, get away from her."

"Katerina, please," Meg said, letting go of Layla's hand. "I just want to talk to you."

"Listen to her, Katerina. She can help you get home," Layla said, and Katerina looked startled.

Katerina put a hand on Layla's head and looked at Meg. "Look, I appreciate what you're trying to do, but I am staying here. I don't remember these people you speak of."

"But—" Meg tried to interrupt as Katerina cut her off.

"No matter how many times you try to describe them to me, that won't change," she said, her voice softening. "I know this isn't what you want to hear, but I think you should go. Come along, Layla."

"Katerina." Layla frowned as her sister pulled her away.

"Layla, come on!" Katerina insisted.

Layla looked back at Meg, tears in her eyes. Meg tried to smile reassuringly, but hope was leaving her as well. She pulled out the hourglass again and her despair deepened. There was only a pinch of sand left. She was not going to make it.

She wasn't the crying type, but if there was ever time to let go, this was it.

She had failed her quest.

Meg sank down into the wet grass and closed her eyes. She was not leaving the Underworld again. She would not become a god. Cassia would grow up without her mother, just like Meg had. She'd never again get to see Hercules's face or apologize for the way she acted the last time they were together. Her last words to him had been cruel. How could she have wasted the time they'd had worrying about whether they were meant to spend eternity together? Why couldn't she have realized how great things had been between them in the moment? She didn't even have the remains of the orchid to remember him by.

Absentmindedly, her hand went to the satchel where she had kept the flower and her fingers brushed across something wooden. Meg pulled it out: Cassia's rattle. The beads inside began to jangle around.

"Katerina?" Meg jumped up and rushed over to the retreating woman. She held out the rattle. "You should have this."

For once, Katerina didn't fight her. Her fingers closed over the rattle in Meg's outstretched hand. Then she turned and walked away.

Meg watched her and Layla disappear into the field, all her hopes carried along with them. Maybe she hadn't been sure of herself at the start of this journey, but as she got closer to reaching Katerina, she had started to believe she could complete her impossible quest.

The old Meg definitely wouldn't have trusted anyone else to help her, would never have believed in leaps of faith. She also would not have been so successful at bargaining with Hades and winning over gods like Athena, Aphrodite, and Persephone. Even Hera had liked her resolution for

Hades and Persephone's love affair. So how could she have come so far and failed?

A breeze picked up and Meg ran her hands over her legs, rubbing them to keep warm. Her fingers grazed Athena's flute.

Unhooking it from the strap, Meg stared at the instrument she'd saved for a god. *You do not play as you once did,* Athena had said, and it was true. Meg's love of music had been wrapped up in her mother and then Aegeus, and after losing them both, she didn't have the heart to play the way she used to. But now she looked at the flute and wondered. Her life was over. Would the flute disappear because she had failed her quest? If it did, would she ever get the chance to try it again?

Meg decided to place the reeds to her lips one last time. As the melody she played took hold, she thought about all this quest had taught her and all the things she'd never do again. The tune shifted into the first song she'd learned for her mother—"The Plight of the Lily." It morphed into the song she had played with Aegeus, the sweet notes lifting into the air, and then the tune changed again. She thought about Hercules's unwavering belief in her, about Mount Olympus and Katerina and this quest, and the notes unfurled into a new song altogether. She let the music take her to another place and time, and for a moment she continued with complete abandon. When she finally took a breath and opened her eyes, Katerina was standing in front of her.

Tears streamed down her face. "That was Aegeus's song," she whispered. "And you're . . . ?"

"Meg—Megara," Meg supplied, her heartbeat quickening.

Katerina sank down on the grass, still clutching Cassia's rattle. "I was married. I had a baby." She looked ashen. "She was so young when I wound up here." She grabbed Meg's hands, her eyes widening. "Her name was Cassia and she already had wise eyes and a playful heart and a cry that cut deep into your soul."

Meg felt her heart stop. "Yes!"

Katerina let out an anguished sob and held up the rattle. "Aegeus made this for our child when I was expecting." She started to cry again. "I remember. I want to go back to my life. I want to see my baby." She looked at Meg in horror. "Am I too late? Can you take me to her? I . . ." She turned around, startled, seemingly having forgotten her sister was standing behind her. "Layla . . ."

Layla reached for Katerina's hand. "You have to go to Cassia. I'll be okay, as I have been before. And we'll see each other again. I can't wait to meet your baby."

Katerina stood and hugged the child fiercely, her face crumbling all over again. "Are you sure? Layla, I . . ."

"Go," Layla insisted. "I promise you, I won't be alone." Layla glanced at Meg before kissing Katerina. Then she ran off over the hill without a second goodbye. It was probably better that way.

That kid really is amazing, Meg thought.

Katerina looked at Meg. "What do we do now?"

Time was running out, and there was no Persephone to speed up the journey. *Persephone.* Meg squared her shoulders, a new thought dawning on her—they needed to get to Persephone. Hera had said she was sending a boat for Persephone's unique *situation*, but she hadn't said the only passenger could be the god of vegetation. Could they hitch a ride? Their stories were entwined, after all.

"Persephone, don't leave without us," Meg prayed. Then she reached for Katerina's hand and prepared to tell the woman to move her legs as fast as she ever had before. But before she could even utter the word *run*, the pair disappeared.

TWENTY-EIGHT: Last Chance

Meg and Katerina materialized at the edge of a dark, rocky dock alongside the river Styx. A voice came to them in the darkness.

"I heard a prayer you wanted to join me on this boat," Persephone said, her eyebrows raised. "So I thought I'd give you a lift. We're leaving soon."

Meg would actually have hugged the god if she didn't think it would offend her. "Thank you."

"Now we're even," Persephone said. She noticed Katerina clinging to Meg's arm. "So is this the ex's new wife?"

Meg nodded. "This is her," she said, but her focus was on Charon rowing his boat toward them, his presence especially eerie in the glow of the torches along the river. She wished he would move faster.

"Where are we?" Katerina trembled as she eyed the large cavern. The stalactites hung precariously above their heads, and the vast cities of the Underworld lay behind them, perched on top of one another like an overgrown tree in need of pruning.

It occurred to Meg that Katerina might not remember this place, let alone even arriving in the Underworld, after all she'd been through. She held tight to the woman's hand, fearing she might bolt. "This is the entrance to the Underworld," Meg told her, "and that boat is coming to take us out of here."

Katerina squeezed Meg's hand as she watched the lost souls swirl about in the dark water. A low layer of fog rolled in. Meg could feel Katerina shaking harder now. *Go faster,* she willed the boat, picturing the last grain of sand shift in the hourglass. *Faster!*

"Hades isn't coming to say goodbye?" Meg asked anxiously. If he appeared, they were done for.

"Oh, no, he'll see me off." Persephone held up a hand to show an ornate snakelike silver band wrapped around her ring finger. "He asked me to marry him." Her dark eyes glowed almost yellow in the darkness, but it sounded as if she was smiling. "My mother is going to flip."

"Congratulations," Meg said, hoping she sounded sincere even as she wished Hades would miss the boat. *Come on, come on,* she begged Charon, who was only feet away. Once they stepped on board, they would be free, right? She didn't want to think about the alternative. She'd gotten Katerina this far. She had to see her through to the end.

Katerina's breath quickened as Charon's boat knocked up against the landing. He held out his oar to hold the boat steady and Persephone climbed in. She turned around and held her hand out to Katerina. Meg practically pushed the woman inside, then jumped in after her.

"Uh, uh, uh."

Hades's voice echoed through the cave. The god of the Underworld was gliding toward them on a bed of smoke, his hands folded calmly.

"Not so fast, Nut-Meg. Per has a get-out-of-jail-free card, but as for you two, I'm pretty sure the time for your little quest is up by now. Which means you've failed, and we have no deal." The yellow in his eyes glowed. "You two belong to me."

Meg's heart thudded. "If we *had* run out of time, we wouldn't even be here, would we?" she said as evenly as she could muster. She could see Persephone watching from the corner of her eye, and she wondered if the god would reveal the truth. "We still have some left."

Hades held out his hand. "Prove it! Show me the hourglass!"

"Fine." Meg swallowed, the thick heat making her ache with thirst. Her fingers trembled as she reached into her satchel for the glass jar. *Please let there be sand left,* she prayed to the gods. *Please! We're so close!* Meg's fingers closed around the vial and she pulled it out, her breath catching in her throat as they all turned to look.

"HA!" Hades roared.

The last sands had fallen to the bottom. It was over.

"You're not going anywhere!" Hades's voice was laced with triumph. Smoke sprang from his hands and headed toward them.

Katerina grabbed hold of Meg once more. "What does he mean? Megara, no. Please, no!" She burst into tears.

Meg stiffened. *Nope. I'm not going out like this.* She grabbed Persephone's arm, instantly regretting the move as Persephone looked down at her hand in surprise. Meg had been rash with a god before, and her mouth had gotten her in trouble. But this time, her words were the only thing left that could save them. She let go and tried to channel calm and diplomacy with every word. "Would you talk to him? He'll listen to you." Persephone frowned, but Meg continued before she could refuse. "We're so close to the end of the journey. I can't send her back now." They both looked at Katerina, who was sobbing. "Please? We're on the boat already. Can't he just let us try to get out of here?"

Persephone pursed her lips. "But if your time is up, the quest is over, no? Even Hera wouldn't let you leave the Underworld if you failed."

"I haven't failed yet," Meg corrected her. "If Hera hasn't stopped this boat from leaving with us on it, she must be looking favorably on us, no?"

Persephone thought this over. "Maybe. Or maybe she doesn't realize what's going on yet."

"I think it means we have an opening," Meg argued. "*Against all odds.* Like your flowers. And if we have an opportunity to get out of here, I am taking it. But I need your help. I gave up my last chance to reach the gods to help you. Can't you do the same for us?"

Persephone looked from Meg to Katerina and was quiet for a moment. After what felt like an eternity, she turned to her fiancé. "Hades, I'm taking them back with me."

Hades's face froze. "Wait—WHAT?"

"I'm taking them with me," Persephone repeated slowly. "Whether the hourglass is full or not, they're already on the boat, so Hera must be allowing it."

"Or she doesn't know what's happening!" Hades's head erupted in blue flames.

They really do think alike, Meg realized.

"Either way, there is no harm in letting them try to leave," Persephone said calmly. "Megara helped us stay together, my love. Shouldn't we offer the same courtesy to her? Doesn't it make for the better story?"

Hades glared at Meg. "No!"

"Well, *I* want to help her," Persephone announced, and Hades's flames died out. "At least let her try to travel to the end of the river Styx. If Hera doesn't allow her reentrance, you'll know. She'll be back." Hades crossed his arms and looked away, his head starting to erupt in flames again.

The sound of water dripping was interrupted by Charon's shifting bones. "Well, are we leaving or not?" he asked, his oar hovering above the water. Meg saw a soul reach for it and Charon swatted it away.

"Hades?" Persephone tried again.

"Fine!" Hades said, sounding annoyed.

Katerina wrapped her arms around Meg and began to weep again. Meg finally exhaled.

"Thank you, my Hades," Persephone said.

Hades's resolve seemed to weaken slightly. "You're welcome, love. I'll see you soon." Hades looked at Meg and his eyes flashed. "As for you, Nut-Meg, the same rules Hera gave to Per apply to you, too—either one of you looks back at the Underworld on your way out, and you're going nowhere."

"Believe me, nothing would make us want to look

back at this place." She glanced at Persephone. "Sorry. No offense."

Persephone shrugged and turned to Charon. "Go already, or my mother will have my head." She sat on the bench and stared straight ahead. "Goodbye, my sweet!"

"See you soon, my pet!" Hades started to laugh. "You too, Meg-let. Now that I think about it, probably in no time at all."

"What does that mean?" Katerina asked, adjusting her seat so that she was facing forward like Persephone and Meg. The ferryman shoved off, moving slower than seemed possible.

"He's just trying to scare us," Meg assured her.

Hades continued laughing. "Wait! Don't you want to say goodbye to your loved ones before you duck out?"

Meg's stomach filled with dread. *What are you doing?* she wondered. She raised her eyebrows at Persephone, who shrugged. "Hey, I just asked him to let you go. He's not going to make it easy. It's not his way." She sighed with a lovestruck, faraway look in her eyes, and Meg inwardly groaned.

"Layla—" Katerina started, but Meg cut her off, taking her hand.

"No matter what happens next, don't turn around," Meg told her firmly.

"But . . ." Katerina said, her voice cracking. "She's so young. She shouldn't be on her own."

"She'll be okay," Meg assured her. "I promise."

Katerina's small nose scrunched up with worry. "How can you promise that?"

Meg attempted a small smile even as her heart started to thud. "Ask me again when we're out of here. Just try to focus on getting home to your baby. Don't listen to anything he says."

Meg felt the boat begin to rock as the souls from the river moaned and begged to climb aboard. Katerina pulled herself in tight, squeezing Persephone, who looked less than thrilled at the loss of personal space. The women remained quiet. If Layla showed up, Meg wasn't sure Katerina's willpower would hold strong. Finally, Charon approached the area where two gigantic bony hands that served as walls opened to reveal Cerberus, who lay still. Katerina gasped.

"Relax. He's out cold," Persephone assured her. "Hades made sure of it." One of Cerberus's heads snored loudly.

The boat glided by and Meg felt her stomach unclench slightly. *It's going to be okay,* she told herself as the guardian's area closed off behind them. Up ahead, she could swear she saw a small light begin to form. *Maybe Hades's threat was just a scare tactic. Faster!* she silently urged Charon, who did not seem to be bothered by their painstaking pace. *Faster!*

"Megara! Megara! Where are you?"

As soon as Meg heard the voice echo through the cave, her blood ran cold. She swallowed. "Mother?"

"So many have told me you're here, but I can't find you," her mother cried out. "Please, let me see you. I've missed you so much!"

Tears flooded Meg's eyes. *How could Hades be so cruel?* Meg couldn't ignore her. "Mother, it's me!" she cried out.

"What are you doing?" Katerina whispered. "Megara, no!"

"Megara! I've found you! Where are you, child? Let me see you!"

"Be strong, Megara," Katerina said, squeezing her hand. "Don't turn around. Think about what's at stake."

Meg's heart beat faster as her tears continued to fall. "I love you so much, but if I show myself, Hades will trap me here forever, and I'm free to go, Mother. I'm free! I have a chance to do something pretty extraordinary with my life. Please don't tempt me to go back and find you, because I love you so much that I'm pretty sure I will." Her voice cracked. An excruciating silence followed. "Mother?"

Had Thea heard? Would she understand? Was she

all right? Meg gripped the bench, tears streaming down her face.

"Mother?" she tried again, more forcefully.

"I understand, my child!" her mother yelled with an anguished sob. "You cannot come back. Be strong and brave like I taught you, my love. You're a big, tough girl. You tie your own sandals and everything."

Meg let out a sob of her own and wrapped her arms around herself to try to remain calm. "I love you, Mother!" she said, but this time there was no reply.

Katerina squeezed her shoulder. "Megara, look."

Meg lifted her head and saw the light.

TWENTY-NINE: The End of the River

"Almost to the end of the river," Persephone announced.

Meg took a few shaking breaths as Katerina patted her back. *Enough tears now, Meg,* she told herself and squared her shoulders. She lifted her head higher. *You need your strength for whatever comes next.*

Meg watched as Charon's boat approached the large opening. Beyond it, she could see the fog that covered the lake at the entrance to Earth. The fog thickened as they neared, and the souls below them began to quiet.

Would Hera let them pass? Or were she and Katerina about to be returned directly to a triumphant Hades? Meg had missed her deadline, but she'd also fought her way out of the darkness and won. Even if she couldn't become a god and be with Hercules, Katerina deserved to be returned to

Aegeus and Cassia. *Please let her live,* Meg prayed to Hera as the boat reached the end of the river. *I understand now what you tried to teach me with this quest. If one truly wants to live, they need to open their heart to others, and I have. No matter what comes next for me, I know now I loved and was loved in return. I will carry that thought with me for the rest of my days if you let me. Just please allow us to pass.*

Charon broke out of the cave into the lake, and Meg felt Katerina's hand slip from her own. Meg watched in wonder as the woman's pale form began to brighten. Katerina's hands and arms started to glow orange along with the rest of her body. Her tan dress faded away, replaced with one as yellow as the sun. Color returned to Katerina's cheeks and then, finally, the woman inhaled sharply, air filling her lungs for the first time in months.

She cried out and looked at Meg in surprise. "I'm alive?"

"You're alive!" Meg shouted, and the two women embraced as Persephone watched them, her eyes sparkling.

And so am I, Meg thought. *Thank you, Hera. Thank you!* She inhaled deeply. The smells of burning and decay were gone. In the distance, she could swear she smelled pomegranate seeds.

"We made it," Katerina said. "Oh, Megara, how can I ever repay you?" She reached out for Meg and started to cry again.

As Meg hugged Katerina, she couldn't help thinking about the fact that she was embracing the very person she'd resented for far too long. Now they were both free. Katerina would get to live her life and be there to watch her daughter grow up. Meg had helped make that happen.

"This is the end of the ride," Charon said as the boat came to a sudden stop.

"Thanks, Charon," said Persephone. "See you in a few months." The ferryman shrugged his bony shoulders. Persephone looked at Meg. "And you. Thank you. For helping Hades and me. And for making things infinitely more interesting."

"You're welcome," Meg responded. "And thank you for making the case for us to leave."

Persephone smiled and held out her hand. "Good luck, Megara."

"You, too," Meg said. "But, um, any chance you can get us to shore before you go?"

"Not a problem." Persephone snapped her fingers and the three of them found themselves on dry land.

Meg felt the grass beneath her feet and the feel of solid ground again and whooped with happiness. The fog started to fade. The river Acheron, where she had toiled for days, started to appear through the mist. She and Katerina hugged again.

"I'm off to see my mother and show her my ring,"

Persephone said, her voice gleeful as she admired it in the light. She looked at Katerina. "You take care of that child of yours. A seedling needs proper love and care. You hear me?"

"Yes," Katerina said. "I will love her with my whole heart."

Persephone nodded, and with one final look at the two women, she snapped her fingers and disappeared.

"Who was that, by the way?" Katerina asked, and Meg couldn't help laughing, realizing with all that had happened, she'd never gotten the chance to explain.

"That was Persephone, the god of vegetation."

Katerina's eyes widened. "We were riding with a god?"

Meg laughed harder. It felt good after ten tough days. And yet, she still couldn't help thinking of what she'd lost during that time, too. She might have been freed from the Underworld, but it looked like she would be staying Earthside. Hercules was hers to love no more. "Come on. Let's get you home."

She looked around, wondering if they could fashion themselves a boat. It was too far to walk. The river had more trials than it did triumphs, and the thought of the Stymphalian birds was enough to make her want to stay at the edge of that shore permanently.

Suddenly she heard a neigh and looked up. Pegasus was flying toward them.

THIRTY: Reunion

"Peg!" Meg cried, rushing to the horse's side as he came in for a landing next to them.

The horse seemed as happy to see her as she was to see him. She patted his mane, smoothing his blue hair and nuzzling her face against his.

"Can you give us a lift to Aegeus's?" Peg snorted again. "We have a ride," Meg told Katerina. "Climb on!"

Peg quickly took to the sky again and Katerina and Meg held on as the horse soared away from that dreaded lake and river and carried them from the mouth of death. With each flap of the creature's majestic wings, Meg breathed a little easier.

Last ride, she thought a bit sadly. After this, Pegasus would return to Hercules, and she . . . she wasn't sure where she'd go, actually. Wherever it was, it most certainly wouldn't have this view.

Meg chortled softy. Could it be after all this time, she actually *enjoyed* soaring above the clouds? She looked down, trying to commit every detail of the flight to memory—how the trees looked like specks and the lakes like splats of blue paint.

Pegasus neighed loudly and they started to dip down between the clouds. Katerina held on tight to Meg's back as they came in lower. Meg could see the coastline up ahead and she felt her breath quicken as Peg dove faster, racing toward the small dot on the hill on the horizon. Finally, he swooped low, his neighs filling the sky as two small figures came running toward them. She could hear their cheering as Pegasus came in for a landing.

"Katerina!" Aegeus cried as he and Phil ran from the house.

"Aegeus!" Katerina sobbed. She scrambled off Pegasus and ran toward him.

Meg watched as Aegeus and Katerina threw their arms around each other and kissed. Seeing them together, she was thankful her heart no longer felt envy. Her heart swelled instead with the joy that came from celebrating someone else's triumph, a love reunited. Who knew such a feeling was even possible?

"Red!"

Meg turned around.

Phil was practically jumping into her arms. "You did it, Red! I can't believe it, but you did it! When you didn't appear on the riverbank on the tenth day, Pegasus and I feared the worst. . . . I kept sending him back on flights to look for you and now here you are." He suddenly looked misty. "I'm so proud of you."

Was the satyr really going to make her tear up again? "Thanks, Phil."

"So tell me everything," he continued, now talking a mile a minute. "What was Cerberus like? Bigger than a Titan? Hades? Does he really burst into flames? How'd you track down Katerina?" He stepped back. "Hey. Why aren't you glowing like Hercules was? Aren't you a god now?"

Meg exhaled. "Phil, there's something you should know."

"There's a lot I need to know! Did you call for Hera yet?" He poked Meg in the arm. "Maybe you need to square things up with her, and then they'll take you up to Mount Olympus."

"Phil . . ." Meg pulled the hourglass out and showed him the gathered sand. "I failed."

Phil looked at the glass bottle and blinked. "Failed? No! You're here!" He looked back at Katerina still embracing Aegeus. "And she's here, too." His face reddened. "How are you here if you failed?" he demanded. "Is this a joke?"

"We got out of the Underworld, yes. But I didn't make it in time." Meg filled him in on everything that happened from the moment she entered Charon's boat: Cerberus, her interactions with Hades and Persephone, what happened when she found Katerina, and how she entered Charon's boat a second time only to find that the last grain of sand had fallen. Phil's jaw dropped when she told him about hearing her mother's voice calling to her on the river Styx. And somehow, Hera had allowed them to return to the land of the living.

"Aww, kid, I'm sorry." Phil shook his head. "I thought you had them beat. I really did." He touched her arm. "Either way, you did good. Real good. Look at those three."

Meg and Phil turned around. Aegeus was holding Cassia out to Katerina. Meg watched as the child hesitated for a split second before reaching for her mother, nuzzling close as if no time had passed. Katerina held her daughter close, and the child laughed and pulled at a lock of her hair.

"Katerina gets to live and Cassia has her mother back," Meg said. "That's what's important. And who knows? Maybe someday Aegeus and Katerina will tell her about the woman who went to the Underworld to reunite them."

"Of course they will." He patted her arm. "Who cares about timing? You finished the race all the same. You're a god in my book, Red."

"Thanks, Phil. I just wish I could see Hercules one last time. His love inspired this whole quest in the first place. And because of that, I was able to get through to Katerina and beat Hades at his own game." Now she felt like she had a lump in her throat. "I don't think I realized how much I really loved the guy till I lost him."

"Maybe you should tell him that."

Meg and Phil turned around. Athena and Aphrodite stood behind them.

"Great gods!" said Aegeus, and he and Katerina knelt down as Cassia continued to wriggle in her arms.

"You have done well, Megara, and acted as a true hero," Athena said. "Even when the path was murky, you found your way."

"And it is clear you have learned what true love really is," added Aphrodite with a bright smile. "Give-and-take, sacrifice, learning to trust in others—it's all a part of it, as you now know."

Meg looked at both gods. "I am thankful for all your guidance."

"As am I."

A third god had appeared on the hillside.

Meg inhaled sharply. "Hera."

"What you did in your hour of need did not go unnoticed," Hera said. "You fought your way to Katerina and never stopped until she remembered the truth about her loved ones. Even when faced with adversity and the choice to save the orchid for yourself or use it to help others, you chose their needs over your own." She tilted her head and looked at Meg curiously. "I thought I had you figured out, but clearly I was wrong. That is why I am here to offer you a gift." Meg looked at her. "Even though you failed to complete your quest before the sand ran out, I will allow you to see Hercules one last time."

Before Meg could even comprehend what was happening, Wonder Boy had materialized in front of her.

"Meg!" he cried, racing toward her and pulling her into an embrace. "You're back!" He kissed her fiercely and lifted her up into his arms.

Meg placed her hands on both of his cheeks, blinking through new tears. "Wonder Boy," she whispered. "I thought I'd never see you again."

He grinned and placed her back on the ground. "I knew you could do it. I just knew it, Meg."

Her smile faded. "But I didn't. Not in the time I was given to complete the quest."

Hercules's brow creased. "But you're here. . . ."

"Yes. It's a long story, but that's not important now." She held him tight, and would as long as she physically could. She had to speak while she still had a chance. "I need to apologize," she said, rushing the words. "I'm sorry for yelling at you when you tried to help with the Stymphalian birds. I was wrong to not accept your help."

"Meg," he tried.

"No, listen to me," she shushed him. "I learned something along this journey. I know now that love means showing up for one another and trusting that the other person always has your back. It means asking for help sometimes, and not thinking that means you look weak. Love means opening your heart to another, no matter the consequences."

"Meg," Hercules said, pulling back to look at her. "What happened down there?"

She smiled sadly. "A lot, and I did good. You'd be proud of me. I saved someone else's love story at the sacrifice of my own." She thought again of baby Cassia and Katerina and Persephone and all those she'd managed to help, even though she couldn't help herself. She felt her voice tighten. "People do crazy things when they're in love."

Aphrodite let out a sob and leaned her head on Athena's shoulder. The other god did not look amused. Even Phil started to cry again. This was it. The end of her love story with Wonder Boy. She knew she'd never find another like him.

"Meg, I don't understand—" Hercules started to say.

"You don't have to," Hera interrupted before Meg could explain further. She walked over to the two of them, beaming. "I can see my son is truly happy with you, and you have more than proven yourself worthy. You have given us what matters most—Katerina." She looked at the babe a few feet away. "Cassia will flourish under her father and mother's tutelage and one day will become a great hero, with Philoctetes's help."

Meg's eyes widened. So that was why the gods had been so keen to get Katerina back to the land of the living.

"My help?" Phil repeated and puffed up his chest. "I guess I could hold off on retirement a *little* while longer."

A dove fluttered into view and landed on Hera's shoulder. In its beak was a small glass bottle, which resembled the hourglass Meg had carried for ten days. Hera took the bottle out of its mouth and offered it to Meg.

"Drink this," she said. "It's ambrosia, the nectar of the

gods. One sip and you will be transformed into a god." Meg couldn't hide her surprise. "I know you didn't complete your quest in time, but gods always find a way to help when a hero shows a true heart." She touched Meg's face. "I have seen yours, Megara."

Meg took the bottle from Hera's outstretched hand and drank its contents without hesitation.

A warmth flooded her as the liquid slid down her throat and spread to every limb. Her body started to glow thistle in color until light emitted from every inch of her. She could feel Aegeus, Katerina, Cassia, and Phil watching her along with the gods, but she only had eyes for one other at that moment.

Hercules stared at her, speechless. "Meg . . ." he started as she continued to transform.

She knew where she belonged now, and it was by Wonder Boy's side. Together, they could do great work.

She put a hand to his lips and smiled, unable to contain her happiness. "Tell me once we're home, Wonder Boy."

EPILOGUE

A few months later . . .

She was getting used to this god business.

There was a learning curve, to be sure, but each time Meg heard a mortal call out for help, her purpose became clearer. Hera had named her the god of vulnerability, and it suited her, even if she bristled at the title at first.

As Wonder Boy kept telling her, she had a knack for hearing a mortal in need, more so than the others. When doubt raised its ugly head, or a mortal acted too proudly, she stepped in and tried to steer them in the right direction.

And Holy Hera, was the feeling rewarding when the mortal actually *listened* and accepted her aid.

Even ol' Zeus, who was less than thrilled to see Meg back on his turf, had to admit she was good at her job.

She seemed to make Hercules deliriously happy, and the feeling was mutual. All the gods were talking about a Mount Olympus wedding, but she and Hercules were taking their time.

She still had some unfinished business she wanted to take care of before she thought about the next part of her own story. And that business took her back to Earth.

Meg appeared there suddenly one afternoon while Katerina was working in the garden, Cassia tucked safely in a basket at her side.

"Hello, Katerina," Meg said.

"Megara!" Katerina stood up quickly in surprise, dropping her trowel.

Cassia screamed with delight at the sight of her, or maybe it was just the fact that she was glowing. Aegeus came running.

"Megara!" he said, looking on in surprise. "To what do we owe this honor?"

"Aegeus, you can forget the formalities. I may be a god, but I'm still me," she said, sitting down on their garden bench and picking up the baby, whom she bounced on her knee. The child had gotten bigger—and heavier—since she'd last seen her. "I am here with some news for Katerina."

"News?" Katerina said, confused.

"Yes." Meg smiled and put Cassia back down in the

basket. "I know the guilt you have about leaving Layla still torments you, especially in the evening when the moon is high."

"It's true," Katerina said, her face crumbling. Aegeus quickly put an arm around her. "I am so grateful for all you have done for me and our family, and I can't imagine not being here to see Cassia's every breath, but leaving Layla is still one of the great regrets of my life. I worry for her."

"I know," Meg said, "which is why I wanted you to know that I was true to my word when we left the Underworld—I promised you Layla would be okay, and she really is. As a matter of fact, why don't I let you see for yourself?"

Meg walked over to the small pond in their garden, and Katerina and Aegeus quickly followed. Meg flicked her wrist and the water in the dark green pond began to swirl. Suddenly an image, much like their own reflection, shone back at them. It was Layla, and she was waving to them.

"Layla!" Katerina cried out and let out a sob on Aegeus's shoulder. "That is my sister," she explained.

Layla held up a basket of poppies to show them, then waved to someone out of sight who stepped into the frame. Meg's heart felt like it might burst at the sight of the two of them together.

"Who is that with her?" Aegeus asked about the woman with the long red hair.

"My mother, Thea," Meg said softly, and the pair looked at her. "Layla and I spoke of my mother in the Underworld, and when she gave you her blessing to leave, she asked me where she could find someone who, too, was looking for love and nourishment in the Underworld. I gave her my mother's location and have since gotten word that the two are inseparable." She looked at Katerina. "Layla has found the surrogate mother she needed to thrive, and my mother finally has the chance to be the parent she never could be on Earth. Persephone checks in on them both, in fact, now that she's returned to Hades, and I'm told they are both quite happy. I thought you'd want to know."

"Yes," Katerina said, smiling through her tears. "Thank you, god of vulnerability. Thank you for this gift!"

They heard a squeal and turned around. Cassia had wriggled out of the basket and was crawling toward them. Katerina scooped the child up and faced her to the fountain so that Layla and Thea could see her.

The image of them looking at one another was one Meg knew she'd never forget.

She heard the tinkling of bells, and Hermes popped up beside her.

"Come along now, Megara! Hercules and Hera are waiting. Meeting starts in ten," he said, fluttering alongside her.

Meg turned toward the family she had helped put back

together and smiled. "I must go, but know that I'm always a prayer away if you need me." The image in the pond disappeared as Meg began to fade away.

The next thing she saw was Wonder Boy waiting with outstretched hands. "Well? Did it go okay?" he asked.

Meg stepped into his arms and kissed him. "It was absolutely perfect."

Read on for a sneak peek at the *Brave* Twisted Tale . . .

PROLOGUE

Merida

Princess Merida of Clan DunBroch squinted, bringing the funny-shaped knot on the tree trunk into focus. When she had been here a fortnight ago, she'd managed to hit it from thirty paces. This time, she backed up *fifty* paces. If she made this shot, it would prove that she was the best archer in all the Highlands. It didn't matter that no one other than her was there to see it.

Merida straightened her shoulders and concentrated on pulling in slow, steadying breaths. She shut out the sounds of the forest critters going about their day. It was just her and the tree. For the next few minutes, nothing else existed.

She homed in on the knot, focusing on the center of it. She reached behind herself and pulled an arrow from her quiver. Merida slightly relaxed her grip on the bow, remembering the instructions her father had given her when she was but a wee lass. Too much tension could send the arrow flying past her target.

She fit the bowstring into the notch on the tail end of the arrow, pulled it back, and—

"Princess Merida!"

"Bloody—" Merida stopped herself before the rest of the curse could move past her lips.

"Princess, where are you?"

She released a frustrated sigh and turned in the direction of the voice.

"Over here, Thomasina," Merida called to the woman, who worked as one of the queen's maids. "What is it?" Merida asked, though she did not need to hear Thomasina's answer. She already knew why the maid was here and who had sent her.

A moment later, Thomasina's covered head crested the short ridge.

"Oh, Princess, there you are," she said, puffing slightly as she climbed the rest of the way. "You must come now. You need to get ready for the evening meal."

Merida frowned. She thought the maid had been sent to call her in for her lessons, not to prepare for dinner.

"Now?" She looked up at the sky. The sun was still high. "We won't sit for a meal for some time."

"The queen wants you washed and dressed in your formal *léine* and DunBroch tartan," the maid said.

Merida drew her head back. "Why?"

She wore her formal léine only on special occasions. Why would the queen want her dressed in it for dinner? So that her three rambunctious brothers could cover it in whatever food the cooks had prepared?

"Do you not remember, lass? The King and Queen of Sinclair Kingdom are in residence tonight. Your mother wants you in your best attire. And for you to be on your best behavior," Thomasina added with no small amount of judgment in her tone.

"Oh, bugger!" Merida exclaimed.

"Princess!" Thomasina shouted.

"Sorry," Merida said. She had completely forgotten about the Sinclairs' arrival, and what would be required of her because of it.

Merida resented nearly every single aspect of being a princess, particularly those as trivial as keeping up appearances. But during her many lessons on her duties as a member of the royal family, her mother had imparted the importance of presenting a united front when visited by the heads of other sovereign kingdoms. Clan Sinclair was as formidable in eastern Scotland as Clan DunBroch was in the north.

At least she would not have to speak all that much at the evening's meal. Her mother would expect her to sit like a docile lamb and eat dinner while the adults at the table discussed boring kingdom business. She would take her cues from her mother, laughing when she laughed and remaining stoic when she did.

That should please Queen Elinor.

One thing that would *not* please her mother was if her daughter smelled like the forest when she sat down for dinner. Merida brushed her fingers through her hair and came away with several twigs.

"Perhaps I could do with a bath," Merida muttered. She gathered her bow and quiver and, with Thomasina trailing behind, headed back to Castle DunBroch.

The castle was brimming with activity by the time Merida returned. She dodged servants carrying armloads of linens, platters, and other items that would be used to adorn the Great Hall. Her mother would insist it had nothing to do with impressing their guests, but Merida had attended enough of these gatherings to know better. Success would be measured by the amount of favorable chatter regarding the dinner that spread throughout neighboring clans.

Merida quickly made it to her room and, after scrubbing her skin to within an inch of her life, sat at her vanity while a maid fussed over her hair and gown. As usual, her riotous curls would not be contained, and after a half hour Merida told the maid to leave them be. She would rather have shown up for dinner with unruly hair than shown up late.

In the end, it did not matter.

Merida entered the Great Hall, head held high in perfect posture, only to learn that the King and Queen of Clan Sinclair had been delayed by weather. They would not be joining them that evening after all.

"Ah, look who got all dressed up for dinner." Her father, King Fergus, laughed as he gestured to Merida with a pheasant leg.

Merida stared at the rest of her family, all wearing normal everyday attire.

"Why did no one tell me that we would no longer have guests?" she exclaimed. Her father only laughed harder.

Merida growled. "I am going to change," she said, turning on her heel.

"Oh, don't be foolish," her mother called. "Come and sit before your dinner grows cold."

"I do not care about eating cold pheasant," Merida said as she marched toward the Great Hall's entrance. "I am—"

"Merida," Queen Elinor announced in her most queenly voice.

Merida stopped. She turned, making sure her expression conveyed her disapproval, but she would not get into an argument over such a trivial matter. When it came to her mother, she knew which battles were worth fighting. Having to eat pheasant in a starched léine was not one of them.

Taking a reluctant seat at the table, Merida dodged a barrage of peas that one of her brothers catapulted at her.

"Boys!" she barked.

"Harris, Hubert, Hamish, not tonight," her mother said.

The redheaded triplets all sat up straight in their chairs, wearing innocent expressions. It was the reason they got away with everything. No one could resist those sweet faces.

Merida picked a stray pea from her hair and started on her dinner. She had to admit that her mother was right; the pheasant, peas, stewed kale, and oatcakes were best enjoyed hot. She shoveled the food into her mouth, suddenly realizing how ravenous she was after an afternoon of archery.

Merida mumbled answers to her mother's inquiries regarding her whereabouts that afternoon, and quickly changed the subject, pivoting to the King of Clan Sinclair. But when the discussion turned to the Sinclair princess's impending nuptials, Merida wished she had just admitted that she had been out with her bow and arrow. She detested all this marriage talk. She would never understand why so many lasses wished to tie themselves down before they had a chance to *live*.

"Are there not better things to discuss at the dinner table?" Merida lamented.

"What could be better than love?" her father asked. He leaned forward, a smile lifting the corners of his mouth. "Did I ever tell you the story of how I met your mother?"

"Please, Dad, not again." Merida rolled her eyes.

"Ah, it's your family history, Merida." He turned to the triplets. "Boys, listen up, this is a great one."

Merida sighed. "You were on the way to Clan MacCameron to deliver a message from the chieftain," she recited under her breath.

"I was on the way to Clan MacCameron to deliver a message from the chieftain of Clan DunBroch," her father said at the same time, lifting the other roasted pheasant leg from the platter before him.

Merida looked to her mother, who returned an indulgent smile as her gaze pivoted to her husband.

"You see," her father continued, a far-off gaze on his face, "Clan DunBroch was under the rule of King Douglass MacCameron at the time. And while we were . . . friendly," he said, gesturing with the pheasant leg as he spoke, "our clans were . . ."

"Not friends," Queen Elinor said.

"We were friendly competitors," King Fergus amended.

Elinor rolled her eyes. "If you say so."

"Where was I?" Fergus asked.

Merida jumped in. "You were on a journey to deliver a message from the chieftain when your horse was spooked by a hare. The horse threw you, you hit your head on a big rock, Mother rescued you and nursed you back to health, and the two of you fell in love. The end."

"No, no. You missed all the good parts," her father said.

Merida sighed. She had been hearing this story since she was a wee lass. It was her father's favorite. Well, his second favorite, right after the one where he single-handedly defeated the sinister monster of a bear, Mor'du.

"It was a sensitive matter of great importance," he continued. "I had been sent because I was the chieftain's most trusted soldier—and his favorite son," he added. "My da knew that I would get word to King Douglass without delay."

"But he did not know that you would be felled by a wee bunny rabbit," Merida teased.

"That's right!" Her father hooted, slapping the table with his massive palm and causing his goblet to teeter. "That little bunny shot from behind a tree like a bolt of lightning. Spooked my horse good. You would have thought the monster from Loch Ness himself was chasing us. I held on for as long as possible, but he still managed to throw me."

"And that's where I first saw your father—sprawled in the grass like a wounded animal," Queen Elinor said.

"But you were brave," Fergus added, pride beaming in his eyes. "She recognized my DunBroch tartan and was ready to put up a fight."

"Until I remembered that we were to be *friendly* to Clan DunBroch," Elinor said.

"She helped me climb onto her horse and brought me to MacCameron Castle. Of course, there were others in her clan who would have left me injured in the forest." Merida's father reached for her mother's hand and captured it in his own. "She nursed me back to health, even though there were others with more skill to do so."

"I felt responsible for you," the queen said.

"I think you felt something else for me," the king said, his eyes twinkling with mischief.

"Oh, Fergus." She slapped his hand, her cheeks turning as red as Merida's hair.

As much as Merida lamented hearing this story over and over again, she always found herself smiling when they reached this part. To look at them, many would say her mother and father were an ill-matched pair. But if there was one thing she was certain of, it was that they loved each other fiercely. And her father loved to tell people about it.

"You will one day have your own husband to contend with," her mother said to Merida.

Merida tutted. "Not if I have anything to say about it."

"It is your duty as a member of this family to marry so that you may begin assuming more royal responsibilities and maintain the peace between the clans. This kingdom depends on it, Merida. It is your fate."

Her mother's voice was resolute, but Merida would not be bullied into something so life-altering.

"Well, I refuse to believe that," she said. "There must be another way to maintain peace without marriage being involved. Besides, I do not see why I must be concerned with any of that. There are others to help with running the kingdom."

Her mother and father shared a look that put Merida on edge, but just as she was about to press harder, Hamish snatched a sweet from a platter and sent the entire thing crashing to the floor.

Chaos ensued. The dogs scarfed down all the cakes before anyone had the chance to rescue them. Harris and Hubert jumped out of their seats and started running around the dining hall, bumping into their caretaker, Maudie, and sending the basket of bread she was carrying flying into the air.

The dogs attacked the bread as fiercely as they had attacked the pastries.

"Boys!" Merida's mother yelled.

Meanwhile, her father chortled, gaily helping himself to another piece of pheasant and a swig of mead.

A typical night at the dinner table in Castle DunBroch. Little did Merida know this rowdy meal with her family would soon be the least of her problems.